A MOST LORDLY LORD

What Lord Nigel Davies wanted, he was very used to getting. His wealth, his title, his good looks and his charm—all combined to make his slightest wish an irresistible command.

What Lord Nigel wanted in a bride was a young woman whom he could mold to fit his ideal of a perfect wife—passionate in private, decorous in public, happy to live in the shadow of his towering stature and bask in the reflected glory of his achievements.

That was what Lord Nigel wanted.

What he got, however, was Courtney—who was determined never to give up her independence. . . .

A MIND
OF HER OWN

Other Regency Romances from SIGNET

A Mind of Her Own

by Anne MacNeill

A SIGNET BOOK

NEW AMERICAN LIBRARY

TIMES MIRROR

NAL BOOKS ARE AVAILABLE AT QUANTITY DISCOUNTS WHEN USED
TO PROMOTE PRODUCTS OR SERVICES. FOR INFORMATION PLEASE
WRITE TO PREMIUM MARKETING DIVISION, THE NEW AMERICAN
LIBRARY, INC., 1633 BROADWAY, NEW YORK, NEW YORK 10019.

SIGNET, SIGNET CLASSIC, MENTOR, PLUME, MERIDIAN AND NAL BOOKS
are published by The New American Library, Inc.,
1633 Broadway, New York, New York 10019

First Printing, September, 1983

1 2 3 4 5 6 7 8 9

PRINTED IN THE UNITED STATES OF AMERICA

— 1 —

"D-don't . . ." Courtney protested softly as she tried to evade her husband's warm, searching mouth. "Mary will be bringing the tea soon."

"Your maid has too much sense to come up here this early," Nigel assured her, nibbling deliciously at her earlobe. "She knows perfectly well we don't want to be disturbed."

A faint blush suffused Courtney's fine-boned features. It was inevitable that the large staff of Nigel's London house would guess how their recently wed lord and lady were occupied that pleasant spring morning. But such knowledge still embarrassed her.

The touch of big, gentle hands along the silken length of her body heightened her self-consciousness. Even after three months of marriage, she was still amazed by how easily Nigel took control of her body. Amazed and resentful.

Yet as his lips wandered down the alabaster column of her throat to the scented hollow between her breasts, she silently admitted that she was far more fortunate than many women. Dimly she remembered the whispered speculations of friends who believed the marriage bed was a place of pain and indignity to be endured as the price for a husband and children. Nigel had put that fear to rest decisively on their wedding night when he woke her to passion with unrelenting persistence she would never forget.

5

Her generous mouth set between a small uptilted nose and a decidedly firm chin trembled as his caresses grew more demanding. A cloud of glistening auburn hair drifted over her slender shoulders. Wide emerald eyes darkened to the velvet glow of forest moss as she gazed up at her husband.

The sheer size and strength of his superbly conditioned body overwhelmed her. As a wealthy member of the nobility who fully participated in the endless round of parties and balls that characterized the social whirl, he might have been excused for a certain softness of flesh. But Nigel was far too vital and active a man to be content with sloth. He rode daily, fenced brilliantly, and had reputedly shown himself quite proficient at the fashionable sport of bare-fisted boxing, which he gave up upon finding it too brutal for his tastes.

The mane of golden hair kept neatly trimmed around his well-formed head set off the silvery glints of gray eyes. His features were too rugged to be considered handsome, but Courtney found she far preferred the chiseled strength of high cheekbones, an angular nose, and a hard mouth to the more classic male beauty society chose to applaud.

At thirty-two, he was the epitome of everything she had dreamt of in a man. But also of more than a few things she had never even imagined. And that, she fully realized, was the problem.

Her eighteen years had been spent mostly in the shelter of her loving parents' London and country homes. Not until she was eighteen, and met Nigel during her first season among the *ton*, did she begin to get even the faintest glimmer of the complex, enticing possibilities that existed between men and women.

Those brief days of their courting had hardly prepared her to confront the reality of his desires. Ever mindful of her youth and innocence, he had kept a strict rein on their physical contact in the months that he courted her. Not until she was formally made Lady

Courtney Davies, marchioness, did she also become a woman in the fullest sense.

A soft gasp escaped her as Nigel's mouth closed over the rosy peak of her breast, tonguing the hardened nipple until she writhed under him. She was powerless to stop the response of her body. Wordlessly she pleaded for the release only he could give her. But still he delayed. Unlike the night before, when upon returning home from yet another party he had abruptly dismissed her maid and taken her still half-dressed thrown across the bed, this time he was clearly bent on languorous seduction.

Courtney had a moment to wonder why he insisted on subjugating her so thoroughly before all thought became impossible. Her husband had so attuned her to his slightest touch that she responded utterly no matter what the setting or her own mood. As his sinewy leg firmly parted her soft thighs, she had no choice but to welcome him completely. A hand slipped beneath her hips to arch her even closer. Their joining was slow and deep, giving her ample time to experience every moment.

When he at last moved within her to bring them both to mindless fulfillment, Courtney's response was unrestrained. All the warmth and passion of her generous nature reached out to him even as she was aware that Nigel withheld a large portion of himself. The long spiral of enthralling pleasure, ending in a shattering burst of ecstasy, left her too drained to more than dimly note his low, utterly male laugh of satisfaction.

Languidly content, she snuggled against her husband as he drew the covers back over them both before nestling her against his broad, hair-roughened chest. "My beautiful wife . . ." he murmured possessively before sleep claimed them both.

She woke several hours later to a gentle rap on the door. A quick glance confirmed that Nigel had taken himself off to his own room and the ministrations of Johnson, his long-suffering valet. Sitting up in bed,

Courtney drew the covers around her shoulders before calling out permission to enter.

Mary kept her eyes scrupulously averted as she settled the tea tray across her mistress's knees. " 'Morning, ma'am. Looks like a pleasant day." The short, plump girl with sparkling brown eyes and a sun-warmed complexion was a model of decorum far beyond her eighteen years. Though Mary had been her abigail only a few months, since replacing her sister in the position upon the latter's marriage, she had already proved herself invaluable. Her skill at hairdressing and fashion was surpassed only by her demure but stalwart good humor and her absolute discretion. She was a tremendous relief to Courtney, who could not have abided a stiff-lipped, disapproving critic of her private life.

As her young mistress expeditiously did away with the warm buttered rolls accompanying her morning tea, Mary pulled aside the floor-length curtains to admit the new day. Golden shafts of light fell across the muted hues of the large Persian rug covering most of the wood parquet floor, over the delicate lines and curves of the *chinoiserie* armoire and chairs, to the massive canopied bed draped in indigo satin.

Only the faintest sniff escaped Mary as she picked up the gown and undergarments carelessly tossed on the floor. Her sharp seamstress eye noted the absence of several buttons and the slight rip in a seam, indicating it had been removed with considerable haste. If it occurred to her that his lordship was responsible for such a precipitous disrobing, Mary gave no sign. She waited patiently as Courtney retrieved her sleeping robe from its neglected position at the foot of the bed.

Decently covered, Courtney slipped from beneath the covers and padded across to the dressing room to make use of the chamber pot and washbasin. Returning, she found Mary laying out her morning clothes.

"Since it promises to be warm today, ma'am, I thought the lavender ensemble would do."

Courtney nodded absently. She knew she was supposed to be interested in fashion, and she did try, but the plain fact was that she was generally content to leave herself in Mary's competent hands. The maid knew what colors and styles best suited her, and didn't hesitate to speak up on the rare occasions when Courtney seemed set on an inappropriate choice.

"That's fine. Just add a shawl in case it gets chilly."

Sitting down in front of the marble-inlaid dressing table, she endured Mary's dabbing at her face with a solution of rosewater and lemon juice as the young maid clucked disapprovingly.

"You went out in the sun again without a bonnet, didn't you? And what have you got to show for it? More freckles, that's what. Just when we were making some progress with your complexion." Putting down the cloth, Mary looked at her sternly. "Begging your pardon, ma'am, but you really must be more careful. What would his lordship say if you ended up all covered with freckles?"

Courtney's emerald eyes widened silently as she considered Nigel's likely reaction. He would undoubtedly insist on counting every one, no matter how inappropriately situated. Trying hard to look as though she was taking the lecture to heart, she murmured, "I will try to do better, Mary. It's just that I don't particularly mind freckles and it's difficult for me to remember that they aren't considered fashionable."

She didn't add that she also despised bonnets, much preferring the feel of wind and sun on her hair. That was just a shade too free-spirited even for Mary's tolerant ears.

Satisfied that she had done everything possible for her errant mistress's abused skin, Mary busied herself dressing the long silken tresses that fell below the marchioness's waist. Considerable brushing was required before the last tangles disappeared, but that was to be expected in view of her ladyship's penchant for leaving her hair unbraided when she slept.

Mary sighed inwardly, wondering how much longer

it would be before the first dizzy bliss of matrimony faded enough for good habits to be reasserted. The slight wave running through the gleaming strands made it easy to brush them high on the back of her head, secured by tortoiseshell combs and softened by feathery curls over each small ear.

Slipping behind a screen, Courtney removed her nightrobe. Despite the unusually balmy spring, there was still a chill in the morning air. She wasted no time donning the white silk *chemisette* with its low square neck and short sleeves. Over it went a matching silk and lace petticoat accompanied by a brief corset which did no more than emphasize the high, firm line of her breasts and the smallness of her waist. Courtney saw little sense to the awkward thing, but even she recognized the futility of trying to fight prevailing fashions in undergarments. The unspoken belief that "decent" women put as many layers as possible between themselves and the world was too strong to combat.

The separate bodice and skirt Mary had selected for her were the last word in fashion. Made of lavender muslin over a cambric lining, the drop shoulders and long puffy sleeves of the bodice flattered Courtney's slender form. A full skirt fit snugly around her slim hips, flaring out below to just brush the pointed toes of her half-boots. Her footwear was the outcome of her only successful stand against Mary's dictates. Left to her maid, Courtney would have been shod strictly in the heelless beribboned slippers favored by ladies who did little but recline languidly in their drawing rooms. In the muddy cobblestone streets of London, they were next to useless. Hence the boots and the grumble with which they were received.

Regarding herself in the mirror after Mary's ministrations, Courtney felt again the spurt of surprise that struck her whenever she caught sight of herself. However much she might privately resent Nigel's unrelenting domination of her body, she couldn't deny that it left her radiant. It was difficult to believe that only a few years before she had been a lanky schoolgirl whose limbs seemed too long for her body and who despaired of ever looking even remotely glamorous.

Now she exuded the unmistakable aura of a sensually content woman. Absently thanking her maid, Courtney took herself downstairs, as much to escape the disquieting sight of herself as to find some useful occupation.

Considering that nothing in her life was to be the same after that day, it started off quite normally. Mrs. Hawkins, the housekeeper, met her on the main landing and respectfully requested a few moments of her time. Courtney inclined her head in acceptance, well aware that the stern metal-haired woman was having difficulty accepting her new and very young mistress. It was only with considerable effort that she had been convinced to defer to Courtney on the major decisions affecting the household.

That morning there was a problem with the staff which Mrs. Hawkins turned over to the marchioness in the evident expectation that she would want no part of it.

"It's Annie, ma'am," she began the moment they entered the sitting room. "She has proved to be most unsuitable and must be dismissed."

Courtney hesitated. The undermaid in question was a new addition to the staff whom she herself had hired to help ease the burden of transforming a bachelor residence into a family home. Granted, the girl was young and had never before worked in a house of such size and grandeur, but she had seemed willing enough.

Cautiously she asked, "What exactly is the difficulty, Mrs. Hawkins? Has Annie failed somehow in her duties?" As she waited for the answer, Courtney ran over in her mind the recent inspections she had made of the town house. It seemed to her that everything was in order. If Annie was not doing her share, someone else was picking up the slack. An unlikely occurrence, considering that the other servants would have no reason to tolerate a newcomer who proved incapable.

"Oh, she does her chores well enough," the housekeeper admitted grudgingly. She smoothed the carefully pressed skirt of her black day dress before adding, "It's her free time that's the problem."

A slight frown marred the ivory purity of Courtney's brow. The servants had almost no free time and were generally too weary to do much with it anyway. What possible mischief could Annie have gotten into?

Sensing the silent question, Mrs. Hawkins went on determinedly. "She's made friends with the butcher's delivery man. They've taken to walking out together on her off day. This week she was late getting back and she's started hanging around the kitchens when he's due even though she may have chores abovestairs. I've spoken to her most sharply, but she's a stubborn wench and persists in seeing him."

The angry glint to the housekeeper's pale eyes left no doubt as to how she regarded such behavior. Like so many of her station, it was impossible if not ridiculous to imagine Mrs. Hawkins enamored of any man. She was a genderless, emotionless factotum existing solely to serve those she resolutely regarded as her betters. Courtney could not begin to conceive of such a life and she was rather glad to hear that Annie too seemed set on different ways.

"I'll speak to her myself," she said quietly, already resolved to take the matter firmly out of Mrs. Hawkins' cold hands.

The housekeeper opened her thin mouth to protest, then abruptly decided against it. No great insight was required to follow the train of her thoughts. Nothing would please her more than to see the new marchioness attempt to settle a domestic problem and fail. Lord Nigel had always taken the tranquillity of his home for granted. If it was upset, he would undoubtedly express his displeasure in terms even his young wife could not mistake.

Ignoring Mrs. Hawkins' obvious intent, Courtney directed that the maid be sent to her immediately. While she waited, she stared out at the garden just beyond the sitting-room windows. The first tulips were already in flower, as were the apple and cheery trees which Nigel had confided were once his favorite playground. Her deep blue eyes gentled as she wondered how long it would be before a miniature version of her husband was once more at play among the trees.

So caught up was she in her thoughts that Annie's timid entrance caught her unawares. It wasn't until she suddenly realized how long she had been standing at the window and turned impatiently to find out what was keeping the maid that she discovered the girl frozen just inside the door, her hands clasped in front of her and her eyes lowered.

"Y-you wanted to see me, ma'am . . ."

Doubt stabbed through Courtney. She had no experience handling such matters. Her mother, the beautiful and renowned Lady Diana Marlowe, would have known exactly what to do. But she was not at hand to advise her daughter. Taking a deep breath, Courtney summoned up everything she could remember about the management of domestic problems in her parents' homes. Lady Diana believed that all people, regardless of station, were deserving of courtesy and respect. So Courtney acted accordingly.

"Please come in," she said gently. "I did ask Mrs. Hawkins to send you here, but there's no reason to be concerned. We're just going to talk."

"T-talk?" the girl stuttered as though the mere thought was beyond her. She managed to take a few tentative steps into the room, but not for the world did she seem able to meet Courtney's concerned gaze.

What she saw reassured the marchioness. Annie looked exactly like an undermaid should. She was plainly dressed in a shapeless gray cotton garment covered by a fresh white apron. Her hair was ruthlessly dragged back from rather pretty features and hidden under a snug cap. Her face was well-scrubbed and shiny, and her hands were chapped from constant immersion in water. At nineteen, as Courtney remembered her age to be, she already had the slightly pinched look of the usual overworked servant.

Seating herself on the edge of the settee so that the pleats of her gored skirt flared out around her, Courtney began carefully. "Mrs. Hawkins is concerned that you may be distracted from your duties here. That is, she is worried that a young man of your acquaintance may be absorbing too much of your time and energy, with possibly unfortunate results. She is anxious about your welfare."

For a moment Annie did no more than stare at her. She seemed at a loss for words until, abruptly, she blurted, "Mrs. Hawkins doesn't care anything about me! She just doesn't want to see anyone with more than she has. Jimmy's a kind, caring man who's good for me. But to hear Mrs. Hawkins tell it, he's a no-good rotter just out for what he can get. I won't let anyone say that about him. I won't!"

No sooner was her outburst over than Annie was clearly appalled by her temerity. She put a hand to her mouth in a futile effort to recall her hasty words. Her eyes were wide and fearful and her thin shoulders trembled.

Courtney, who thanks to her mother's tolerance was accustomed to a household in which servants spoke their minds when necessary, saw nothing amiss except Annie's own reaction. Quickly she moved to soothe her. "Of course you don't want to hear anything against your young man. No one would. But you must realize that however Mrs. Hawkins may feel, *I* at least am concerned about what's best for you. It ... it isn't unheard of for a young girl to ... be taken advantage of ...." Aware that she was fumbling, having only the vaguest notion of what dangers might or might not confront the unwary female, Courtney broke off.

"Jimmy isn't like that," Annie exclaimed, taking courage from her mistress's unexpected tolerance. Later she might stop to ask herself how she had found such daring, but just then she wanted nothing so much as to express the convictions that were rapidly becoming the cornerstone of her life.

"He works so hard, all the time almost. And he doesn't waste his earnings on cards or drink like a lot of the other lads. He has dreams, Jimmy does." She leaned forward slightly, all the strength of her slight body pouring from her. "Someday, Jimmy's going to have his own shop. The biggest and finest in London. Then it'll be his wagons pulling up at the great houses with deliveries, his meat that's served at the best parties. You'll see. He'll make it, I just know he will."

"I'm sure he will," Courtney murmured placatingly. "But in the meantime, surely you can understand that he mustn't interfere with your work." Gently but firmly she insisted, "You must stop trying to be in the kitchens when he comes here if you have duties abovestairs. And you mustn't come back late on your off days. Such behavior is grounds for dismissal."

Her simple statement brought an unexpected reaction. Annie turned white, the color fading even from her lips as she contemplated a fate that was the stuff of nightmares.

"Oh, no! Please don't say that, ma'am! We need my wages, Jimmy and me do. If we're ever going to be able to get married and open our shop, I have to keep earning. Let me go from here and I won't be able to get a good job anywhere. Why I . . . I might as well go out on the streets, that's how hard it'll be to earn a farthing!"

Courtney colored painfully. She understood of course the reference to being "on the streets." Sometime in recent years she had registered the awareness that the intimacies she associated strictly with marriage were in fact also provided by certain . . . professionals who . . . There her thoughts broke off. She simply could not go any further. The idea of sharing such experiences with another man, let alone a whole host of them in return for payment, was repulsive to her.

"Don't exaggerate," she snapped, momentarily forgetting the lofty calm that was supposed to characterize her position. "You are not in any danger of losing your position here, provided that you perform your duties properly. That is all we ask."

"You mean," Annie ventured hesitantly, aware that she had angered her mistress, "that I don't have to stop seeing Jimmy?"

"Not as long as you confine such meetings to your off hours and do not let them interfere with your responsibilities."

A moment passed before Annie believed what she had just been told. The relief that slowly spread through her was almost painful to witness. "Oh, thank you, ma'am! Thank you! You won't be sorry, I promise. No one will have a better undermaid. You'll see!"

Uncomfortable with such fervent gratitude, Courtney nodded dismissively. "That's fine, then. Off you go. I'm sure there's much to be done."

Annie couldn't leave without yet another round of thanks, but she did eventually depart in a shower of relieved tears and more devout promises. When she was gone, Courtney sagged against the settee. All in all, she thought she had handled the interview well. But she couldn't deny her distaste for interfering in other people's private lives. Certainly Annie had a perfect right to pursue her fondness for the butcher's assistant. No matter what the difference in their positions, she and Courtney were alike in their desire for a husband and family. No one had suggested to her that she should not see Nigel when they were courting, so why should anyone dictate to Annie?

In the back of her mind Courtney knew full well the two situations were not the same. The birth and affluence of her family and Nigel's provided a certain presumption of privilege. Whereas for Annie and her Jimmy, every tiny assertion of independence and humanity was won at great cost. In the case of the maid, it was the fear that she would be thrown out on the streets.

Courtney shuddered inwardly, thinking of the other girl's suggestion of what that would mean. Surely she was mistaken? This was the London of Turner and Keats and Byron. The center of the civilized world, the hallmark of all that man could aspire to. The glittering regency capital of 1819 was far too refined and enlightened to misuse any young girl. Wasn't it?

Such worrisome thoughts had no place in a clear, balmy day bright with the promise of spring. Putting them resolutely aside, Courtney made her way to the small family dining room where Nigel breakfasted. His blond head was in a copy of *The Times,* but he looked up at her entrance.

"There you are. I wasn't sure you were planning to join me."

Rising, Nigel kissed his wife fondly if lightly, with appropriate regard for the nearby footman, who suddenly evinced great interest in the ceiling.

The interview with Annie was forgotten as Courtney felt the brush of her husband's powerful arm against her. Beneath the light broadcloth of his brown frock coat and white linen shirt, she could feel the sculptured strength of his broad shoulders. Casually dressed for a day in town, he wore soft moleskin trousers tapering from the knee downward to his gleaming boots. A cravat of snowy silk was elaborately secured around his neck, undoubtedly by the indomitable Johnson, who would have tried but failed to convince his master that a stiffly pointed neckcloth was also *de rigueur.*

Unlike the dandies who so enlivened the court, Nigel wore no jewelry except a signet ring emblazoned with his family's crest. Courtney glanced at it, thinking of the gold pocket watch engraved with the same design that she had commissioned for his birthday. Thanks to the considerable allowance specified in her marriage contract, she had no concern about how to pay for it without ruining the surprise.

Waving the footman aside, Nigel pulled out a chair for his marchioness. "Are you hungry?" he inquired. "The kidneys are still warm."

Courtney shook her head. "Mary brought me some of those French rolls and tea. I'm quite full."

The arch look Nigel shot her had Courtney holding her breath. He had already teased her several times about her appetite after making love, and she feared he intended to do so again despite the footman's presence. But discretion won out and he merely nodded.

"Probably a good idea to save your appetite. Don't we have another party this evening?"

"At the Mountjoys', and we mustn't be late because Prinny is going to be there." It still surprised Courtney that she could refer so casually to His Royal Highness, Prince George, Regent of England, Ireland, Scotland, Wales, and a host of lesser possessions. But she managed it with aplomb. Never mind that he was a short, round man devoid of wit or wisdom who had sorely disappointed her from the moment she was first presented to him. He was still the closest thing Britain currently had to a monarch, and as such, he stood at the virtual hub of society.

Nigel grimaced slightly. "I suppose we have to go."

"Why, of course," Courtney exclaimed, surprised that he should even suggest otherwise. It simply wasn't done to miss any of the season's major parties, let alone one at which the Prince himself was in attendance.

"It's just that . . ." Nigel began, only to break off as he rather glumly considered the remnants of his tea.

"Just what?" Courtney persisted gently.

"The same people go to all these things, night after night and year after year. I suppose it still seems exciting to you, but frankly I'm beginning to feel a bit bored."

Not certain that she understood him, Courtney shook her head slightly. "But everyone goes. . . . It's what one does. . . . I mean, if you didn't go to the parties and balls, what would you do?"

"I don't know," Nigel admitted. "There really doesn't seem to be anything else." He was silent for a moment before suddenly smiling. "Don't mind me, I'm just a bit down this morning. Have to see the old factor today, go over the accounts. Bores me to tears, but it can't be helped."

"There's nothing wrong, is there?" Courtney inquired politely, already knowing the answer. Her father was far too meticulous a man to have allowed her to marry into any family with less than impeccable finances. She had no concern about Nigel's wealth, but she did worry at his apparent restlessness.

"Nothing," her husband readily confirmed, "except that I can think of far better ways to spend such a lovely day." A positively devilish smile lightened the silvery glints of his wide-set eyes. "For instance, we might have gone for a stroll in the park, taken a look at the new plantings, found our way into a secluded copse . . ."

Courtney blushed painfully. She lowered her eyes as the memory of a certain day in the Bois de Boulogne swept over her. But they were honeymooners then and in France, where even the most shocking behavior seemed cause for no more than a Gallic shrug. This was England, with decorum the cornerstone of all comportment and the nobility expected to provide an example to the lower classes. Surely not even Nigel would violate that?

"Then it is fortunate we are both otherwise engaged, my lord, else we might lead each other astray."

"I can think of worse fates," Nigel grumbled before recalling himself. Stalwartly he inquired, "What are you planning to do today? Shopping?"

Courtney wrinkled her nose. "My mother dragged me to every modiste in London before our marriage. I have enough clothes to last a lifetime, or at least to next season, when the styles will undoubtedly change. No, I'm meeting Sara. We're going to the circulating library and several of the galleries." A faint wistfulness entered her voice as she added, "She seems to be the only one of my friends who enjoys doing things like that."

Nigel regarded his young wife sympathetically. He was distantly aware that she possessed rather more intelligence and perception than the general run of woman. That had in part influenced his desire to marry her. The thought of a lifetime spent with one of the simpering maidens who thronged to Almack's terrified him. Courtney at least was someone he could talk to, although he had to admit that since their marriage he had found rather different occupations to share with her.

He was not at all surprised that she felt hard pressed for congenial company, and was glad to know that she and Lady Sara Drake were such close friends. Together they could keep each other amused and out of mischief while he was otherwise engaged with the usual manly pursuits of his station. Or so he believed. . . .

—— 2 ——

"I'm so glad we chose today to go to the library," Lady Sara said as her friend was handed into the open phaeton. "I have nothing left to read."

"You could visit the library daily," Courtney teased, "and still have nothing to read. I've never seen anyone so devour a book."

"You go through them rather quickly yourself," Sara reminded her, "or at least you did before your marriage." A teasing gleam entered her violet eyes set beneath arching brows the same shade as her glossy chestnut hair. "I suppose now you have better things to do."

Courtney knew her companion far too well to be surprised by her frank reference to the distractions of the married state. Sara had a decided penchant for speaking her mind, but never had she heard her say anything to deride or hurt.

"Wait until you're wed," she advised sagely. "You'll find yourself falling behind in a multitude of pursuits."

Sara indulged in an unladylike snort as the phaeton picked up speed, turning the corner near St. James's Park. "I'm in no hurry. I have yet to encounter a gentleman with whom I wish to spend more than a few hours, let alone the rest of my life!"

"You will," Courtney averred, her confidence based only in part on the natural instinct to share her own happiness. Sara's distinctive good looks, far removed from mere prettiness, set her apart in any crowd. Taller than Courtney by several inches, she had a willowy figure perfectly set off by a day dress of pale yellow bombazine, the cotton-and-silk blend well suited to the season. Some might think that her mouth was a shade too large, but with the sensitivity of a woman lately awakened to pleasure, Courtney guessed many men would find it enticing, particularly because of the tiny mole nestled in one corner.

Though Sara was no more scrupulous about protecting herself from the sun than the young marchioness herself, her apricot-tinged complexion was just as lovely. She carried herself with an instinctive grace that to one who had known her for many years, as Courtney had, seemed indicative of her whole approach to life. Sara was a naturally serene, giving woman who would make a superb wife and mother. To find her the right partner in such an endeavor was high on Courtney's list of things to accomplish soon.

But just then there were more immediate matters to discuss. Casting a quick look at the coachman, fully occupied with handling the spirited pair of hacks, Courtney murmured, "Have you finished it yet?"

Sara nodded, her lovely face abruptly serious. "I have, and it's magnificent. Far and away the finest book I've read in a long time. There's really nothing I can say to prepare you for it except that it's the product of an extraordinarily original mind. And to think that a woman wrote it! No wonder it has sparked such disapproval. We aren't supposed to have an original thought in our heads, but be content to let the men tell us what to think and do."

Ordinarily Courtney would have been pleased to discuss the merits of women taking more initiative and control of their own lives. It was one of Sara's and her favorite topics, at least when there were no disapproving ears nearby. But the book her friend had promised to lend her was uppermost in her mind. "Then you brought it?"

Sara nodded. Reaching into her reticule, she withdrew a small cloth-bound volume and handed it to Courtney.

Though Mary Shelley's *Frankenstein* had been privately published only the year before, this copy was already dog-eared. It had made the rounds of certain more free-thinking ladies and gentlemen eager to read the tale by Lord Byron's friend. The day might come when it would be generally available, but just then the story of a man destroyed by a monster of his own creation still held the breath of scandal. Courtney looked forward avidly to reading it even as she resolved not to mention the book to Nigel. He would be all too likely to object. The thought of him bringing the same determination he showed in the conquest of her body to the pursuits of her mind chilled her.

The fare at the circulating library to which they both belonged was far blander. Leaving the coachman beneath a spread of poplar trees framing the wide cobblestoned street, they ventured inside. Most of the library offerings consisted of soppy, sentimental tales of young love or, alternatively, pious enlightenment. They were interspersed with horrifying gothic tales of ruined castles and heart-stopping perils confronting innocent heroines. Courtney had found them tedious as a child; now they were utterly intolerable. Passing through the more popular sections swiftly, she and Sara found the few shelves of poetry, essays, and "serious" novels.

Courtney had read a delightful book by an American writer several months before. She hoped to find Mr. Washington Irving's *Knickerbocker* for Sara, and was not disappointed. With that and a copy of Sir Walter Scott's *Ivanhoe* safely in hand, they felt the trip had been worthwhile. Never mind that its true purpose had been to exchange Mary Shelley's work. If anyone asked about their visit, they could display the borrowed books in good faith. The clerk who checked out their choices thought to mention that new copies of the *Lady's Magazine* had arrived, but since both were subscribers, they saw no reason to linger.

"So," Lady Sara began when they were once again settled in the pheaton, "am I correct in thinking you and Nigel are getting along well?"

"Oh, yes," Courtney assured her quickly. "Nigel is an excellent husband." This, at least, was true, though it hardly represented the sum total of her feelings. His generosity and gentleness would be envied by many women burdened with callous, selfish spouses. If only he weren't so . . . overwhelming. . . .

"Did you know before you were married that you would do well together?" Sara quizzed with the persistence of one to whom the matrimonial state was still uncharted territory.

Courtney nodded hesitantly. "It's hard to explain exactly, but right from the moment we met I felt quite drawn to him. There was none of that awkwardness, not knowing what to say, not really understanding each other." She laughed softly, remembering. "I'm afraid a few people were shocked at how swiftly we came to seek each other out, but neither Nigel nor I had any patience with what passes for flirting and coquetry. We just enjoyed being together too much to go through all that."

"I suppose you talk about all sorts of things," Sara ventured.

Thinking about that, Courtney hesitated. In truth, she and Nigel had talked far more before they were married than they did now. Except for sharing her bed each night, when conversation was hardly uppermost in his mind, they were rarely alone together. Nigel was taking a greater interest in politics these days, going so far as to occasionally occupy his seat at the House of Lords and attend a few political meetings. His club, horses, and male friends kept him busy the rest of the time. That was all well within Courtney's expectation of what marriage would be like, but she couldn't deny an ill-defined wish that things were somehow different.

Feeling rather churlish for not appreciating all that she had, Courtney reminded herself that a husband was hardly the same as a friend. She couldn't imagine having the sort of conversations with Nigel that she did with Sara, since they spoke frankly of all manner of subjects. Nor was she certain she would want such closeness with a man. A male presence so firmly enmeshed in the inner workings of her life might destroy what little confidence and self-assertion she possessed. It was probably just as well that men and women moved through different spheres of existence, coming together only in predetermined situations where each knew both how to behave and what to expect.

Somewhat surprised by her own thoughtfulness, Courtney pinned on a bright smile as she firmly changed the subject. Nodding toward the fluted-columned edifice of the Strand Theater they were just passing, she said, "I have read that Edmund Kean will be performing in *Richard III* this season. Perhaps we could go together."

Sensitive to her friend's unexpected withdrawal from what was apparently a touchy subject, Sara courteously followed her lead. It was not her way to intrude on anyone's privacy, even when their acquaintance was of years' standing. "I would like that. The only play I have seen him in was *Macbeth*, which I still remember most vividly."

Talking on about the theater and various players they admired brought the young women to the gallery that was their final stop. Mr. Turner's house in Queen Anne Street was abominably cold and drafty even on so pleasant a day, but the discomfort was considered a small price to pay for viewing his works. Though he exhibited frequently at the Royal Academy, the bulk of his new paintings were kept at his private gallery. There were rumors that he intended to leave soon for Italy, having become enamored of the special quality of light he had found there on an earlier trip. Courtney, who had fallen in love with Venice on her honeymoon, hoped he would do so and that the results would be everything his earlier work promised.

Mindful of the passing time and the fact that they both had to dress for the Mountjoys' soirée that evening, the young ladies stayed only briefly at the gallery. As they were leaving, with Sara deep into an amusing if unflattering anecdote about Prinny, a disturbance on the street distracted them.

A crowd was gathered around the phaeton, at the center of which stood their coachman arguing with a "street keeper," the district policeman charged with daytime patrols, and a flashily dressed man in his middle thirties who was making what could only be described as threatening gestures at something beneath the carriage.

Drawing her most patrician air about her, Sara stepped forward. "What is the meaning of this? Has there been some accident?"

The hapless coachman she addressed shook his head. "Begging your pardon, ma'am. It's no accident. There's a child hiding under there and she won't come out no matter what we say or do." He nodded toward the irate man still prodding beneath the coach with a stout walking stick. "This gent says she belongs to him, run away from somewhere, and he wants her back."

The police officer, who had been waiting with ill-concealed impatience during this explanation, interjected to assure the obviously noble lady that the matter was well in hand. "Nothing to worry about, ma'am. We'll have her out from under there in no time." He, too, joined the other man in reaching beneath the carriage, their combined efforts bringing an anguished cry from the fugitive.

While all this was going on, Courtney had bent down to get a better look at the cause of all the turmoil. Her eyes widened in shock as she beheld a small, skinny girl-child of not more than twelve years dressed in rags and cowering in terror like a helpless animal brought to bay.

There was a livid bruise on one side of the child's face and the marks of tears on ashen cheeks pulled tautly over delicate bones. Her sea-green eyes were sunken and hollow, ringed by dark shadows that spoke of both hunger and pain.

A gasp of outrage broke from Courtney as she took in the evidence of abuse far beyond anything in her previous experience. Instinctively she reached out to the little girl, her voice low and soothing. "There, now, love, don't be afraid. I won't hurt you. Come to me, now, there's a good girl."

The child did not look inclined to obey. She continued to crouch beneath the carriage, her attention now riveted on Courtney with mingled wonder and fear. Only when the flashily dressed man leaned down and made a concerted effort to grab her did the child spring to life. With a cry, she hurled herself away from him, straight into Courtney's outstretched arms.

The touch of the tiny, trembling body against her own stirred the young marchioness deeply. Everything warm and maternal in her nature rose up in an irresistible need to protect. "Get away from her, you ruffian! Lay one hand on this child, and you'll answer to me!"

Glaring at the man, Courtney rose with the girl clinging to her. Her slight weight was hardly a burden, though the desperate grip of her tiny hands was a bit painful. Ignoring the discomfort, Courtney kept both her arms around the child, unconsciously sheltering her with her own body.

The would-be assailant sneered, looking her up and down with what could only be described as definite disrespect. "And who are you to be telling me I can't have my own property?" he demanded angrily. "Leave her go or you'll be the sorrier!"

A large hairy hand lashed out to try to enforce his order, only to be stopped by the coachman snapping his whip down with impressive accuracy. "You can't talk to her ladyship like that," he snarled. "Remember your place!"

The crowd, pleased that the confrontation had passed beyond mere words, pressed forward for a better view.

But the police officer, awakened at last to the dangers of allowing the gentry to be discomfited by a dandified ruffian who should never have ventured out of the East End, called a halt. Interposing his considerable bulk, he drew out his billy club. "That's enough! We'll settle this peaceable-like." Turning to the irate man, he demanded, "You say the girl's yours?"

"Damn right she is! I'd like to know what we're coming to when a man can be denied his own property!" He turned toward the crowd, as though soliciting its support. "None of you would stand for something like that, would you? So why should I?"

There were a few murmurs of agreement, firmly overridden by Sara. "We have only your word for the girl's being any connection to you at all. Certainly she does not seem disposed to go with you."

"That's right," Courtney agreed. Bending her head close to the child's, she murmured, "You can't just stay out here. Will you come home with me?"

Sara, overhearing her, stared in surprise. It was one thing to intervene to protect an abused child, but quite another to assume responsibility for her. She doubted Courtney understood the full ramifications of her offer.

"Are you sure . . . ?" she began tentatively, only to be stopped by her friend's determined nod.

"Absolutely. I wouldn't leave an animal in a situation like this, let alone a child. Besides, the house is certainly large enough. We won't even know she's there."

Nigel will know, Sara thought silently. Not to mention the servants, who would be scandalized. Being distantly acquainted with the punctilious Mrs. Hawkins, she had no difficulty anticipating the frosty climate about to descend on that household. But there was no dissuading Courtney, who faced down the outraged protests of the girl's self-declared "guardian," as well as the genuine concern of both the police officer and the coachman.

"If you really do have a legal right to this child," she informed the man icily, "then produce proof of it to my husband, Lord Nigel Davies, and we will release her to you. Otherwise, don't let me hear of you trying to come near her again."

"There's no law that supports what he had planned for the chit," the coachman muttered, casting the policeman a meaningful look. The officer nodded silently, well aware of how the man had intended to make use of the child. He was accustomed to the darker side of London life, but what the ladies would say when they discovered exactly what they had prevented, he could not begin to guess.

With a regal tilt of her head, Courtney swept back into the phaeton, the urchin still nestled against her. Sara had no choice but to join her friend, nodding to the driver to continue on his way.

She tried several more times to make Courtney realize the impropriety of what she proposed, but the young marchioness would have none of it. As the child watched mutely, her terror-filled eyes moving back and forth between the two grand ladies who seemed like beings from another world, her fate was firmly settled.

By the time the carriage drew up in front of the Davies' town house, Sara was reconciled to the futility of arguing further. However, she had no desire to witness what was certain to be a domestic debacle. Aware that she could learn all the details of what transpired when they met again later that evening at the Mount-joys', she took her leave.

Courtney was too distracted by the child to see anything precipitous in her friend's departure. Grasping a small filthy hand in hers, she swept into the house, ignoring the openmouthed stare of the footman, and proceeded immediately to the kitchens.

The staff was hard at work when she entered. Mrs. Williams, the stout, florid-faced cook, stood over the cast-iron stove preparing a pudding for the next day's luncheon. Two scullery maids worked nearby peeling vegetables and kneading dough. Annie and another upstairs maid were ensconced in a corner, ironing linens.

Somewhat removed from the rest of the staff, as befitted their position as personal servants to the lord and lady, Mary and Johnson sat at a large table. She was stitching at dainty lace undergarments as he polished a pair of riding boots.

At the opposite side of the room, Mrs. Hawkins busied herself at the desk which she considered to be the true nerve center of the house. Her pen scratched laboriously over the menus she was preparing for the following week.

The well-ordered scene continued for several moments after Courtney entered, until one of the scullery girls caught sight of her and her extraordinary charge. A shocked gasp alerted the rest of the staff.

An instant of stunned silence followed as each struggled to come to terms with what had all the earmarks of a mirage. Proper British ladies simply were not seen in the company of street urchins. But there was their very own marchioness actually touching one of the filthy things.

Johnson recovered first. Rising, he approached his mistress nervously. "Ma'am . . . is something . . . wrong?"

Courtney regarded her husband's valet tolerantly. Johnson was of indeterminate age and possessed no distinguishing characteristics. His very blandness might have him set apart were it not for the success with which so many other servants pursued such anonymity. In the months they had shared the same house, she had never seen him exhibit the least emotion. From the top of his unobtrusively groomed head to the bottom of his quietly shod feet, he presented an inviolable facade, quite in keeping with his seemingly tireless, flawless dedication to his craft.

That being the case, it was difficult to know who was the more shocked—Johnson at the apparition suddenly appeared before him or Courtney at the sight of so perfect a servant struck dumb with horror.

He looked so stunned that she was hard pressed not to laugh. Only the knowledge that she faced a difficult situation and had better make an immediate start at handling it caused her to restrain her natural impulses. Very calmly, in the tone of one who takes it for granted she will be obeyed, Courtney said, "The child needs something to eat and a bath, as well as fresh clothes. I thought it best that we take care of all that down here."

The reason was obvious. Now that they were indoors, there was no mistaking that the little girl positively reeked. When she had last felt water on her skin, if in fact she ever had, was impossible to determine. Courtney shivered slightly, wondering what parasites the poor thing harbored. But she beat that thought down as both useless and uncharitable.

Mary did not agree. Dropping her sewing, she squealed, "Lord, ma'am, you can't mean to have her in here! Why, she must be crawling with vermin. She'll give us all sorts of diseases!"

A look Courtney's old nanny would have recognized passed over the lovely marchioness's face. Angrily she snapped, "There's no reason to embarrass the child. It isn't her fault that she's dirty. I'm sure she'll clean up just fine."

Mrs. Hawkins did not see it that way. A hand pressed to her flat bosom, she rose unsteadily. "Th-this can't be happening. A child like that . . . in this house . . . It's . . . it's unheard of!" Her knuckles were white as she gripped the back of her chair. For an unguarded moment the full depth of her dismay, and her poor opinion of any lady who would do such a thing, showed clearly on her stern face.

Courtney frowned. She was all for the servants having opinions of their own, but this had gone quite far enough. Frostily she repeated her instructions regarding the child's needs. When still no one moved to obey, she stamped her foot angrily.

"Are you all suddenly deaf? Or perhaps your wits have fled? Surely I can find no other reason for such incompetence."

At a loss as to how to handle the extraordinary

situation, the servants stared at each other dazedly. Only Annie managed to break through her own surprise to react sensibly.

Stepping forward, she gazed at the little girl as she said, "I'll take her, ma'am. You . . . you shouldn't stand too close to her, just in case."

Though she was touched by the maid's courage, Courtney did not appreciate her suggestion. "Nonsense. I brought her here, so she's my responsibility. Just prepare some food and a bath for her and I'll take it from there."

Annie privately thought that was one of the more foolish assertions she had heard in her short life, but she was too well schooled to say so. As the rest of the staff still appeared incapable of action, she put water on the stove to heat before fixing a plate of sliced ham and bread still warm from the oven. Setting that on the table, she stood back and nodded to the girl.

"Come and wash your hands. Then you can eat."

Eyes riveted on the food, the child struggled only slightly as Annie cleaned the worst of the grime from her fingers. Released, she still held back, as though fearing some trick, until Courtney gently encouraged her to sit down.

Once placed in front of the meal, hunger got the better of her. She seized hunks of the food and stuffed them into her mouth, heedless of the mess she made. A moan of dismay broke from Mrs. Hawkins, who turned abruptly and fled, followed quickly by both Johnson and Mary. Mrs. Williams took shelter behind her stove, where she wrung her hands forlornly and inquired of no one in particular what she had ever done to have such a calamity inflicted on her.

It was left to Annie and the scullery maids to fill the large tin tub. While they did so, Courtney tried to coax the now replete child out of her filthy clothes. But the moment she began to unbutton the tattered bodice, a howl of protest went up.

Baring her teeth, the little girl kicked out desperately.

Only Courtney's swift reaction saved her from being bruised. Dumbstruck, she stood at a safe distance surveying the huddled, whimpering form.

Annie, who, though slightly younger than her mistress, had a somewhat more realistic view of life, bit her lip. She thought the problem was all too clear, though she had no idea how to handle it. Only the memory of that morning's interview and the gratitude she felt to her mistress caused her to act.

Grasping the child by the shoulders, Annie turned her firmly to face her. In a low, firm tone she ordered, "Stop that. There's no reason to be afraid. We're only women here, and none of us will hurt you." When the girl still appeared doubtful, she added, "You're in a grand house, full of proper people. We don't want anything except to get you clean and into fresh clothes. That's not so terrible, is it?"

The child shook her head, but flinched when Annie tried to touch her. The maid considered the situation carefully before suggesting, "I think you might try again, ma'am."

This time Courtney's ministrations were accepted, albeit with wide eyes and trembling shoulders. When the child stood naked before them, neither woman could resist an appalled gasp. Ugly welts covered her narrow back and buttocks. Her ribs and small pelvic bones showed clearly through skin shrunken by malnourishment. A multitude of bruises darkened her neck and torso, extending even to the tiny buds of her burgeoning womanhood.

Easing her into the water, Courtney tied an apron around herself before beginning to gently soap the child's matted hair. As she did so, she asked, "What's your name, little one?"

The whispered response was so faint as to be barely heard. "P-Peggy . . ."

"That's a pretty name. And how old are you?"

A frown of concentration ruffled the girl's brow above

curved brows. "I . . . I don't know for sure . . . twelve, I think."

That was Courtney's guess, allowing for the effects of malnutrition. By normal standards, the tiny body could easily have been mistaken for eight or nine, except for the small breasts and the faint wisps of hair beginning to hide her sex. That the child was aware of her approaching maturity was evident. As Courtney and Annie carefully washed her, she tried vainly to keep her hands and arms over her private parts.

A sigh of relief escaped her when she was at last lifted from the tub and enveloped in a large warm towel. Clasping it tightly, Peggy offered no further resistance as her hair was rubbed dry and brushed. There were no clothes available to properly fit her bony shape, but Annie managed to improvise an outfit by cutting a half-foot off the bottom of a spare servant's uniform and nipping it in with a leather belt of her own. From the child's reaction, the result might have been the loveliest creation ever. She stood in the center of the kitchen, reverently touching the folds of crisp, sweet-smelling cambric as tears formed in her thick-fringed eyes.

"Oh, my," she breathed shakily. "It's so soft, like a kitten's fur." Looking up, she gazed at the women in amazement. "Is it really mine to wear?"

"Of course," Courtney murmured, deeply touched by such thankfulness for garments that were scarcely serviceable. Some faint understanding of what the child's life had been to date was beginning to form in her mind. She swallowed thickly as Peggy beamed a radiant smile that transformed her pinched little face into genuine beauty.

The glimpse of what the girl could be surprised both women. For the first time they saw the promise beneath the evidence of deprivation and cruelty. Peggy's slim, graceful build and satiny skin predisposed her to loveliness. Added to them were perfectly formed features set off by startlingly large green eyes that gave her the look of an enchanting forest sprite. Properly cared for, she would be breathtaking.

But just then she was no more than an exhausted child in desperate need of sleep. "Where can she . . .?" Courtney began, knowing she didn't want to put the girl somewhere alone; yet uncertain how welcome she would be in the servants' quarters.

"There's an extra bed in my room," Annie said. She smiled reassuringly at Peggy as in an undertone she added, "If she comes in with me, I can keep an eye on her. Help her adjust to being here and make sure she doesn't get into mischief."

Courtney nodded gratefully. "That's an excellent idea. For a while at least, I don't think Peggy should be doing any chores. But eventually there will be much she has to learn. I wonder what skills she may have. . . ."

Annie listened to her mistress silently, hoping that in fact there had been no time to teach Peggy the skills for which she had undoubtedly been destined. The child still retained a certain aura of innocence that suggested her "guardian" had only recently acquired her from one of the orphanages or workhouses overflowing with urchins. Or her own parents might have sold her for the price of a bottle of raw gin and the temporary oblivion it would bring.

Not for the first time, Annie reminded herself that she was infinitely fortunate to have her present position and must do everything possible to retain it.

Realizing that Peggy was having trouble keeping her eyes open, Courtney decided any further questions could wait. Taking the child by the hand, with Annie holding the other, she led her from the kitchens. They reached the entry hall to the sound of angry voices. Nigel had just arrived home from his club, to be confronted by an irate Johnson and a hysterical Mrs. Hawkins. He was trying vainly to make some sense of their tirade when he spotted his marchioness.

"What on earth is the meaning of this?" he demanded gruffly. Out of temper by virtue of a bad hand at cards and a particularly tedious meeting with the factor, he positively glowered. Looking very large, very male, and very angry, he stepped forward threateningly.

Courtney, caught up in the need to soothe her husband, did not realize the effect he was having on the child. Nor did Annie, who was too busy wondering how to absent herself. Not until a terrified scream reverberated from the high molded ceiling did anyone notice that Peggy had torn herself loose and was hurling herself through the open door toward the street with desperate haste.

3

"Then what happened?" Lady Sara demanded breathlessly. Leaning closer to Courtney along the bench they shared, she strained to catch every word above the din of the raucous crowd.

"She was stopped, thank God. A man saw her run from the house and heard me shout. He caught her and brought her back." Courtney sighed wearily, remembering the fright of that moment when Peggy disappeared out the door. "His name is Sir Lloyd Paterson. He's here tonight . . . somewhere." She craned her neck slightly, trying to see over the milling guests intent on their champagne and gossip.

"I've heard of him. Isn't he some sort of social reformer?"

"He might be. Certainly he seemed to . . . understand about Peggy." Courtney stared off into the distance, no longer seeing the gloriously plumed lords and ladies crowding the Mountjoys' opulent ballroom. She was back in the hall, cradling a terrified Peggy, who could not bring herself to even look at the men. A few brief questions were addressed to Courtney by the tall, angular lord whose eyes held such gentleness. Her answers must have told more than she realized, for both Nigel and Sir Lloyd appeared very grim as they spoke quietly together.

The upshot was that her husband agreed that Peggy would remain in the house under Annie's care. Before the child was led upstairs, he bent down beside her and spoke very gently. His words, and the significance Courtney hardly dared to give them, still haunted her.

"I know you're very frightened," Nigel had said softly, "but there isn't any reason to be. No one here is going to hurt you or ask anything bad of you. As far as we're concerned, you're just a little girl who needs looking after. You'll sleep upstairs with Annie, and when you're feeling stronger, you'll learn to sew and cook and do other things you'll be proud of. Do you understand?"

Peggy had only managed to nod mutely, still not daring to meet his eyes. When she was led away by Annie, Nigel addressed the valet and housekeeper. His tone made it clear he would stand for no further objection from either of them. "I expect the child to be treated kindly, Mrs. Hawkins. There are to be no further references to her being unwelcome in this house. You needn't deal with her directly if you don't care to, but neither are you to do anything to make her unhappy."

Turning to Johnson, he added the instructions that most puzzled Courtney. "Explain the situation to the rest of the male staff. Tell them to keep out of the child's way until she realizes she truly is safe."

The valet had seemed to understand perfectly; at least he nodded and made some appropriate response. A stiff-lipped grimace was the only sign of his continued displeasure as he went upstairs to lay out his master's evening clothes.

A somber-faced Mary had come to fetch Courtney just then, reminding her she had to dress. She excused herself as Nigel invited Sir Lloyd to share a glass of sherry with him. The low murmur of their voices followed her upstairs.

"Do you have any idea why she tried to run away?" Sara asked, recalling the marchioness from her thoughts.

"I'm not sure. . . . She seemed to be settling in all right until Nigel came home. The servants were agitated, and he got angry. He frightened Peggy somehow."

Sara frowned, wiggling her feet beneath the wide skirt of her pink gauze-and-silk gown. She despised the color, believing incorrectly that it did nothing for her, but was restricted to such modest shades until she married. "There's nothing particularly frightening about Nigel," she mused. "Oh, I imagine he could be terribly dangerous if ever really angered, but he doesn't give the impression of being able to hurt someone without extreme cause."

"I know," Courtney agreed. She moved her fan absently to cool the satiny skin above the low V neckline of her rose taffeta. The dress was cut far more daringly than anything she had previously worn. Only the knowledge that it was the *dernier cri* in fashion had given her the nerve to wear it. Normally she would have been a bit self-conscious despite Nigel's obviously sincere reassurances that she looked glorious. With her thoughts fully occupied by Peggy, she had lost all awareness of herself and of the admiring glances cast her way by the male guests.

"Perhaps it wasn't Nigel himself that scared her," she ventured. "She was also very frightened of Sir Lloyd. I think she may just react that way to any man."

"Because of her experience with that brute who was claiming to be her guardian?"

"I . . . I think there may be more to it than that," Courtney murmured, still not quite willing to put her misgivings into words. She broke off as Nigel and Sir Lloyd returned with the champagne ices they had thoughtfully fetched for the ladies. The light, cool confection was particularly welcome after the usual leaden supper of soups, fish, cold meats, roasts of beef and fowl, stuffed pastries, and grandiose desserts each sweeter and stickier than the last.

The Mountjoys' kitchen staff was clearly adept, but most food was cool before it reached the table, with sauces showing the inevitable tendency to congeal. The seemingly endless stream of dishes left an uncomfortably stuffed feeling no matter how much care was taken to select small portions of some offerings and skip others entirely. Awash with copious quantities of claret, brandy, and Madeira, it was no wonder that many of the guests had difficulty bestirring themselves to dance afterward.

But neither Nigel nor Sir Lloyd had that problem. Observing their new acquaintance, Courtney realized he shared at least one quality with her husband. Both were moderate men who instinctively avoided excess. The brown-haired, hazel-eyed Sir Lloyd was a few inches shorter than Nigel and his frame was sparer, lacking the broad shoulders and powerful torso of the marquess. But he carried himself with the same easy grace and looked more than capable of handling anything the world might choose to throw at him.

Sara certainly seemed to agree. She had barely taken her eyes off the young peer since they were introduced at the start of the evening. Sir Lloyd gave every evidence of returning her regard. As Courtney watched with a satisfied smile, the couple departed once again for the dance floor.

She and Nigel followed them shortly. Drifting in her husband's strong arms to the soaring strains of a waltz, Courtney thought she should have felt utterly content. She had everything in the world a woman could ask for: youth, beauty, position, security, and most of all a loving husband who was easily the most attractive man at the ball. His black evening coat worn over a white waistcoat, pleated shirt, and black silk cravat emphasized the breadth of his shoulders. White breeches of the fashionable heavy cotton fabric called *Marseilles* set off the powerfully lithe line of his legs.

Compared to many of the other men in attendance, his dress was simple. Along with the extravagances of fabric and tailoring the dandies found irresistible, Nigel also eschewed the growing custom of crimping men's hair into elaborate swirls and sideburns. His blond mane was neatly trimmed, brushed back from his broad forehead in the way that gave him the least trouble and left it to look much as nature had intended it.

Nestled against him at rather less than the one-foot distance propriety decreed, Courtney breathed in the intrinsically male scent of sandalwood soap, brandy, and tobacco. To her it was the headiest perfume. Lost in the sensuous pleasures of the dance, she was disappointed when the music ended and her husband indicated it was time to pay their obligatory respects to Prinny.

The bulky, jovial custodian of the throne stood surrounded by a group of eager syncophants whose only purpose in attending was to bring themselves to his notice. What good, if any, that might do them was impossible to predict, for Prinny was known to make spur-of-the-moment judgments that were equally likely to lead to unexpected benefices or penalties.

Most of the court "blades" and "whips" were there— the supercilious young gentlemen distinguishable only by their preferred pastimes of fencing and riding. So also were many of the high-spirited ladies who shunned the company of their husbands and made no secret of their view that marriage was no more than a formality that did not restrict the all-important pursuit of pleasure.

In tacit recognition of the high regard Prinny showed them, the crowd parted respectfully as Nigel and his lady approached. Though neither had made any particular effort to win royal esteem, they were nonetheless its unwitting recipients. The Regent made no secret that he liked Nigel immensely. Had the two men been of equal rank, such affection might have been transformed into jealousy. But sheltered by both birth and vaunting self-opinion, it never occurred to Prinny to be envious of anyone. He went along blithely convinced that he was the wittiest, handsomest, most congenial of fellows, who could well afford to extend the hand of friendship to those lucky few he found worthy.

A benign smile puckered his small round mouth set between ruddy cheeks as he caught sight of them. "Nigel, old bean! I was just wondering where you'd gotten to. Couldn't imagine you missing this turn-to, what with such a lovely lady to show off."

The honor of a slight bow was directed toward Courtney. She curtesied deeply in response. "You are so in demand, your Grace, that we have not been able to get near all evening."

The Prince chortled indulgently. "Know what you mean. There does get to be quite a press. Can't imagine why they all want to talk to an old stick like me."

An expectant pause followed, into which Nigel slipped smoothly. "To bask in your radiance, of course. How often do mere mortals have the opportunity to share such exalted wisdom and erudition?"

Courtney could not quite suppress a shudder at such blatant sarcasm. She held her breath, thinking even silly old Prinny would have to realize he was being mocked. But the Regent's vanity was a bulwark nothing so subtle as irony could overcome.

"I do try to make myself available," he intoned solemnly. "After all, my subjects need me."

And I need some fresh air, Courtney thought anxiously. She tugged surreptitiously on Nigel's sleeve, in the type of signal wise couples developed for just such encounters. He took her meaning, assuring the Prince that they were grateful for his time but could not monopolize him, and withdrew expeditiously.

"Whatever were you thinking of?" Courtney demanded *sotto voce* as soon as they were out of royal earshot. "I know we all like to think Prinny is just a pompous oaf, but he can make a bad enemy."

Nigel sighed wearily, running a hand over his patrician features. "I'm not sure what provoked me," he admitted. "I was just suddenly fed up with all the posturing around a buffoon who, were it not for the accident of his birth, I wouldn't trust to clean out my stables!"

"Not so loud! Do you want that getting back to Prinny before this evening is out?"

"I suppose not. . . . But when I think of it, the worst he could really do would be to bar us from society, and frankly I can think of more terrifying fates."

"More terrifying than what?" Sara inquired, coming up with Sir Lloyd to join them.

Perceiving that he had already upset his young wife more than enough, Nigel adroitly deflected the question. "Than being forced to do without more of that excellent champagne. May I get you some?"

Laughing, Sara shook her head. "I think I've had quite enough already, thank you. My head feels quite full of bubbles."

That remarkable statement coming from her usually sedate friend pleased Courtney no end. If she read the situation correctly, Lady Sara's giddiness had only one cause, and that was standing right next to her in the person of Sir Lloyd, his usually grave visage festooned by what could only be described as a doting smile.

Delighted at the progress of her plan conceived the moment she had seen what a perfect couple Sara and the young peer made, Courtney decided it was time to inflict a little deprivation on the gentlemen. "And my head feels full of pins." She sighed, touching a hand to her elaborately coiffed tresses. "It's these dreadful curls. Do come with me to the cloakroom and see if you can make sense of them."

Sara cast a wistful glance at Sir Lloyd, but friendship required that she comply. Tugged off by a grinning Courtney, who met her husband's knowing glance without a blush, the ladies made their way out of the ballroom and down the wide marble staircase lit by a brace of enormous crystal chandeliers to the suite of rooms set aside for the comfort of female guests.

Several ladies were ensconced on lounges easing their weary feet and chatting desultorily. A young girl, on her first season in society, was bemoaning the slight stain on the skirt of her frock, close to tears as she claimed it had perfectly ruined her evening. A long-suffering mother listened to her silently while making soothing motions with a sponge.

Flopping down at one of the dressing tables, Courtney waved aside Sara's offer of help with her hair and ruthlessly pulled out all the pins holding the confection in place. Long auburn strands tumbled in riotous disorder down her bare back. She sighed with relief, shaking her head in abandon. "Thank heaven! I couldn't have endured that another moment."

Sara eyed her with a tolerance not shared by all the other women in the room. There were several slightly shocked looks, evidence of the prevailing view that a woman's hair was a temptation to men and should therefore be kept firmly under control at all times. "I'm sure you're more comfortable that way, but whatever are you going to do with it now?"

"I have no idea," Courtney acknowledged, finding a brush in the small velvet reticule secured to one wrist. She began to vigorously untangle the gleaming mass even as she asked, "Are you enjoying the party?"

A soft smile curved Sara's generous mouth. "Oh, yes. It's quite the best I've been to all season."

"Does that have anything to do with the fact that it seems to be the first one Sir Lloyd has attended?"

The color that flowed into Sara's cheeks was quite becoming. Lowering her eyes, she murmured, "Perhaps. . . ."

A gleeful giggle greeted her shy admission. "I knew it! The moment I saw the two of you together, I thought you would make a pair."

"We're nothing of the sort!" Sara protested agitatedly. More faintly she added, "At least, not yet. . . ."

Courtney waved aside even the hint of hesitation. "You're going to be, I can tell. You look at each other just the way Nigel and I did."

"That may not mean the same thing," her friend cautioned softly. "Sir Lloyd is very . . . serious. He has a great deal on his mind. I don't think he's given any thought to forming . . . personal ties."

"That can change. Given the right encouragement, just about any man will begin considering marriage. The trick is to make him believe the whole thing was his idea." Smiling unrepentantly, Courtney murmured, "You know what they say. A man chases a woman until he is caught."

"You didn't chase Nigel," Sara pointed out. "As I recall, he did all the pursuing."

"Not exactly. I took care to be where I knew he would see me, to attend those events which interested him. Once his attention was engaged, I certainly offered no evasions." She sighed, remembering the hours of advice she had been forced to listen to from her worried mother. "I suppose there was a certain risk in seeming too available, but I just couldn't hide the fact that I liked him very much. Fortunately, not all men want a coquette. Sir Lloyd, for instance, strikes me as far too intelligent and honorable for such silliness."

"I hope so," Sara allowed, "for as you well know, I have no skill at flirting."

Courtney nodded pensively, trying to work some order from her hair. She could hardly return to the ballroom looking as if she had just emerged from a tumble in bed. Nigel might appreciate the thought, but he undoubtedly would not approve of the ideas it might provoke in others. Sara had secured a length of velvet ribbon from a maid and was helping Courtney effect a more comfortable arrangement when they were distracted by the conversation of a group of ladies seated nearby.

Not even the most courteous regard for the privacy of others could block out the high-pitched complaints of a thin, tense matron who shrilled, "I cannot believe she has the gall to come here. Why, there was a time when Katherine Hampson would not have been allowed in the same room with decent women, let alone be tolerated at a social gathering attended by the Prince himself!"

"*Lady* Katherine Hampson," another of the women

corrected caustically. "Since she got herself married, she has to be accepted everywhere."

A memory flickered dimly in the back of Courtney's mind, something about a scandalous marriage between a lady of questionable character and Lord Philip Hampson, one of the wealthiest and most respected peers of the realm. Because it had occurred during her own wedding trip, she was not familiar with the details. But it was easy enough to imagine the furor such an alliance must have caused within the acutely status-conscious *ton*.

Sara and Courtney were glancing at each other devilishly, amused by the ladies' protestations, when their smiles abruptly vanished. "You can hardly expect proper behavior from a wanton who spent most of her early life in a brothel," declared one of the women. She lowered her voice minutely to an outraged hiss. "Why, I have heard she was one of the highest-paid child whores in London from the age of ten on. The Lord only knows what depravity she's seen!"

Whatever else the more wordly and spiteful ladies had to say was lost on the two friends. Sara's eyes were wide with shock as she confronted a possibility that in all her sheltered, innocent life had never even occurred to her. Courtney, to whom the same thought had come several hours before as she watched Peggy become panic-stricken at the mere sight of a man, trembled at the confirmation of what she had tried to tell herself could not happen in a civilized country. It was one thing to tacitly accept that certain grown women made a business of intimacy; it was quite another to know that children were being used to provide the same services.

"I think," she managed at length, "that we should return to the ball."

Sara nodded mutely. She looked almost ill with shock and revulsion, a fact which did not escape Sir Lloyd. His sensitive features tightened with concern as he caught sight of her. Though Sara protested faintly, he insisted on rounding up her mother and younger brother, to whom he had been presented earlier in the evening, and escorting them home.

Courtney and Nigel left shortly thereafter, the marquess in no way misled by his wife's valiant attempt to hide her own disquiet. He could not be certain of the cause, but he was reasonably sure of what thoughts and suspicions had come painfully together in her mind. Given the events of the morning, when she rescued Peggy, and later, when she witnessed the child's seemingly unprovoked terror, it was inevitable that she would realize what he and Sir Lloyd had known from the beginning.

For men of the world such as themselves, child prostitution was a venal but undeniable fact of Regency life. He could have wished, however, that his wife had been spared such awareness. Reluctantly Nigel warned himself she was far too intelligent and inquisitive to let the matter drop there. Still, he was not prepared for the question Courtney flung at him the moment they were alone in her room.

"Is it true that some men like to lie with little girls?"

The breath was knocked from him. He gaped at his wife in shock, unwilling to believe such blunt, harsh words had come from her sweet lips. When after several moments the question continued to hang in the air between them, he gathered himself sufficiently to reply, "Uh . . . I don't think that is something we should really be talking about."

"Why not?" Courtney demanded, dropping her cloak on the dressing-table bench and turning to face him, her slender body stiff with outrage and determination.

"Well . . . it just isn't. . . . You are, after all, a lady and there are certain matters that aren't fit for your ears." The excuse was offered in a bid to gain time, not out of any real hope that Courtney would desist.

His marchioness's patience proved even shorter than he had thought. With a derisive snap of her head she insisted, "My ears work every bit as well as yours, and my mind is no less capable of grappling with the less savory facts of life. Whatever you may think, the admittedly sheltered existence I have led to date has not turned me into a blithering idiot!"

"I didn't think it had," Nigel shot back, his own anger beginning to rise. He hardly relished being put in such an untenable position. Had Courtney turned to him for comfort and guidance, he would have managed nicely. But to be confronted with a bald demand for facts about the intimate practices of the more disordered members of his sex was a bit much.

"We will not discuss this," he declared firmly, pulling off his cravat and frock coat with an irate yank that would have made Johnson wince. With the consideration that was second nature to him, the marquess had long ago established the practice of not having personal servants wait up for him. The valet was safely abed, as was Mary, who was thereby spared the sight of the delightfully liberated coiffure her mistress had concocted with the assistance of a velvet ribbon and a modicum of pins.

The seemingly unrestrained tumult of gleaming curls had caused quite a stir upon her return to the ballroom. But she was far too absorbed in matters vastly removed from the vagaries of fashion to notice.

Nigel had thought the style delightful, so much so that he was seized by a now familiar but nonetheless intense need to take his wife to bed. Her insistence on such an unseemly discussion had somewhat stilled his ardor, but he had by no means given up the idea. Plucking the ivory-and-gold stays from his waistcoat, he eyed her cautiously.

She made an enthralling picture with her emerald eyes blazing, her cheeks aglow, and agitation causing the low, snug bodice of her gown to rise and fall most distractedly. His attention focused on the ripe swell of her partially exposed breasts, the marquess made swift work of his shirt.

Courtney automatically turned around so that he

could undo the buttons of her gown and loosen her stays. The touch of his hands through the thin silk of her chemise made her momentarily forget her train of thought. But she recovered quickly and persisted.

"If you won't tell me, I shall be left to my own conclusions, which are that as revolting as it may sound, there are men making such use of girls no more than children. That was to be Peggy's fate, wasn't it?"

A deep sigh escaped Nigel. He sensed fatalistically that there was no graceful way to end the matter. Either he steeled himself to explain an utterly repulsive and rather embarrassing matter to his wife, or he lived with the knowledge that she might well seek such information elsewhere. He could not imagine where she might secure it, but that was not a risk he was willing to run.

Taking her hand, he sat down beside Courtney on the edge of the bed. They were close enough for their thighs to touch and the warmth of their bodies to mingle, but she would not have to meet his gaze unless she chose to. It was the same setting he had used to gently but matter-of-factly explain the fundamentals of sexual intercourse before making love to her for the first time. That had worked quite well; perhaps this could be handled as smoothly. His goal was to get the whole thing over with as quickly as possible and put it out of her mind for good.

Accordingly, he began, "All right, I will answer your question. But don't expect me to go into any great detail. As I hope you know, it is not a matter within my experience."

Courtney had never imagined it might be. Nigel was far too decent a man to be anything but revolted by such perversity. Though she could claim no knowledge of the intimacy men and women shared beyond what he had taught her, her every instinct proclaimed that his sexual appetites were thoroughly healthy. Wherever her husband had acquired his remarkable amatory skills, it had been in the company of fully grown, willing women. In the past, she might have resented the idea of him in anyone else's arms. But compared to the alternative she had just become aware of, she could only be thankful for both his normality and ability.

In a very low voice, evidence of the distaste he felt, Nigel went on, "There are brothels in London catering to men with a preference for children. It is my belief, and Sir Lloyd's, that Peggy escaped from such a place. The man you prevented from reclaiming her was most likely not the proprietor himself. They generally keep well away from the public eye. He would have been an employee charged with . . . breaking in the new arrivals, making them docile and submissive to what would be required of them."

"Th-then you think Peggy was . . .?" Courtney choked.

"No," Nigel assured her quickly. "It is likely the child escaped in time, for had her . . . instruction actually begun, she would have been far too closely confined to allow any hope of flight. However, it seems clear that she is well aware of what would have been done to her. Hence her quite understandable fear of me."

Tears filled Courtney's eyes and trickled down her petal-soft cheeks as her tender heart recoiled from such horror. Her throat tightened painfully as she asked, "Why doesn't anyone put a stop to it? Surely the authorities could do something?"

Nigel knew full well that the wealthy, powerful backers of the brothels kept them insulated from legal action. But he wasn't about to reveal such a brutally cynical fact of life to his young bride. Instead, he said gently, "It would be best for you not to think about this anymore. I have explained all I think proper for you to know. Beyond that, I will not go. Be content that you saved Peggy, and put this matter from your mind."

Courtney was tempted to argue that she should be allowed to decide for herself how much she should know about any topic. But having so lately passed from the sheltering care of her father to that of her husband, she wasn't even sure how to phrase the thought.

She kept silent as Nigel eased the remainder of her clothes from her. Aware of her troubled spirit that left her unusually tired and vulnerable, he did not persist in his desire to make love with her. Instead, he merely turned off the gas lamp and slipped into the bed beside her. Holding her tenderly, he brushed away her tears. "Go to sleep, love." A slight smile curved his hard mouth. "You want to look your best for the Carlisles' house party, don't you?"

Courtney sighed. Another party. This one lasting days and packed with all the hectic distractions the *ton* so adored. She had been looking forward to it for weeks, but now her eagerness was replaced by weary lassitude. The conviction grew in her that she was changing in some fundamental way, beyond the usual adjustments that could be expected after marriage. The woman she was becoming was still a shadowy figure, but in the last moments before sleep irresistibly claimed her, Courtney thought she could see glimmers of what was to be that were both exciting and alarming.

—— 4 ——

The country seat of the Duke and Duchess of Carlisle
lay some fifteen miles west of London amid rolling hills
and verdant glens. Built on the site of the high stone
keep from which the duke's Norman forebears had so
effectively controlled all the surrounding countryside,
the house was a sixteenth-century masterpiece of carved
stone and sturdy tile deliberately intended to resonate
with the echoes of bygone times.

In building the palatial manor house to which their
descendants would make only the most minor and necessary additions, the lords of Carlisle had shunned the
gentler, more gracious lines of Elizabethan homes. Even
from the distant perspective of the massive stone gates
which heralded the border of the demesne, the twin
towers looked immense. Connected by a gallery dotted
by leaded windows, the towers framed a large wood-
and-brass doorway set beneath a stone arch. Pendants
flew from the tower peaks, proclaiming that the lord
and lady were in residence.

Courtney had heard about the Carlisles' extraordinary home, though she had never before visited it.
Were it not for their reputation of impeccable hospitality,
she would have expected accommodations as brooding
and uncompromising as the manor itself. But inside,
the fortresslike setting gave way to a gracious, well-
appointed home.

The magnificently proportioned entry hall glowed

warmly in the summer light. Oak wainscoting was polished to a high gleam. Crossed lances and swords were hung above heraldic shields along the walls and up the full length of the wide stone staircase. Priceless oriental rugs lay scattered across the flagstone floor.

The butler's footsteps, as he came to greet them, were soundless. Bowing from the waist, the frock-coated man intoned, "My lady, my lord, you are very welcome. Their Graces are in the drawing room. If you would like to freshen up before joining them . . ."

The slightest incline of Nigel's head was enough to signify his approval. As footmen hastily unloaded the luggage under Mary and Johnson's watchful eyes, the butler conducted them upstairs to the west wing, where a large guest suite had been put at their disposal.

Wall and ceiling moldings stained a rich dark brown were interspersed with white lathed and plastered walls which together gave the rooms an unusually large, lofty air. Casement windows fronted on the formal gardens beyond which a sparkling stretch of river could be seen. Geese and swans floated regally along as peacocks sunned themselves on the banks. Roses, irises, daisies, and chrysanthemums were all in bloom, their heady fragrance wafted on the soft breeze.

The furnishings, though large and ornate, were as comfortable as anyone could wish. Courtney was bouncing on the side of her bed, under the indulgent eye of her husband, who had no intention of sleeping in his own chamber, when Mary bustled in.

"Put those there," the maid directed as harried footmen deposited a trunk and several smaller pieces of luggage. Turning her attention to the undermaid sent by the housekeeper to inquire if anything further was needed, she snapped, "Hot water for a bath, plenty of towels, and a light snack, if you please." Glancing round the room, Mary sniffed audibly, making it clear that ducal residence or not, she expected her own standards to be met.

Courtney and Nigel suppressed a grin. Hearing Johnson issuing his own orders in the next room, his lordship resignedly took his leave. The crotchety valet would be like a bull terrier worrying a bone until he was allowed to undo the damages of the road and restore his master to accustomed elegance.

An hour later, suitably refreshed by a hot bath, fresh clothes, and a meal of thinly sliced cucumber and ham sandwiches, their lord and ladyship proceeded downstairs to join the rest of the house party.

"Do you have any idea who else is here?" Courtney asked softly as she and Nigel were escorted to the drawing room.

"I'm not sure, but I think it's less than the usual mob. Philip said something about keeping this weekend rather more manageable."

"That's a change. Lately it has seemed that everything we do involves a crowd." She blushed faintly. "Well, almost everything."

Nigel chuckled appreciatively before he said, "There may be a reason for not inviting certain people this time. I believe Philip and Elizabeth had some concern about how one of their guests would be received."

"Really? Why ever?" The hint of something untoward sparked her interest. House parties were generally lacking in any but the most ordinary amusements. Even the routine switching of bedrooms that went on between ladies and gentlemen bored with their mates was hardly worth a raised eyebrow, so commonplace had it become. But Nigel's cryptic statement suggested the possibility of that rarest of all treats, controversy. Debating if the mysterious guest might be a statesman of questionable views or an actor cloaked in the disreputable glamour of the stage or even an Irish firebrand who would quote Gaelic poetry and make the case for his homeland's freedom, Courtney swept into the drawing room.

A quick glance around left her feeling decidedly let down. Of the dozen or so ladies and gentlemen gathered there, she saw no one the least bit unconventional. Certainly the Duke and Duchess of Carlisle were everything they should be. His Grace, Lord Philip, was tall and spare with dark brown hair and aquiline features. He had the self-composed air of a man accustomed to authority, just as Nigel did. But at thirty-five, after ten years of ruling his considerable inheritance, he also possessed a gentle, tolerant air that put Courtney instantly at ease.

His wife, Lady Elizabeth, was some ten years younger and less restrained in either manner or appearance. Small enough to come no higher than her husband's shoulder, her figure was slender but well rounded. Dark blond hair was swept back from pert features set off by mischievous hazel eyes. She smiled warmly as Lord Philip greeted them.

"Nigel, old boy! Glad you could make it. It's been an age." The two men shook hands sincerely. They had been at Harrow together, enduring the endless cold baths, Latin chants, and rugby wars that were to turn them into gentlemen. Later still they had served in the same regiment under Wellington and had fought together on the bloody field of Waterloo. It was not an experience either ever spoke of, but it bound them indelibly in a way that went far beyond the ordinary ties of blood and class.

"I'm so sorry we were unable to attend your wedding," Lady Elizabeth said when the other guests were greeted and Courtney had sat down beside her. She glanced at her husband tenderly. "Our son had just been born. I could not travel and Philip was unwilling to leave me."

"That's quite all right," Courtney assured her, remembering the stories she had heard of Lady Elizabeth's close brush with death during her confinement. Looking at the vivacious young woman beside her, it was difficult to believe she had almost lost her life just a few months before. Lord Philip, who loved her dearly, was said to have almost gone out of his mind in the long days he knelt beside his unconscious wife, beseeching

God to spare her. It was no wonder that they had been little in society since then. After such an experience, their own company would be more than sufficient for quite some time.

"I would like very much to meet your son," Courtney added a bit shyly. Some people thought it wasn't proper for any young lady, even a married one, to show too great an interest in children. Prevailing wisdom had it that they were better left to nurses and tutors until reaching the age when they could be expected to behave properly. But Courtney, who already looked forward to the sons and daughters she would give Nigel, felt no such distaste. She sensed in Lady Elizabeth a companionable spirit and was not disappointed.

The young duchess fairly beamed as she said, "You are welcome to accompany me when I visit the nursery." Blushing slightly, she admitted, "I go to see him several times a day, especially when he wants to be fed."

This was unusual behavior indeed. After the distastefulness of pregnancy and childbirth, few noblewomen wanted anything to do with the physical care of their offspring. Courtney did not share that view, since her own mother had played a strong role in her upbringing and that of her brothers. But she was well aware that her attitudes were unfashionable. So, too, it seemed, were those of the duchess.

Fortunately, none of the other ladies present seemed to find such free thinking at all offensive. The half-dozen peeresses, ranging in age from thirty to sixty, were all known to Courtney. She was struck by the fact that none was considered particularly stiff-necked or dogmatic. They were all unusually intelligent women with generous, kindly spirits. Remembering Nigel's warning, she realized this could hardly be a coincidence.

The afternoon passed pleasantly as the ladies played cards and the gentlemen debated the merits of horseflesh. Lord Philip took the male guests on a tour of his stables to show off the Arabians he had just purchased and to discuss the hunt planned for the next day. The

ladies visited the nursery, where they cooed over the
infant heir snuggled complacently in his crib, then felt
free to indulge in a little gossip noteworthy for its
unusual lack of viciousness. Courtney had thoroughly
enjoyed herself when the time came to return upstairs
to change for dinner.

As Mary slipped her into a corselette and ruthlessly
tightened the lacings, she thought she heard a coach
arriving. Only good breeding stopped her from peering out the window for a glimpse of the mysterious
guests.

Dressed in a gown of ivory satin highlighted by emer-
alds which matched her eyes, Courtney felt more than
able to hold her own. But she was disappointed to
discover there was no sign of the late arrivals in the
parlor where everyone else gathered for drinks before
dinner. Lord Philip explained that a problem at the
Home Office had caused their delay, then deftly turned
the talk to cricket. Even the ladies had firm opinions
about which teams had the best chance for a champion-
ship. Conversation was getting just a bit heated when a
movement at the parlor door brought them all up
short.

The man who stood there dwarfed the footman who
hastened to announce him. Though he was well past
forty, he was as lean and muscular as a much youger
man. Black hair sprinkled with silver was neatly trimmed
around weathered features. His gaze, at once inscruta-
ble and uncompromising, swept the gathering intently.

But impressive though he was, it was the woman at
his side who held all eyes. Courtney caught her breath
as she stared at beauty far beyond any she had ever
before seen. How had she managed to miss her at the
Mountjoys' ball? Lady Katherine Hampson would stand
out in any crowd.

Unusually tall for a woman, she was at once graceful
as a willow yet ripely curved to a degree not even her
modest gown could hide. Hair like spun moonbeams

was pulled back to reveal the purity of her oval face and long, slender throat. Beneath thick lashes, her eyes were hidden. Except for a glimpse of violet depths, they gave no clue to the lady's thoughts.

The duke and duchess rose together to greet their guests. Their welcome was quiet and warm, so much so that Lady Katherine barely hesitated when Elizabeth took her hand and led her over to the other ladies. She acknowledged the introductions calmly, mindful of her husband's protective stance not far away.

Whatever other skills they might possess, their graces were expert as judges of character. Not an eyebrow was raised, not a cheek flushed as Katherine was welcomed into the circle. She had met several of the other ladies before and acknowledged them politely. For the others, there was just the briefest hesitation before she realized there would be no condemnation. Tension eased from her, becoming noticeable only by its sudden absence. Smiling slightly, she glanced toward her husband, who shot a look of gratitude at Lord Philip.

With the briefest interruption, the party continued.

Dinner was, as expected, excellent. Turtle and mush-room soups were followed by thinly sliced salmon, roast capon, leg of lamb scented with rosemary, potatoes, cauliflower, pea soufflé, savories, ices, and finally sweets and cheese. Washed down by a sparkling chilled hock ideal for the warm summer night, the meal left every-one relaxed and congenial. Contrary to usual custom, on which Lady Elizabeth made no secret of frowning, the gentlemen did not leave the ladies for their port and cigars. Instead they paid them the ultimate compli-ment of including them in the political talk which inevi-tably followed.

As a bulwark of the Home Office and one of the most powerful landowners in the kingdom, Lord Hampson might have been expected to be staunchly conservative. But he surprised Courtney by expressing a degree of dissatisfaction with the Corn Laws.

"I opposed them when they were first instituted," he said, "despite the arguments that they were necessary to protect our home markets from the intrusion of cheaper foreign-grown grains. But the result has simply been that our poor must pay higher and higher prices for often inferior goods while much land once given over to crops is now deliberately left barren in order to force the cost even higher." He shook his head regretfully. "There is genuine hunger in this country now, which, given the level of our wealth, is inexcusable."

"It isn't the Corn Laws alone that are causing the problem," Nigel ventured. "They are iniquitous enough, but when the ever-increasing burden of taxation is added even on such necessities as candles and tea, the poor are hard-pressed to get from day to day."

"You hardly sound like a Tory," Lord Philip challenged. "If I didn't know better, I'd think we were harboring a Whig."

The guests laughed at the absurdity of such a thought. No man born to the highest levels of the aristocracy with the birthright of immense wealth and power associated with the opposition party, which had gone so far as to suggest that a man without property or position should still be permitted some say in the future of his country. Such radical policies were too extreme even to mention, but they made Lord Philip's sally all the more amusing.

Nigel took it good-humoredly. "I've never involved myself in politics, so I cannot claim to be a great partisan of either party. But only a complacent fool would believe everything is as it should be. We live at a time of great change that is bound to affect all our lives."

"You wouldn't think so when you consider how most people behave," Lady Elizabeth observed. "They seem bent on losing themselves in an endless round of parties and balls. It's as though they sense that if they just slow down for a moment, they will be forced to confront some very unpleasant realities."

Courtney, having just come face to face with the harsher side of life, had to agree. But she did so silently. The frank, serious conversation was beyond her usual experience. She was accustomed to after-dinner chatter more vapid than thoughtful. But she considered closely what Lady Elizabeth had said and was still mulling over it when the last port was downed, the last cigar snuffed out, and the sleepy guests took themselves off to bed.

The next day dawned damp and gray, but with the promise of improved weather in the thin rays of sunlight peering through the leaden clouds. Nigel and Courtney rose early despite the interruption of their sleep occasioned when she woke crying from a nightmare.

The dream, something involving Peggy and the man who had chased her, so frightened Courtney that she woke sobbing convulsively. Her husband's arms were instantly around her, his broad, hard chest warm beneath her cheek. He held her gently, murmuring reassurances, until her fear dissolved. When, exactly, gentleness turned to passion, neither knew. Their lovemaking was swift and consuming. Courtney fell asleep again drowsily replete, without the strength to resent the embarrassing ease with which he controlled her body.

The pack was already out when they reached the courtyard. As justly famous as his horses, Lord Philip's hunting dogs were renowned throughout the kingdom. It was said that let just one catch the merest hint of a fox and they would all be off in a tireless heat across the roughest country until their quarry was brought to ground.

Seated on her own well-behaved hunter, brought along with Nigel's favorite mount, Courtney smoothed the skirt of her burgundy habit. The close-fitting jacket emphasized her small waist and high, firm breasts. A neat plumed hat protected her hair, and gloves kept her hands from direct contact with the reins. Her riding boots, though polished to an impressive shine, were well worn and comfortable. She had ridden since childhood and felt utterly relaxed and at ease in the saddle. But she could not claim any great fondness for hunting and was relieved that the pace would be sufficiently fast to let her drop back from the kill with honor.

The guests toasted each other from the hunting cup of mulled wine potent enough to hold off the chill of even the dankest morning. Hunger was staved off with thick slices of meat pie. As Lord Philip ordered the dogs let loose, the servants and farm laborers assembled to watch the hunt cheered lustily. Freed from the keepers' reins, the hounds began a deafening clamor. Courtney exchanged a rueful grin with Lady Elizabeth, resplendent in a soft yellow riding habit which complemented her glowing complexion. This was her first hunt since her confinement, and she meant to enjoy it thoroughly.

A dog was sent into the untouched wood every serious huntsman maintained on his property, and within minutes a fox was flushed from cover. Bayiny hounds and the trumpet call of the hunt master singaled the beginning of the chase.

Heedless of the rough terrain dotted by high fences, trenches, and springs, the lords and ladies put the spurs to their horses. Clods of earth flew up from pounding hooves as superbly conditioned mounts were given their head. Courtney, who disliked using the spurs, hung back. Her well-behaved mare could be expected to keep a decent speed without undue persuasion.

Nigel rode at the front with Lord Hampson and the duke. Courtney lost sight of them as they vanished over a hillock with the rest of the hunt in close pursuit. The sun, emerging at last from behind the last stray clouds, warmed her enough to undo the high collar of her white silk shirt. She kept a light hand on the reins until a fence cut across her path. Other riders might have sought a gate to go around, but with instincts honed from childhood, Courtney preferred to accept the dare. Crouching lower in the saddle, she urged her mare on. The ground sped by in a blur, then fell away as the powerful horse lifted high into the air, carrying them both smoothly over the fence.

"Good girl! You enjoyed that as much as I did, didn't you?"

The mare whinnied in agreement. Laughing softly, Courtney slowed her to a trot until her breathing returned to normal, then headed her once more in the direction of the hunt.

Two more fences proved no obstacle to the combined skill of a powerful horse and a confident rider. Content with her private contest that involved no hapless fox, Courtney was looking around for another jump when she spied a high stone wall.

Innate caution caused her to ride over and examine it before deciding whether or not her mount could take it. Though larger than anything she could remember attempting before, the wall was surrounded on either side by firm, flat ground that would provide good traction for taking off and landing. There was no danger of the mare coming down in a ditch which would twist her legs under her and possibly risk a break.

Cantering back a distance she judged to be more than adequate, she spoke reassuringly to the horse, letting it sense her own excitement. Only when she could feel the powerful haunches heave under her did she gently urge her forward.

The horse's speed was everything she wished. The sure grace of its lithe form seemed the very embodiment of animal strength. A heady rush of exhilaration filled her as the wall approached. The clear sky hung like a cobalt canopy above her. The distant shouts of the hunt rang through the crystal air. The pristine purity of the summer day combined with her own overriding sense of well-being to banish the faintest suggestion of doubt.

Without a thought of hesitation, she stretched forward in the saddle. The mare's silken mane tickled her cheek, the familiar scent of horseflesh filled her nostrils. Courtney was smiling as the ground rushed up to meet her.

She was never exactly sure afterward what had happened. One moment she was taking the wall with complete confidence, the next she was lying on the other side dazed and winded, her head throbbing painfully and the mare whinnying in dismay.

Rising unsteadily, Courtney managed to reach the horse. Years of training compelled her to see to the animal's need before her own. A moan broke from her as she bent over, running her hand over each of the mare's legs before she was reassured there was no serious damage. At most a tendon might have been pulled. The horse could certainly walk, though it might be wise not to ride her.

Her own condition was rather worse. Her hat had come off in the jump, lost somewhere on the other side of the wall, and her hair hung in disarray around her shoulders. Blood from a cut to her forehead trickled down her ashen cheek. One ankle ached badly and her shoulder felt as though a fully loaded wagon had slammed into it.

Sighing, Courtney realized she had little chance of getting help. The hunt was far away by now. Nigel, accustomed to her aversion to the kill, would not think to look for her for some time. There was no sign of a farmhouse or other habitation where she might go for assistance. The manor house, miles behind her, was her only hope.

Cursing her own foolishness, she took the mare's reins and began slowly to trudge across the field. Before she had gone very far, Courtney realized she had underestimated the extent of her injuries. Pain stabbed through her head so severely as to almost blind her. Warm blood continued to trickle down her face. Her ankle gave way beneath her, sending her to her knees with an agonized whimper.

The mare neighed sympathetically and nuzzled her shoulder, sending fresh waves of misery through her. Tears rose in Courtney's eyes as she contemplated her plight.

It was getting late. She had not stayed to the course set by the hunt but had veered off, following her own impulses, so tracking her would be difficult. The clouds that had so congenially vanished were reappearing, bringing with them a chance of rain.

Sniffling, Courtney told herself not to be lily-livered. She had gotten into this mess on her own, and would get out the same way. But any hope of that faded abruptly when she tried to rise and found that she could not.

The full realization of her peril made her tremble. Were she on her own lands, she would have some hope of the horse finding its way back to the stable and at least alerting others to her need for help. But on a strange manor, the mare might wander for days before being found. And by then she could be well beyond all assistance.

Gritting her teeth, she tried again to rise. A red mist rose before her. On the verge of fainting, Courtney gave up. She sagged against the ground weakly, overcome by pain.

How long she lay there, she had no way of knowing, but when she was next conscious she thought she must be delirious. Through the haze of her exhaustion she thought she heard the mare snorting as another horse approached.

A cool hand touched her forehead. "Lady Courtney, can you hear me? Please try to tell me where you are hurt."

Forcing her eyes open despite the pain, Courtney stared into the worried gaze of Lady Katherine Hampson. She blinked, certain she must be imagining this vision of beauty and safety. But the image did not vanish. On the contrary, it grew clearer, until she could see the concern filling violet eyes and the compassion making lovely features all the more enthralling.

"I . . . I feel . . . Jumping the wall . . . My head . . ."

Lady Katherine nodded quickly. Gentle, skilled hands touched her brow, moved down across her shoulder, and lingered briefly at her rapidly swelling ankle. Leaving her briefly, she dipped a handkerchief in the cool water of a nearby spring, then returned to bathe her wound. Pulling a silk scarf from around her neck, Lady Katherine fashioned a sling for Courtney's injured arm, then gently urged her to stand.

"Just for a moment, long enough to get you on my horse. Otherwise, I'll have to leave you here while I go for help, and I'd rather not."

Courtney heard her as though from a great distance. A hammer was beating dully inside her head. She was swept by a nearly irresistible desire to give in to the spreading numbness and lose herself in blissful unconsciousness.

Well aware of the dangers should she allow that to happen, Lady Katherine was determined to keep Courtney awake. Since she could not sit the horse alone, they had to ride in tandem, with the mare following behind. As they crossed the fields back toward the manor, Lady Katherine kept up a determined stream of conversation.

"Whatever were you doing out there alone? Did you get separated from the hunt?"

"Wh-what . . .? Oh, no, I just . . ." Courtney hesitated. She was reluctant to admit her aversion to hunting even to acquaintances of long standing. But she couldn't quite remember why she should feel that way. ". . . I hate to see them kill the fox. . . . It seems so cruel and senseless. . . . So I always go off on my own. . . . Nigel understands. . . ."

An unexpected sense of affinity swept over Lady Katherine. She sighed softly. "I share your dislike, but in my case I thought it was because one had to be born to the hunt to appreciate it. William is quite accustomed to my disappearing as soon as the chase begins."

"W-William . . . he seems very nice . . . not at all int . . . intimidating."

"Why ever would you expect him to be?"

"Because he's so important," Courtney explained, wishing she didn't have to talk but sensing somehow that she should not stop. ". . . So powerful and respected . . . I remember my father always speaking of him almost with . . . awe."

Behind her, Katherine grimaced. "It is just as well he held such a high position," she murmured. "Otherwise he could never have acted as he did and survived."

She hadn't really thought Courtney would understand her words and was surprised when the younger girl said, "You mean because of your marriage? Yes, almost anyone else would have been ostracized. But . . . even if he had known that would happen . . . Lord Hampson would still have done the same. . . . You have only to see how he looks at you to know that. . . ."

Dimly she wondered when she had become such an authority on the behavior of great lords, but that did not shake her certainty that she was correct. Lord Hampson was clearly passionately in love with his beautiful, courageous wife. Whatever horrors Lady Katherine had known in the past, he would not let them touch their life together.

"I suppose many people refuse to receive you," she went on, aware that she was babbling but unable to stop, "but you mustn't let that bother you. They aren't worth your concern. The people who really do matter wouldn't act like that."

Startled to hear her husband's words echoed by the injured girl, Lady Katherine swallowed hard. She was unaccustomed to honest kindness, except from Lord William, and was not quite sure how to deal with it.

She remained silent as Courtney went on, "Those women at the Mountjoys'—they make themselves as ugly as their words. . . . I wouldn't have listened to them except for Peggy. . . ."

Distracted from her embarrassment at what the women must have been saying, Lady Katherine murmured, "Who is Peggy?"

"The little girl I found. She was hiding under Sara's coach. So ragged and filthy . . . terrified . . . that horrible man was trying to get her. I didn't understand . . . never heard of such places . . . didn't know until I heard those women talking. Then I realized why she was running away . . . why she was so frightened of Nigel . . . Sir Lloyd . . . any man."

"What did you do with her?" Lady Katherine asked sharply, swept by horror at the thought of another child being made to endure what she herself had lived through.

"I took her home, of course." Courtney smiled faintly despite her intense pain. "Servants didn't like it . . . but I insisted. My house, after all . . . mine and Nigel's. He talked to her . . . reassured her . . . He's good at that. She'll be safe there and she can grow up as she should."

A long sigh of thankfulness escaped from Lady Katherine, followed swiftly by astonishment that there were other members of the nobility besides her husband who were capable of acting with generosity and compassion.

"But there are so many more children," Courtney mumbled, her voice growing slurred. "So many . . . Need to do something . . . help somehow . . ."

Lady Katherine barely heard her. Gazing ahead through the gathering dusk, she was immensely relieved to see the high towers of the manor house over the next hill. Though she was reasonably certain that Courtney was not critically injured, she knew the young marchioness had to be gotten to bed quickly. When she caught sight of the horsemen galloping toward them from the house, she almost cried out in relief.

5

"I'm not trying to discourage you, Courtney," Sir Lloyd insisted. "I am simply concerned that you may not grasp what you're getting into."

"How can I when I've only just become aware of the problem?" Courtney countered softly. Glancing from the young peer to Sara, she asked, "Surely you understand? I saw the look on your face when you realized what would have happened to Peggy if we hadn't intervened. But she is only one child, and there are countless more no one is helping. Do you want that to continue?"

Sara shook her head sorrowfully. Seated beside Sir Lloyd in the drawing room of the Davies town house, she looked the picture of a lovely, serene English maiden. Not a hair was out of place, not a wrinkle marred the grace of her pale blue day dress of delicate merino wool trimmed with lace. She was the perfect complement to her friend's more vibrant beauty. But beneath her unruffled facade, Sara's thoughts were in turmoil.

For almost a fortnight, since her return from the Carlisle house party, Courtney had talked of nothing except what could be done to help the unwanted children of London threatened with Peggy's fate. Nigel had been surprised but not particularly displeased when she announced she wished to form a Ladies' Aid Committee to look into the problem. He was too relieved by her quick recovery from the riding accident to deny her much of anything. Besides, he was well accustomed to noblewomen involving themselves in good works. Since his lovely young wife seemed unable to amuse herself with fashion and gossip, he could well understand that she would need some pursuit to keep her from becoming bored.

So far, so good. But the marquess was too busy with his own occupations to notice what Sara could no longer ignore. She was deeply concerned that Courtney intended to throw herself headlong into what at best would be a frightening situation and might actually become dangerous. Hence Sir Lloyd's presence and his quiet efforts to fulfill Sara's request that he somehow rein in her friend.

"I wish," he continued gently, "that you would reconsider my suggestion of a house in the country. It would do these children a world of good to be taken out of London."

"I understand why you say that," Courtney said. "But aren't several organizations already running such houses outside the city? They are able to reach only a small percentage of children, and they have no effect at all on the actual neighborhoods where the problem is rooted."

She did not offer the source of this information, correctly presuming her friends would believe she had heard it in some drawing room. In fact, her knowledge of the country houses came from Lady Katherine. The day after Courtney's fall, when she was sufficiently recovered to have calmed a distraught Nigel and received permission to have guests, the two women had spoken long and earnestly in her bedchamber. Once convinced that the marchioness was no longer delirious and that she was sincerely horrified by Peggy's plight and wanted to do something to prevent it from happening to other children, Lady Katherine unbent to offer what help she could.

Her own charitable efforts were absorbed by the refuges in the countryside which Lord Hampson funded and which provided an outlet for her overriding need to help without drawing her into areas of the city that still had the power to terrify. Therefore, her assistance to Courtney amounted primarily to advice. But because she spoke from a level of experience no other woman of her rank could match, what she said proved invaluable.

Quietly, without the slightest surrender to self-pity, Lady Katherine outlined the course of her life up to the time she met her husband. She explained to a white-faced Courtney how children came into the brothels and, glossing over the details, told what happened to them there. She aslo offered some insights into why so little had been done to stop the appalling practice of child prostitution, including how the suspicions of the poor made even the most well-intentioned efforts difficult.

Any ideas Courtney had about what really constituted a lady crystallized as she listened to Lady Katherine. Looking at her, it was impossible to guess the degradation she had suffered. Only the glimpse of sorrow lurking in her violet eyes, which no amount of happiness would ever fully erase, gave evidence to what her life had been. Lord Hampson's insistence on marrying the woman polite society thought should never have been more than his mistress had been a rare act of courage. Courtney silently applauded him even as she vowed to do everything she could to stop Katherine's story from being repeated in other innocent lives.

Watching her, Sir Lloyd sighed. Not for the first time he reminded himself of the futility of underestimating the beautiful marchioness. For a man who prided himself on being without prejudice or preconception, he was having a hard time accepting the idea that so lovely a woman possessed a keen mind and strong will many men would envy.

Studying her as she sat across from her guests on a satin-and-brocade settee, the soft late-spring light filtering through gauze curtains to frame the perfection of her oval face and glorious hair, he felt a stab of envy for Nigel. It dissolved beneath his awareness of the quiet young woman seated beside him and of all she was coming to mean to him.

Aware that he was about to earn Sara's displeasure, Sir Lloyd said, "Very well, if you are decided against a country house, then I suggest you consider using your funds to purchase a property in the East End."

"Wh-what?" Sara gasped, her stomach plummeting at the sight of Courtney's quick nod.

"That's exactly what I've been thinking," the marchioness stated. "We could create a sanctuary in the middle of that human desert. Give people a safe, hospitable place to come for food, shelter, help in finding work, all sorts of essentials. And for every person we aid, we will be creating a living testimony to our effectiveness that others in the neighborhood won't be able to help but see."

"Surely Lloyd doesn't mean we should actually be right in the East End," Sara ventured in the faint hope that she had misunderstood. "Wouldn't somewhere on the edge, near enough but still in a good area, be more suitable?"

"No," Courtney and the young peer said together. He courteously deferred to her explanation.

"It will be difficult enough to convince these people to come to us without forcing them to leave their own neighborhood and venture into places where they feel distinctly unwanted and uncomfortable. Moreover, it will be much harder for us to understand their needs and provide accordingly if we maintain such distance between us. To help the greatest number of people possible, we must be right in there among them."

"Nigel will never agree," Sara began, only to be stopped by the firm look that flitted across the marchioness's face.

"It is not Nigel's decision." Courtney purposefully ignored the shocked looks of her friends, who were only beginning to sense the full depth of her determin-

ation. In truth, her firmness surprised even herself.
Never before had she made such a serious choice with
a view to sticking to it no matter what opposition she
might encounter. Not even the thought of Nigel's inevitable anger, disquieting though it was, could dissuade
her.

Deep inside, she understood that if she gave in on an
issue that affected her so profoundly, she would never
be able to take any measure of true responsibility for
herself and her own fate. For a variety of reasons
which she suspected had to do with events since her
marriage, particularly the discovery of how easily Nigel
could control her physically, it was essential that she
reclaim some portion of herself without delay.

Her resolve had only strengthened when she and
Sara met again several days later to accompany Lloyd
on a tour of the property he had, despite second
thoughts and much hesitation, found for them.

The ladies wore their plainest, most durable clothes,
left their reticules at home, and took care to be shod in
heavy boots. But despite such precautions, they were
not at all prepared for the onslaught of filth, noise, and
despair that assaulted them the moment they entered
the infamous East End.

For all the ressemblance it bore to the London she
knew of wide boulevards, vast parks, and wealthy, secure men and women, the scene before Courtney might
have come straight out of hell.

The sun itself seemed not to come near this cesspool
of human suffering. The ramshackle wood and mortar
buildings were constructed so closely together over the
narrows streets that they blocked out almost all light.
Perhaps the lack of visibility was somewhat merciful,
for what little she could see spoke of degradation beyond
imagining.

Men, women, and children alike were all dressed in
filthy rags through which rancid, sore-infested flesh
could be glimpsed. Mounds of garbage were piled
everywhere, the stink of their rot adding to the all-

pervasive odor of urine and feces in the open sewers. Rats too bold to wait for nightfall browsed among the waste, challenging scrawny dogs and pitiful children for a bit of gristle or bone.

As though it were not enough for the eyes and nose to be so assailed, the din was incredible. So many people clustered so intimately together created a clamor that seemed to reach to the very heavens and an impervious god who gave no sign of hearing them.

Sara shrank against Sir Lloyd as a gap-toothed beggar reached out a grime-encrusted hand to her. "Got a ha'penny, miss?" he croaked.

Their guide, who had sensibly brought several hulking grooms along, waved the man off. But not before Courtney said, "Surely we could give him something . . . ?"

"If we do," Sir Lloyd warned, "we'll have a hundred like him down on us in a moment. When you come here, you have to make choices. Do you react to the natural horror and sympathy you feel and try to give immediate help, or do you concentrate on something larger and more lasting?" Not unkindly, he added, "Decide now, because you will have to go on as you begin."

Courtney gazed at the beggar, who lacked the will to keep his attention focused on them more than an instant. He had returned to sucking the empty gin bottle cradled in his scrawny arms.

"If we give him money," she asked quietly, "will he spend it on drink?"

"Most likely," Sir Lloyd said. "The people here are hardly insensitive to their plight. They know full well the horror that surrounds them. Many seek oblivion from it at the bottom of a bottle."

Keeping her face rigidly expressionless, Courtney passed on down the street. Only her deep green eyes showed the extent of her compassion and distress.

The building Lloyd had found for them was at the center of the squalid district. Once it had served as a small warehouse, but with the decline of the neighborhood it had been abandoned by its owners and had decayed into little more than an empty, barren shell. Lacking even interior walls or a serviceable roof, it was one of the few empty buildings in the area that did not attract squatters. For a fairly modest fee to the city, paid through Lloyd in his capacity as business representative of the Ladies' Children's Aid Committee, the property was secured for their use.

"The men are digging drainage ditches and laying a water pipe," Sir Lloyd explained, gesturing to a group of laborers. "Tomorrow they'll patch the roof and refit the windows. Beyond cleaning out as much of the grime as possible and whitewashing the walls, that's about all we have funds for right now."

Courtney nodded, well aware that the essential repairs were stretching their slim budget to the limit, leaving little margin to hire staff. For a time at least, the shelter would have to be run by volunteers. "We will manage," she assured him rather more confidently than she felt. "I am hopeful that some of the ladies who have joined the Aid Committee can be persuaded to volunteer their time here."

Sir Lloyd was privately doubtful such would ever be the case. Very few women had Courtney's and Sara's courage. They might be willing enough to attend a few meetings in elegant drawing rooms and contribute a few pounds from their extravagant personal allowances. But he found it difficult to imagine many would agree to come anywhere near the devastating reality of the East End. Nor did he truly believe Lord Nigel would be agreeable to the idea of his wife working among such squalor and depravity. In this, he proved eminently correct.

Courtney had only just returned home, white-faced and shaken after her trip, but still resolute, when she was confronted by her outraged husband.

"Where have you been?" Nigel demanded grimly the moment she set foot in the entry hall. Ignoring the startled look of the footmen, he went on relentlessly, "I

heard some ridiculous story about you visiting the slums with Sir Lloyd and Sara. Just what the hell is going on?"

Courtney sighed warily. It wasn't difficult to guess who had told Nigel. A glimpse of Mrs. Hawkins scurrying down the kitchen steps with a malicious smile on her prune-shaped face was enough to tell the tale. The housekeeper would have taken considerable pleasure in informing the marquess of his wife's activities. She had hoped to tell Nigel herself, in her own way, and bring him round to at least tolerating her efforts. But now it seemed she was too late. Glaring down at her, hands on his lean hips and his high cheekbones slightly flushed, he was in a foul temper.

Acutely aware of the servants, who though discreetly out of sight were still undoubtedly listening, Courtney said, "May we discuss this upstairs?"

Nigel frowned, but agreed. His anger did not abate in the short time it took to reach their quarters. Slamming the door shut behind them, he confronted his wife.

"Now, tell me what you think you're doing. How could you be so foolish as to go into that cesspool?"

Confronted by such scornful disapproval, Courtney snapped, "That *cesspool,* as you call it, is filled with people who need help. Someone has to go there."

"Not my wife! Don't you have any idea at all of what is proper for one of your position?"

"Don't you care about anything but propriety?" Courtney countered, her own temper rising to meet his. "Those are human beings there, who need many of the same things we do but who do not even have the most basic requirements for a decent life. You may be willing to ignore that, but I am not!"

"I'm not ignoring it! I said you could form that Ladies' Aid Committee, didn't I? I didn't complain about all those damn meetings, in fact I wrote a rather large check at your request. Why the hell can't you be content with that?"

"Because it isn't enough! You can't just salve your conscience by giving money. The problem is too severe for that. Unless compassionate people intervene personally, the horrors of the East End will never even be lessened, much less eliminated."

Facing off in the center of the bedroom, the marquess and marchioness stared at each other furiously. Each was absolutely convinced of what was right, and neither would unbend an inch.

Finally Nigel shook his head disbelievingly. "You're still such a child. You have no real idea of what you're dealing with. You just think you can go down there playing Lady Bountiful and everything will be all right."

Indignant at what she considered his negligent dismissal of her intelligence, Courtney sputtered, "I don't think any such thing! I know how difficult it will be to accomplish anything of worth. But at least I am willing to try. You won't even do that!"

"Because the situation won't change!" Nigel exclaimed. "If you had any sense at all, you would know that. We live in a world where power and wealth inevitably breed corruption. That's just the way life is."

"You mean that's the way you want it to be!" Pacing back and forth, Courtney clenched her hands so tightly that the nails bit into her palms. Dimly she told herself she was being foolish. She should be making every effort to placate Nigel. But instead, her nerves, already strained by the horrors she had seen in the East End, were closer than ever to breaking.

"Tell me," she demanded harshly, "some of the men who make use of children like Peggy, do they belong to your clubs?"

Taken by surprise, Nigel hesitated. "I don't know. . . . Perhaps."

"Do you play cards with them, debate the merits of horseflesh, lay wagers on votes in the Lords?"

"Courtney, I don't see any point to this."

"Then you condone their behavior, if only tacitly! If you would refuse to be seen with such perverse excuses for men, if they were barred from society and held up to public condemnation, you would see how long such practices continued."

"That's ridiculous!" Nigel insisted. "Such things have always existed and always will. If you were better informed about the world, you would know that."

"I could be the sagest person in existence, and I would still never accept such an obscenity!" Coming to a stop before her husband, Courtney gazed at him entreatingly. "Oh, Nigel, don't you understand? Little girls like Peggy are being robbed of far more than their bodies. Their very souls are being shattered. It's bad enough when such things happen to grown women. But to children! They're completely helpless and vulnerable. How can anyone stand by and let them be so brutally hurt?"

Touched by her obvious sincerity, Nigel relented a bit. His hands caressed her shoulders gently, one finger stroking the smooth line of her jaw. "I don't like it any better than you do, believe me. But there is nothing to be done. If there were, it would have happened already."

He hoped she would accept this and let the matter drop. But Courtney had a strength of will neither of them had really begun to suspect. Determinedly she shook her head. "If everyone has given up the struggle before it even begins, then of course nothing will change. Public outrage must be aroused . . . an end brought to the conspiracy of silence that protects these villains—"

"Stop right there," Nigel ordered. "Whatever you may think, these *villains* are among the most powerful and in some cases the most respected men in the kingdom. What they do privately is strictly their own affair. I will not have you even contemplating any effort to expose them."

"Then you do wish to protect them! Where do you draw the line between actually taking part in such loathsome practices and merely tolerating their existence?"

"I draw the line," Nigel snarled, his voice becoming dangerously low, "in my own bedroom with my own wife! I will not be taken to task by you or any other woman! The dealings of men are beyond your provience, thank God, and will forever remain so!"

In her agitated state, it seemed to her that he could not have made himself clearer: her husband had only contempt for her convictions and was willing to cynically tolerate practices she found evil beyond belief. There seemed only one course left to her.

Drawing herself up, Courtney faced him stalwartly. "Then it seems we have nothing more to say to each other, my lord. Please leave."

"What!"

Marching over to the door separating their bedrooms, she thrust it open. "I said to leave. I will not have you near me. Not while you tolerate such foul perversity as a mere quirk of behavior among your peers!"

For a moment, she thought he intended to refuse. Nigel stalked over to her, holding on to his temper by the merest thread. In that instant she became aware for the first time of just how large and threatening he could be. If he chose to enforce his husbandly rights, she did not have a prayer of stopping him. Her stomach tightened with fear.

Staring down at her, his eyes glittering with silver fire, Nigel growled, "Be very sure, wife. Once I leave this room, I will not easily return. You will have to beg for my touch."

Rage washed out dread. "Never!" Courtney hissed. "Nothing on earth could make me want such a cynical, callous man who gives his approval to the worst depravity!"

"Fine sentiments!" Nigel sneered. "We'll see how well they keep you warm. Just remember, you made this choice and you will live with it. God help you if I hear you try to assuage the passion of your nature that I know so well with any other man. For then you will truly learn what cruelty means!"

In the instant before he slammed the door, Nigel

added ruthlessly, "However, since this absurd estrangement is of your doing, there is no reason for the same restriction to apply to me. The congenial ladies I thought I had said farewell to are about to renew my acquaintance!"

6

By the end of the following week, Courtney was ready to admit that Sir Lloyd's unspoken doubts about the help she could expect from the noble ladies of her acquaintance were proving true. Try though she did, she could not convince any to help out at the shelter. It fell to her and Sara to organize the meager kitchen, unpack and shelve what supplies they were able to gather, set up the beds, and generally make the place habitable. Each night she dragged home aching in muscles she had not known she possessed.

Exhausted as she was, sleep proved elusive. Hour after hour, she lay staring up at the silken bed canopy, her mind torn between worries over the shelter and her growing despair over Nigel. He had not come near her since the night she ordered him from her room. The few times she had been home for dinner, he was out. Were it not for the occasional sounds of movement in the next room, always very late at night, she would have thought he had ceased to live under the same roof.

Over and over she fought down the desire to try to heal the breach between them. Nigel must realize that right was on her side. But somehow knowing that did nothing to ease the ache deep within her that intensified with each passing day. She longed for the sound of his voice, the touch of his hand, the warm security of his arms. Fruitlessly she struggled against memories of the passion they had shared. His threat to seek his pleasure elsewhere was a constant source of pain, despite the contradictory feelings she had always had about his mastery of her body.

Where was he now? she wondered as yet another night slipped away in deadening worry. At his club playing cards and drinking with men who also saw no reason to go home? Or was he involved in more private pursuits? Pain stabbed through her as she recoiled from the thought of her husband in another woman's arms. Yet if he was, could she completely blame him? Wouldn't at least some of the fault be hers?

Sighing, Courtney gave up her efforts to sleep. She lit the silver gas lamp beside the bed and reached for a book. It was a treastise on social reform that Sir Lloyd had recommended, with the warning that like most of its kind, it was pedantic and boring in parts. "But it's worth wading through," he assured her. "There is some practical discussion of meeting the needs of the poor which you may find helpful."

Courtney hoped so. The effort required to keep her mind on the long, turgid passages ought to reap some reward. At the very least, she thought with a faint smile, it might cure her insomnia.

It did not. She was still wide-awake an hour later when a sudden sound from the corridor brought her bolt upright in bed. The heavy thump of wood against flesh was followed by a muted curse.

Nigel! Without stopping to think, Courtney tossed back the covers. She covered the distance to the door in quick steps, flinging it open in time to find her husband rubbing his shin and scowling at the offending piece of furniture that had gotten in his way.

Wearing an ebony silk cape over a black velvet evening coat and startling white silk shirt, with his golden hair rumpled and his cravat askew, he looked devastatingly handsome. Her throat tightened as she took in the wide sweep of his shoulders and chest, the tapering leanness of his hips, the sinewy strength of his thighs.

He was so uncompromisingly male, so familiar to her in the most intimate ways. Yet he might have been a perfect stranger for all the interest he showed her.

"What the hell are you doing awake at this hour?" Nigel snapped. Icy silver eyes wandered over her contemptuously, barely hindered by the thin silk of her nightgown, through which the rosy tips of her breasts and the slender, gently curved outline of her body could be clearly seen. "Can't you sleep, dear wife?" he drawled derisively. "I thought the pure and righteous never had that problem."

The contempt in his voice tormented her. Reeling under its impact, she instinctively lashed out in response. "I thought you might have been hurt and needed some help. But I can see I was mistaken. It would take more than a few bruises to make you feel anything!"

Whirling, she started back into her room, intending to close and lock the door behind her. But Nigel was too swift. A steely hand gripped her arm, pulling her back.

"So you think I don't feel? Your memory must not be very good. Or don't you want to remember all we felt together?"

The accusation was so close to the battle she had waged with herself only a short time before that Courtney flushed. Trying vainly to get free, she hissed, "My memory is fine! I have no trouble recalling your promise not to come near me again unless I asked you. In fact, you didn't say *ask*, did you, my lord? Your vow holds until I *beg* for your touch, which will be never!"

"Indeed?" he murmured, bending his proud head to nuzzle the silken skin of her throat. "Do you really want a lifetime without this . . .?" His large warm hand cupped her breast, the thumb just brushing her nipple to bring it to urgent life. "Or this . . .?" His mouth closed over hers, hard and demanding, taking her by surprise just long enough to force open her lips. The moist velvet heat of his tongue plunged within. Long, deep strokes reminded her forcefully of the other, far greater joining they had shared.

Courtney responded helplessly. Even as her mind cried out that she would not let him do this to her, her body answered with a will of its own. Arching against him, she moaned softly. Her lips parted further in a tiny gesture of submission that was instantly rewarded by even more enthralling caresses.

He knew so well how to move her. The wild, unabashed sensuality of her nature, which he had first awakened and then finely tuned to himself alone, overrode all thought and reason. She became a creature of sensation, swept along by the undulating ripples of pleasure he unleashed within her.

Until an unexpected awareness penetrated the haze of her delight. The cloying scent of tuberoses filled Courtney's breath. She drew back slightly, not yet fully conscious of what caused her unease but sensing something was very wrong. The perfume, clinging to Nigel's evening cloak, struck her again, abruptly bursting the bubble of giddy bliss.

"Stop it!" she cried out painfully. "How dare you do this! If you think I want the leavings of some whore, you are badly mistaken!"

"Hell's fire, what are you talking about!" Pulling back, Nigel stared down at her angrily. Hard lines were etched into the sculptured planes and angles of his face. His mouth narrowed tautly. As she watched wide-eyed, a muscle jumped along the ridge of his jaw, faintly shadowed by a night's growth of beard.

It took all her willpower to remember the skillful trickery with which he had brought her almost to the point of surrender. After already slaking his lust with another woman!

"If you have any discretion at all, my lord," she said frostily, "you will require your paramours not to wear such powerful perfumes." A sneer distorted her lovely mouth as she struggled to hide her pain. "You fairly reek of it. I can't think what Johnson will say. He may be well advised to simply burn that cloak."

So caught up was she in her own suffering that Courtney failed to note the look of mingled shock and anguish written clear in her husband's eyes. Before the tears she could barely hold in restraint swamped her rigid self-control, Courtney fled. Nigel tried again to stop her, but being dazed as much by her joyful responsiveness as by the stunning accusation which followed, he was slow in his efforts. Even as he called her name, his marchioness disappeared into her room, leaving him alone in the dark, chill corridor.

Sir Lloyd was a worried man. Though the East End Children's Shelter continued to make surprisingly good progress, he was beginning to suspect that he had inadvertently embroiled Lady Courtney in a matter which could bring her only unhappiness.

That conclusion was not reached lightly. In the fortnight since the shelter began to attract the first of what quickly became a slow but steady trickle of desperate children, he had watched the lovely marchioness carry on stalwartly despite an inner turmoil that only the most insensitive could miss.

Violet shadows lay like bruises beneath her eyes. Her face was pale and rigidly composed. She was losing weight, to the extent that the simple dresses she wore to work in hung on her increasingly slender frame. To the children and the few adults who ventured in, she was kind without being cloying, offering sensible help free of either pity or condemnation. He had seen her bathe the infected scabs of an infant, remove the lice from a little boy's hair, and bandage the rat-bitten arm of a little girl, all with quiet calm that could only stem from the greatest self-discipline.

The restraint she was putting on herself and the almost desperate way she worked to exhaustion each day convinced both Sara and Sir Lloyd that something had to be done. Their friend's estrangement from her husband was now hardly a secret. With Courtney spending every possible moment at the shelter, she and Nigel were no longer seen together socially. That alone was enough to give rise to rumors about the well-being of their marriage. But added to it was the marquess's frequent attendance alone at the more raucous affairs where the only ladies present were of the *demimondaine*.

The man's a fool, Sir Lloyd thought caustically even as honesty forced him to admit such was not his impression of Sir Nigel. On the contrary, the peer had struck him as unusually intelligent and capable. He and Courtney seemed admirably matched and, until a few weeks ago, gave every appearance of being genuinely fond of each other. Such relationships were rare enough without seeing one destroyed by what must surely be a misunderstanding.

"If we leave it up to them," Sara had insisted as she and Sir Lloyd snatched a rare moment of quiet at the shelter to converse privately, "things will only get worse. I love Courtney like a sister and I am very fond of Nigel, but they are both as stubborn as mules. Neither will bend an inch, unless someone pushes them."

It came as no surprise to Sir Lloyd that "someone" was supposed to be him. Incapable of denying the lovely Sara anything, he gave in resignedly and girded himself for an interview with Sir Nigel.

White's Club, to which they both belonged, was the obvious choice for a meeting place. Sir Lloyd made his way there on a promising spring morning when the trees already hung heavy with a hint of the approaching summer and the drone of flies clustering about the sturdy carriage horses and sleek mounts that crowded St. James's Street gave a slumbering air to the usually bustling city.

True to form, the club's bow windows fronting on the street were crowded with the usual assortment of whips, rips, blades, and dandies passing languid comments about the passersby. Sir Lloyd guessed correctly that he would not find the marquess among them.

Instead, he sought him first in the gaming rooms, which despite the balmy weather were already crowded. In addition to the betting on cards and horses, numerous wagers were put down on every manner of contest, from who would be the next man to walk into the room, to the likelihood that a particularly notorious lady was breeding, to the possibility that it would rain three weeks from Saturday.

Sir Lloyd sighed inwardly. It was difficult for him to believe he had once been like them, too bored and directionless to do anything but seek amusement. Ten years before, while in his early twenties, he had made a deliberate choice to break with that life and devote himself to pursuits that, thankless though they might be, had the advantage of occasionally resulting in an actual accomplishment. His birth and position continued to guarantee him membership in the most elite of London's clubs, but he still felt out of place there.

Rather to his surprise, Nigel was not to be found in the gaming rooms. Aware that he could spend several hours wandering through the rambling club in search of his quarry, Sir Lloyd summoned one of White's older and more discreet servants. A quiet word ascertained that his lordship was indeed on the premises, but in the library.

Sir Lloyd's eyebrows rose precipitously. The library? It was the one room in the club usually guaranteed to be empty. A slight smile curved his mouth as he considered that this might be its attraction to Nigel. The poor chap must be feeling quite unsociable.

With something akin to the sensation of bearding the lion in his den, Sir Lloyd pushed open the heavy wood-and-brass doors and stepped inside. At first he could make out little in the shadowy chamber crowded with overstuffed couches and chairs, shelves of musty books donated by long-forgotten members, and dust-covered magazines dating back to the previous reign.

But as his eyes adjusted, he spied a lone figure slumped in one of the chairs, booted legs stretched out before him and a glass of brandy, clearly not his first, clasped carelessly in a large hand.

"Sir Nigel?" he ventured softly.

No response. The man before him might have been in another world. Only the slow rise and fall of his powerful chest beneath a somewhat rumpled frock coat and the fixed stare of silvery eyes attested to the fact that he was indeed alive.

Determinedly Sir Lloyd tried again. "Pardon me, Sir Nigel, but I would like to have a word with you."

This got somewhat greater effect. Nigel straightened very slightly, glancing briefly at the intruder before looking away again. "I doubt we have anything to say, sir, and I would greatly prefer to remain undisturbed."

"That may be, but nonetheless I believe a few moments of your time are not too much to ask for a matter that concerns you deeply."

So saying, Sir Lloyd stepped forward, close enough to observe the full effect of his words. The color drained from Nigel's face as he grated, "Courtney—has something happened to her?"

"No . . . at least not as of a short time ago when I left her. However, I am surprised you bother to ask."

"What is that supposed to mean?" Nigel growled, all pretense at uninterest gone. He straightened in the chair, glowering at Sir Lloyd, who observed him calmly.

"Only that Lady Courtney is obviously not eating or sleeping properly. She appears weighed down by some considerable burden that is sapping even her indomitable spirit. Since work at the shelter is proceeding quite well, I can only presume the problem lies closer to home."

"You *presume* a great deal. Since when have private matters between husband and wife been the stuff of conversation?"

"Since you chose to hold a gentle and gracious lady up to public speculation and scorn," Sir Lloyd snapped, abruptly out of patience with the self-absorbed lord who seemed little concerned with the havoc his actions were wreaking on his wife. He sat down across from Nigel, making it clear he did not intend to leave until the matter was settled.

"I don't know how this trouble between you began, but I do perceive its effects. Courtney is miserable. Oh, she tries to put up a brave front and she is not the sort to speak of such personal matters even to close friends. But to those who know her well, it is obvious that—"

"How well?"

The curt question interrupted Sir Lloyd's train of thought. "What . . . ?"

"I asked," Nigel repeated quietly, "how well you know my wife." Although he did not appear to have moved in the deep chair, Sir Lloyd had the uncanny impression that the large, powerfully muscled body was throwing off its relaxed pose. Strength and determination, undercut by something perilously close to anger, surged to the fore.

Cautiously the young peer said, "Lady Courtney and I have not been acquainted very long, but we have worked together under very difficult circumstances in which people tend to get to know each other swiftly. I would say, therefore, that I am sufficiently familiar with her to be concerned about her present state."

The answer did not appear to satisfy Nigel. Straightening, he set his brandy snifter on an adjacent table and regarded the other man from beneath hooded gray eyes. The silence between them drew out tautly. Sir Lloyd was the furthest thing from a coward, but he could not deny a faint shiver of apprehension as he met his lordship's steely gaze. A warning sounded deep within his mind. The mask of civilization was slipping. Despite the quiet, restrained setting, the propriety of their position, the lack of any overt threat or challenge, emotions recognizable to the most primitive male were seizing control.

Nigel leaned forward slightly. His big hands, lightly tanned and callused from his disinclination to wear gloves while riding, were clasped before him. As Sir Lloyd watched, the knuckles whitened.

"Whatever differences there may be between my wife and myself," his lordship said slowly, "do not give any man leave to become *familiar* with her. Her sudden infatuation with 'good works' is bad enough, but I am prepared to wait that out." This was not quite true, since Nigel was privately uncertain just how much longer he could endure his present mode of life. His estrangement from Courtney was growing increasingly intolerable. But he gave no hint of his quandry as he continued, "However, there is a limit to my patience. You would be foolish to overstep it."

It took Sir Lloyd a moment to fully grasp what his lordship was suggesting. When he did, the young peer was torn between shocked outrage and a treacherous desire to laugh. He had never before considered jealousy a positive emotion, but now he could see it had some definite advantages.

"My lord," he ventured when he was certain his voice would not betray his amusement, "it appears that there is some misunderstanding between us. While it is true that your wife and I have become friends because of our shared concern for the children of the East End, that friendship could not have reached its present level so swiftly were it not for the affection and esteem we both have for Lady Sara Drake. It was Lady Sara who brought about my involvement with the Aid Society. While I would have supported such a worthwhile endeavor under any circumstances, it is because of her that I have devoted so much time to the effort." He hesitated before confiding, "It is my hope to persuade Lady Sara to become my wife."

The change in Nigel's demeanor was nothing short of farcical. As understanding dawned, so did embarrassment. His aristocratic features reddening, he murmured, "It appears I have made a mistake. . . ."

Not one to miss the chance of driving home a point, Lloyd nodded cordially. "Perhaps more than one."

Nigel eyed him warily. The long nights of frustration, concern, and just plain male pique had taken their toll. He was in no condition to bandy words. "Courtney and I do seem to be at an impasse," he admitted.

"But not one that need be insurmountable. If you would permit my advice . . ."

Nigel's acquiescence was silent but nonetheless unmistakable. He paused long enough to summon a tray of coffee before giving all his attention to the peer.

As the gentlemen bent their heads together and spoke in low tones, Courtney was embroiled in a scene of a far different sort. Some two dozen children clustered around the long trestle tables set up in the shelter's kitchen. They ranged in age from those barely able to toddle to twelve- and thirteen-year-olds with the too-wise faces of those burdened early on in life by the most adult cares. All were dirty, poorly dressed, and marked by the gauntness of perpetual hunger. They shifted nervously on the benches as fragrant soup was ladled into bowls and large loaves of bread were sliced.

With the ingrained habit of obedience reinforced by a swift cuffing for even the slightest transgression, none made a move toward the food as it was carried to the tables. But neither did any of the two dozen pairs of eyes glance away for even an instant as what appeared to them very much like a feast was set before them.

It fell to Peggy to finally break the spell. "Go on, then," the little girl instructed briskly when a bowl was set before each child. "Ain't going to bite you."

No further encouragement was required. In a single motion, the half-starved children fell on the food. Spoons were extraneous as eager hands lifted the warm, hearty fare to hungry mouths. Courtney stood by silently, thinking that the youngest might need some help to get their share. But that was not the case. After the first avid swallows, the older children remembered their younger sisters and brothers.

Those who were having trouble managing their bowls

were gently aided. Hunks of bread were broken into smaller pieces for tiny mouths. The few able to recognize the different sorts of vegetables sharing space with morsels of chicken in the hearty broth shared their knowledge with the others. Such strange words as "carrot," "green bean," "marrow," and "pea" were whispered ear to ear by those whose usual diet was confined to half-rotted potatoes, lard, and black bread adulterated by all manner of indigestible sweepings.

The meal Courtney had thought barely adequate was received with solemn courtesy befitting the masterpiece of a great chef. Fighting down the thought of the immense quantity of food wasted by the lords and ladies of her acquaintance, she smiled at the little girl who stood so gravely beside her.

"You are doing very well, Peggy. I can't think how we would manage without you."

The child flushed becomingly. Several weeks of proper care had worked wonders with her. Her green eyes sparkled with the glow of good health. The ashen pallor was gone from cheeks that were no longer hollow. The small amount of weight she had gained made her long, slender limbs now appear to fit her body. Dressed in a neat yellow serge skirt and white blouse covered by an apron, with her ebony hair caught back by a bright lemon bow, she looked altogether a different person from the terrified urchin who had hidden beneath the wheels of Sara's phaeton such a short time before.

Courtney doubted that the faint shadows of pain lingering beneath her young friend's thick lashes would ever be completely erased. But in Peggy at least the brutal experiences of childhood were transformed into determination to help others. Already she had shown a decided talent for winning the confidence of the often shy, fearful children who had to be coaxed into the shelter. She was, in a sense, still one of their own, yet risen vastly above them to a world they could not even imagine. To Peggy, therefore, fell the duties of a mediator who bridged the vast gap between the aristocratic sponsors of the Children's Aid Society and their bedraggled recipients.

"I'm glad to be here," Peggy averred. She touched the soft, clean fabric of her skirt pensively. "Though I can still hardly believe this is happening to me."

The hint of anxious disbelief that hung about her, as though she feared her life of the last few weeks was only a beautiful dream from which she must shortly wake, saddened Courtney. She put an arm around the little girl's slight shoulders. "It is happening, Peggy, and nothing will change that. You will never have to go back to the life you once knew."

That was a promise she could make with clear conscience. To no one's surprise, the child's self-described "guardian" had not dared make any effort to reclaim her. Nor did Peggy's dim recollections of her parents suggest they would interfere in her new life. So far as she could remember, her father had died shortly after her birth, and was replaced by a series of men who sired the assortment of half-brothers and half-sisters fighting for what little food and shelter their gin-sodden mother could provide.

Early on they found their way to the streets, propelled on their own or, if they were less fortunate, sold for the price of another bottle. Peggy had no way of knowing their fates for certain, but she suspected some were sent into the notorious "flash houses" where young thieves were trained, others to the brothels that would have been her prison, and a few to the gangs of professional beggars who found a youngster, particularly one they deliberately mutilated, useful to their scams. It was from those same grim ends that they were struggling to save the children gathered under their roof. The battle promised to be difficult.

"I wish we could convince more to come," Courtney sighed, even as she had to wonder where they would get the food to feed a larger group. After the first flush of enthusiasm, contributions were slow. The plain fact was that most of the ladies she and Sara knew were far more concerned with the latest fashion and gossip than with the tragedy of the East End. Most of the funds for the shelter were coming from the two friends' personal allowances, which were rapidly proving inadequate to the task. Courtney had considered applying to Nigel for help, but had so far not managed to face him. The mere thought of her husband set off such waves of mingled longing and anger that she sought some immediate distraction.

"I'm going to sort through the clothes that came in today. Before the children leave, I'd like to be able to give each something better to wear."

Peggy nodded understandingly. Though she was privately grateful that the only man who spent much time at the shelter was the quiet, soft-spoken Sir Lloyd, to whom she was slowly becoming accustomed, she could not help but feel sorry for her young benefactress, who so clearly missed her husband. Why any woman would long for a man, she could not imagine. But her near-reverent admiration for Lady Courtney convinced her there must be some good reason. Frowning slightly, Peggy puzzled over this as she guided the children in cleaning up after their meal.

In a quiet corner of the shelter, partitioned from the rest by a battered screen, Courtney began to undo the bundles of castoffs that had arrived that morning. Her friends might be reluctant to part with money, but they were only too pleased to have someplace to dispose of the endless piles of garments no longer considered fashionable. A sigh escaped her as she began to separate the frivolous ball gowns, riding habits, and fragile day dresses from the few items that would be useful to the children.

She did not get very far before a disturbance on the street caught her attention. A child cried out in fear, followed swiftly by the angry exclamation of a man and the sound of a hard hand striking flesh. Dropping the ruffled lady's cape she held, Courtney ran toward the windows. She had not quite reached them when a trembling, breathless Peggy collided with her.

"It's him!" the child burst out. "Getting into a carriage. He's got a little girl with him. I know it's him! Do something!"

Grasping her shoulders gently but firmly, Courtney forced herself to speak calmly. "It's *who*, Peggy? I can't do anything until I know what you're talking about."

Peggy's slight chest rose and fell frantically as she gasped, "It's the man who bought me for the house. He's getting into a coach outside with another child. She doesn't want to go. She tried to get away but he grabbed her and hit her. Oh, please, my lady, don't let him escape! Once she's locked up, she won't have a prayer!"

Shocked into silence, Courtney could only nod. She stood rooted in place, struggling to grasp the fact that the appalling scene with Peggy was being repeated right outside her door. When her mind had at last communicated this to her body, she exploded into action.

Heedless of Sara's warning cry, Courtney raced from the shelter. She spied the burly flashily-dressed man instantly. Without a thought to her own safety, the marchioness hurled herself at him.

"Let her go!"

Startled, the man was caught unawares. His grip on the child loosened enough for her to wrench free and dart away. But the shock of being assaulted by a beautiful young lady in the midst of the East End was quickly overcome. An ugly grin revealed broken teeth as his hand closed bruisingly on Courtney's arm.

"It's you again! By God, my luck's in! I swore I'd find some way to pay you back, and now I 'ave!"

Courtney barely heard him. Kicking and scratching, she was intent only on inflicting as much damage as possible to one she considered beneath contempt. So great was her rage that she was unaware of either the fact of the child's escape or her own predicament until she felt herself lifted off the ground in the direction of the waiting carriage.

"So you don't want me to take the chit, do you?" the man growled. "Fine with me. You'll fetch a damn higher price anyway!" A guttural laugh broke from him as he observed the color drain from Courtney's cheeks.

"Didn't think o' that, did you? No 'ighfalutin little bitch gets the better of Jake Donal! You'll make a welcome addition to the best whore'ouse, where it'll be my pleasure to teach you proper manners!"

Now fully alerted to her dire circumstances, Courtney redoubled her efforts to get free. Twisting around desperately, she managed to sink her teeth into Jake's hand and was rewarded by a grunt of pain. But any satisfaction she might have felt faded instantly as he struck out in retaliation.

The blow hit Courtney just beneath the right ear, stunning her into immobility. Waves of pain washed over her. Her eyes opened wide, seeing not the street but only spirals of colored lights and fast-closing darkness. Her anguished moan followed her into unconsciousness.

— 7 —

Courtney returned to consciousness slowly. Her mind was enveloped in a languorous mist from which she was reluctant to emerge. Vaguely she sensed that on the other side of that mist lay pain and fear, but she could not imagine why.

Not even the gradual perception of her surroundings intruded sufficiently to concern her. The room she occupied was small and bare of all furnishings but a narrow iron-frame bed and a small table. The single window was covered by heavy shutters which blotted out all but the faintest light. Her eyes, the pupils contracted to pinpricks, had difficulty seeing anything. But that didn't matter. She was quite content to drift free of all thought or worry.

A dazed smile curved her mouth as she gazed down the length of her body. How peculiar. She must have forgotten to put on her nightrobe. It was fortunate Mary wasn't about. Her mistress's natural state unimpeded by any sort of cover would undoubtedly provoke the maid's disapproval.

Courtney could almost hear her. *Whatever are you thinking of?* Mary would demand. *Get under the covers before you catch your death of cold.*

Actually, that might not be a bad idea. She was a bit chilled. Stirring slightly, Courtney tried to reach for a blanket, only to discover that both her hands were securely tied to the bedpost above her head.

A soft giggle escaped her. How silly. Who would do such a thing? Someone very thorough, she observed an indeterminate time later when the mist again parted sufficiently for her to notice anything. Her ankles were similarly fastened, one to each side of the bed. Struck by a vague desire to test her bonds, Courtney tried to close her legs. Impossible. The ropes were of velvet, so they did not damage her sensitive skin. But they nonetheless held her firmly. Until someone chose to untie her, she was trapped.

Oh, well. That didn't seem very important. Offhand, she couldn't think why she should be stretched out naked on a bed, the alabaster perfection of her skin glowing translucently against the dark mattress. But there must be some reason. For a brief time she tried to think of it, only to do that required too much effort. With a little sigh, she closed her eyes and sank back into dreams.

When she woke next, Courtney was no longer alone. Two women had entered the room. One was middle-aged with pitch-black hair that looked as though it might have been dyed in a futile effort to hold on to her youth. She wore a dark blue silk gown lightly touched at the neck and cuffs with lace. Her companion was younger and more extravagantly dressed. Courtney's eyes widened as she took in the woman's bright pink taffeta gown cut so low as to expose the ample curves of her breast to the nipples. Her blond hair was worn up in an elaborate arrangement of curls and waves. She wore a beauty patch at one corner of her wide mouth, and a heavy scent rose from her rouged and powdered skin.

Both women frowned when they saw she was awake. "I still say," the older insisted, "that Jake was out of his head to snatch her."

The younger one shrugged. "Maybe so, Mrs. Hammond, but there's no denying she'll bring a good price. When was the last time you saw a body like that?"

With professional detachment the black-haired woman

looked Courtney over. She noted the long, slender legs flowing from small pink-tipped feet to lithe thighs separated by a tangle of auburn curls which matched the luxurious tresses falling from a simple coiffure. The waist was small enough to be spanned by a man's hands, its narrowness accentuating the gentle curves of supple hips and high, firm breasts whose rosy nipples puckered in the cool air.

Silently running over her client list, Mrs. Hammond was reassured that the risk she was taking in auctioning the wife of a peer of the realm was worthwhile The men who patronized the exclusive brothel at the edge of the East End were far too dissipated to take part in the usual social round of the *ton*. They might have heard of Lord Nigel Davies and his beautiful young wife, but the chances that they would recognize her were remote. Anyone who did so could easily be convinced to keep silent by threatening to bar him admittance to what was easily the most luxurious, degenerate, amoral pleasure house in London, where literally anything could be had for the right price. Were it not for the lady's rank, there would be nothing at all remarkable about the night's sale except the extraordinary loveliness of the object offered for bidding. Beautiful girls went on the block frequently at Mrs. Hammond's, without her ever giving a second thought to their fates.

"Look at that skin," the younger woman mused admiringly. "There isn't a mark on it."

"No, and there won't be if I have anything to say about it. I'd have to be crazy to let Jake break her in, angry as he is at what she did."

Leaning closer, she smiled at Courtney encouragingly. "Cold, love? Don't worry, you'll be warmer soon." The soothing voice hardened as she turned to give instructions. "Cat, tell the maids to come in. I want her ready by this evening."

The two young girls entered the room. They were plainly dressed in the gray cotton uniforms typical of maids throughout London, but there the similarity ended.

Even in a city where human ugliness was by no means rare, the girls seemed especially unfortunate. One was severely pockmarked, the other's back was disfigured by a slight hump. But through their occupation, they had learned to appreciate their homeliness. They were fed, sheltered, and paid a small wage in exchange for merely working eighteen hours a day. Compared to much they had seen beneath Mrs. Hammond's roof, that seemed the rarest of good luck.

Scurrying about their tasks, the maids set out various supplies on the table before approaching the bed where Courtney lay tied. Pleasantly curious about these two new arrivals whose ugliness did not penetrate the fog of her contentment, she smiled slightly. The girls ignored her. Each matter-of-factly poured a small amount of oil into her hands and began gently but thoroughly to rub it into the beautiful marchioness's skin.

Courtney had enjoyed massages before, but this was different. There was an unexpectedly sensual quality about the way her body reacted, not to the girls' touch but to the oil itself. The fragrance of jasmine and patchouli filled her breath. The honey-thick liquid seeped into her skin, evoking a gentle warmth. Courtney sighed contentedly. She offered no protest when the maids briefly untied her, long enough to turn her over before resecuring her bonds. With brisk, efficient hands they continued to stroke the oil over her back and thighs.

The warmth slowly increased. What began as an enjoyable sensation of well-being similar to that experienced when being touched by a light summer breeze gradually changed. Courtney shifted languidly as ripples of heat moved through her. What little awareness she retained of herself became focused on the shivering, titillating glow that spread steadily everywhere the oil touched. Undulating waves of need uncoiled from deep within her. She moaned softly, arching on the bed. Nothing seemed to matter except satisfying the hunger which was quickly becoming ravenous. Whatever achieved that would be welcomed unrestrainedly.

Mrs. Hammond observed the effects of the oil without surprise. She had ordered its use several times before when the subject of the night's entertainment was expected to be willing. On other occasions, with other audiences, a different sort of amusement was offered for which terrified young girls were preferred. But for this evening and this clientele, Courtney must be utterly compliant, even eager to perform anything required of her.

When she was assured such would be the case, she motioned to the maids. "That's enough. Get her dressed."

The ropes holding her in place were discarded. Helped from the bed, Courtney swayed slightly. One of the maids kept a hand on her as the other brushed the glorious auburn silk of her hair into the appearance of sensual disarray. A slight touch of vermilion cream with some of the same properties of the oil used on her body was applied to the marchioness's lips. They tingled for a moment before pouting soft and full.

Mrs. Hammond judged that no further artifice was required to complement the lady's face. But for the rest . . . She glanced at what Courtney was to wear, then gave instructions to the maids. More of the cream was applied to the high, firm nipples so that they shone darkly through the thin gauze of the gown that was to be her sole garment.

Made of transparent silk as finely spun as a cobweb, the robe fell straight to Courtney's slim ankles. Long, full sleeves perched on the edge of her shoulders. Little more than a tantalizing film over her body, the gown was cut low enough to bare the full swell of her ripe breasts. As she moved, it clung gracefully to her small waist, slender hips, and long, shapely legs. Barefoot, Courtney giggled softly as she caught sight of her toes peering from beneath the hem.

Her amusement wrung a tolerant smile from Mrs. Hammond. "Come along, dear," she murmured encouragingly. "There are some gentlemen downstairs who are eager to meet you."

How odd, Courtney thought dimly. She couldn't remember ever going to a party in her nightgown. But there must be some good reason for it. Obediently she was led out of the shuttered room and down a short flight of stairs.

Cat hung back long enough to have a word with her employer. "There's quite a crowd this evening. Word got out that you would be offering something special."

"Did most of the regulars make it?"

"Yes, and one or two I don't recognize."

A slight frown touched Mrs. Hammond's brow. "Problems?"

Cat shrugged. Instincts honed through years of experience with all manner of human villainy made her hesitate. "I'm not sure. . . . There's a big chap, keeping to himself. He's wearing a mask."

Mrs. Hammond laughed shortly. While listening to Cat with half her attention, she had calculated the evening's probable take from this one offering alone. The result brought a rare flash of good humor. "I'll warrant he isn't the only one."

"That's true. Quite a few gentlemen like to hide their identity, or at least they like to think they do. But we almost always know who's behind the masks. All I'm sure of in this case is that I haven't seen him before."

The inherent caution that had carried her so far in her profession dimmed Mrs. Hammond's joviality. "Tell the muscle to keep an eye on him," she instructed. Very rarely was it necessary to evict a patron from premises where just about any behavior was not only encouraged but also avidly procured. One of the very few transgressions that could result in ejection was failure to settle accounts. Still, it was good business to keep several strong-arms on hand to dispose of any problem which might arise. If the gentleman in the mask proved to be difficult, he could count on at least a few bruises and perhaps a broken limb or two.

Satisfied that her precautions were adequate, Mrs. Hammond told Cat to wait in the corridor with Courtney while she went inside to prepare the gentlemen. It never hurt to put an added edge on their eagerness before unveiling the night's sport.

The hall was damp and a bit chill, but Courtney did not feel it. Under Cat's worldly eye, she hummed softly to herself, turning round once or twice to enjoy the feel of silk against her limbs. Her behavior convinced the other girl that no further doses were needed of the cantharis-laced wine and hashish-based confections with which her present dreamy state had been achieved. As always when administering such drugs, a fine balance had to be struck between docility and unconsciousness. A too heavy hand could make useless even the most delectable creature, whose appeal could be speedily lost to coma or even death.

Trust Mrs. Hammond, Cat thought wryly, to know exactly how much to give. The old harridan had come up the hard way, and had forgotten none of the lessons of her early years. Perhaps she was right to believe the risk they were taking was worthwhile. Certainly few managers of brothels would have shown the audacity she did in purchasing the marchioness from Jake. If her identity became known ...

Cat shivered slightly. Not for the first time, she thought of the hoard of cash she was slowly accumulating. There was almost enough for the country inn she had a mind to buy. When that day came, she would be gone from the likes of Mrs. Hammond forever. But until then, she could only hope nothing went wrong.

From the sounds drifting out of the viewing room, there was no need to be concerned. The gentlemen, though well pleased with the amusements so far offered them, were now ready for something more than brandy, opium, and lissome dancing girls and boys performing nude for their enjoyment. They listened attentively as Mrs. Hammond described the charms they were about to witness, offering encouragement in the form of hoots and shouts, which grew more explicit as the commentary continued.

At last, when she was convinced their excitement had reached a fever pitch, the signal was given to bring Courtney out. Cat took her hand, murmuringly soothingly, as she led her into the crowded room.

The noise died abruptly.

Touched by the faintest flicker of puzzlement, Courtney glanced round curiously. It was a nice-enough room, although rather overdone for her taste. Heavy red brocade curtains covered any windows there might be, as well as the walls and ceiling from which they fell in graceful folds reminiscent of an Arabian tent. To further the impression of oriental luxury, heavy rugs lay over the floor and the fragrance of incense rose from copper braziers. Low, pillow-festooned settees offered seating for the half-dozen or so gentlemen who lolled about on them regally, looking just a bit out of place in their frock coats and breeches.

The gentlemen, whoever they might be, seemed to be having a good time. She wondered momentarily, as the laughter and conversation broke off, if something might be wrong. But the clamor broke out again even more raucously than before, with compliments shouted at Mrs. Hammond that made even that stern-faced woman beam.

"God's breath! Is she real?"

"Where did you find her? She's magnificent!"

"Turn her around! Let's get a better look!"

Guided up to the small stage, Courtney was slowly turned in each direction so that the gentlemen could fully appreciate the impact of her beauty. Foreheads beaded with perspiration and suddenly dry lips were licked absently as each man contemplated the pleasures that might await him. *If* he could afford the price.

When she judged the preliminary exhibition to have accomplished its ends, Mrs. Hammond coughed discreetly. "Gentlemen, the bidding is open."

All eyes were abruptly fastened on her. There was a moment's silence, the deep inhalation of many breaths, and then . . .

"One hundred guineas!"

"Hundred-fifty!"

"Two!"

The bids came so quickly that it was not possible for some time to determine who was ahead. But at last, when the exorbitant sum of four hundred guineas was reached, half the gentlemen were forced to drop out. Those still in the bidding glanced at each other warily, then looked back at Courtney as though to convince themselves such extravagance was merited.

Mrs. Hammond well understood the meaning of this pause. Her strategy for dealing with it was proven in long practice. Smiling faintly, she drew Courtney closer to the edge of the stage. Almost—but not quite—near enough for some of the gentlemen to touch her.

Pushing the gown from one creamy shoulder, she allowed it to fall away, exposing the perfection of a single breast. As the audience pressed nearer, Mrs. Hammond said quietly, "Surely such loveliness deserves only the highest accolades. You gentlemen are known for your discerning appreciation of feminine beauty. I trust I have not misjudged you. . . ."

So saying, she slipped the gown from the opposite shoulder, baring the marchioness fully to the waist. A low groan broke from the appreciative audience. Surprised by the touch of air against yet more skin, Courtney instinctively raised a hand to cover herself. Only to be stopped by Mrs. Hammond, who firmly seized and lowered her arm. "Now, now, dear," she crooned, "you don't want to disappoint our guests."

Unable to remember quite what she had intended to do, Courtney desisted. She stood obediently as the bidding resumed.

"Four hundred and fifty."

The crowd gasped, now almost as excited by the sum on the table as by the girl herself. But the gasp turned to a near-shout of amazement as a quiet voice from the back of the room said, "Five hundred."

It was the first bid from the stranger in the mask.

Her small eyes narrowing yet further, Mrs. Hammond surveyed him sharply. She could see why Cat had noticed him. He was an unusually big man, broad of shoulder and long of limb. Whereas the other gentlemen had long ago unfastened jackets and loosened shirts in the warmth of the smoky room, he remained engulfed in a black cape matching the rest of his attire. Even his head was fully covered, as was his face, by the black leather mask.

An aura of danger emanated from him, due only in part to the sinister somberness of his garb. This was not a man to cross, Mrs. Hammond decided quickly. But that did not mean he wouldn't turn out to be a perfectly good customer. She cast a quick look at the chief of her security force, who lounged against one wall in a deceptively casual attitude. As he rubbed the knuckles of his right hand, slightly bruised while convincing Jake to take his money and leave, the man scrutinized the stranger carefully.

Deciding the situation was under control, Mrs. Hammond repeated the bid. "Five hundred guineas. A generous offer, but hardly remarkable. Come, gentlemen, can you not do better?" In fact, the bid was above the top price she had considered attainable. But that did not prevent a hardheaded businesswoman from seeing if the price might be driven yet higher.

To encourage the remaining bidders, who were lagging behind, she drew the gown below Courtney's waist until the delicate curve of her hips was fully revealed. Faintly disturbed by this, the lovely marchioness tossed her head back, sending the heavy waves of her hair into even greater disarray. A slight frown appeared to mar the ivory smoothness of her brow.

There were limits to even the most ardent gentlemen's rashness. When this further revelation failed to provoke a higher bid, Mrs. Hammond knew greater action was needed. A slight motion of her hand was enough to send the pool of silk to the floor, leaving Courtney completely unclothed. Her lips parted in a soft moan of distress, which went unnoticed by the older woman.

"Gentlemen, are you so unmoved by the sight of such loveliness? Surely you can tell by simply looking at her that this exquisite creature is fully prepared for you. See how her eyes and lips are shining, how her breasts beckon your hands. The lucky man who buys her services will experience the most enthralling ecstasy. This beautiful thing will do your every bidding, she wishes only to please you. You will find her not only utterly submissive but also eager, imaginative, skillful beyond your wildest dreams."

Actually, she had no idea what amatory skills the marchioness might or might not possess. But before being turned over to the winning bidder, she could easily be drugged again. Under the influence of cantharis and hashish, even the most reticent woman proved astonishingly inventive.

This was sufficient to inspire the bidding higher. But the resurgence was brief, ending when the price reached six hundred guineas. This amount, again offered by the stranger, appeared to be the final bid. Resigned to accepting a fee considerably above her highest expectations, Mrs. Hammond smiled at him benignly. Her expression was intended to soften her words. "I am impressed by your determination, sir. Now, if you will kindly convince me also of your sincerity, the lady will be yours."

The gentleman stepped forward, through the path swiftly cleared for him. The other men might be far gone with drink and lust, but they were still alert enough to avoid what had all the appearances of potentially deadly trouble. A few held out the hope that he would not be able to pay, in which case they could enjoy the sight of him being beaten to a pulp before the bidding began again. But they were doomed to disappointment. In a gesture noteworthy for its economy of movement, the dark man tossed a sack onto the stage in front of Mrs. Hammond. It landed with a resounding clunk.

"I think this will satisfy you."

She bent hastily to retrieve it. A quick glance inside assured her the deal was set. The comforting weight and shine of gold won a smile far more sincere than any that had gone before. "Indeed, and I trust you will be as well pleased." Raising a hand, she gestured to Cat.

The end of the auction was also the signal for the men in her employ to position themselves unobtrusively near the room's only exit to assure that none of the disappointed bidders took it in his head to protest. That had happened occasionally, but this time the combined effect of the dark man's aura of intrinsic danger and the girl's stunning beauty, plus the sheer magnitude of the price he had paid to possess her, kept the others frozen in place. By the time a few recovered sufficiently to grumble, other less exorbitant amusements had arrived to distract them.

Led from the room, Courtney stumbled slightly. Something was wrong. There was too much she did not understand. Where was she? Why was she dressed only in the black cape slipped round her by the dark man who, though she could not recognize him, seemed somehow important to her? What was he saying to Mrs. Hammond?

"I don't want her given more drugs. I prefer a woman awake and aware."

"Yes, of course, sir. But in this case, there may be a small problem . . ."

Mrs. Hammond was not about to insist on the drugs. She sensed it was not wise to insist on anything with the stranger. But neither did she relish the thought of a violent scene in which he would undoubtedly damage the marchioness. Once he was through with her, it was her plan to sell the lady to a certain merchant of her acquaintance who transported young women out of the country to places where their fair-skinned beauty was highly valued as exotic and provocative. If she was badly bruised, the sale would be delayed. A perilous complication in view of the search that would undoubtedly be undertaken for her.

A sardonic smile touched the stranger's hard mouth beneath the mask. "You mean she may not be willing?"

"Exactly. If you do not wish her drugged, may I suggest she should be bound to the bed? Just a precaution, you understand."

She was about to go on to assure the stranger that his purchase could be trussed up in such a way that would not interfere with the many and varied acts he might care to enjoy. But her rather nervous chatter was forestalled when he shrugged dismissively.

"It matters not. I'm sure she will serve me well either way."

Serve him? Courtney shook her head slightly, trying to clear enough of the fog from her thoughts to determine what those words might mean. Did he think her a servant? Remembering the plain skirt and bodice she had worn to work in the shelter, she thought perhaps her dress had misled him. But glancing down, she saw only the folds of his cape, which further jarred her sensibilities.

Whatever was she wearing? And why was she barefoot? The stone floor of the corridor they were passing through was cold beneath her feet. She stopped abruptly, overcome by the conviction that something was hideously wrong.

"I . . ." At the sound of the marchioness's voice, hesitant though it was, Mrs. Hammond turned swiftly. She took in the expression of perplexity giving way to fear and knew at once that the drugs were wearing off. If they were not to be readministered, something had to be done at once.

The stranger had also noted his purchase's return to consciousness. He placed a hand on her arm, speaking to her softly. "Come along, there's nothing to be afraid of."

Impressed by his management of the girl, Mrs. Hammond nonetheless thought it wise to get them safely sequestered in a room as quickly as possible. Since they had reached the area of the brothel with the most luxurious accommodations, certainly to be expected by a man who had just paid six hundred guineas, that was no problem. Pushing open the nearest door, she beckoned him inside.

"I trust this will be satisfactory."

Still holding on to Courtney, who had begun to strain against his touch, the man glanced round uninterestedly. The lavish decoration did not impress him. His gaze settled on the huge canopied bed and the velvet ropes already thoughtfully provided at each corner.

"This will do fine."

The finality of his tone made it clear he expected Mrs. Hammond now to withdraw. She hesitated an instant, wishing she could stay long enough to be sure the marchioness was securely restrained. But the man's impatience was tangible. It was not wise to linger. With a slight bow in deference to his gold, she left the room.

Alone with the stranger, Courtney breathed in sharply. Her knees felt weak and her body trembled as it cast off the last effects of the drugs. The muscles of her stomach clenched painfully. Her mouth was dry and her nipples and loins ached. But it was the fear that struck her most savagely.

What was happening to her?

The room told her nothing, except that she was someplace where she did not belong. The man, who strode over to the windows the moment the door was closed, revealed even less. She watched with widening eyes as he tore loose the concealing curtains and stepped back to study the locked and bolted shutters.

The sudden appearance of something long and lethal in the man's hand rent the final remnants of Courtney's drug-induced haze. A scream bubbled up in her throat. But before it could emerge, the stranger turned back to her, caught her expression, and moved swiftly.

Steely arms closed round her, forcing her against a

huge, hard body that seemed to her terrified senses to be made of stone. "Be silent!" he growled, covering her mouth with a firm hand. "The last thing I need is for the charming Mrs. Hammond and her cohorts to come rushing to your aid." An unpleasant laugh broke from him. "Although, come to think of it, I suppose there's little danger of that. They'd just think I was getting my money's worth!"

Stunned by terror more profound than any she had ever known, Courtney was very limited in what she could think and feel. Whearas before there had been blissful contentment, now she knew only soul-shattering fear. Beneath the black cape, she was naked. Weakened by the cantharis, which turned her muscles to jelly, and robbed of will by the hashish, she could barely stand. The conviction grew in her that she was in greater danger than she had ever imagined possible and that, just as the man said, no one would save her. She was alone and helpless, trapped by a captor who had paid well to use her body in any way he chose.

Tears flooded her luminescent green eyes, spilling down her alabaster cheeks. The man cursed softly. He seemed about to speak when the creak of a carriage outside distracted him.

Shaking his head regretfully, he pulled one of the velvet ropes free from the bed and quickly tied both her hands behind her back. From beneath his black coat he pulled a white silk cravat, which he used to gag her. As Courtney tried vainly to kick out at him, he dropped her onto the bed and used another of the ropes to lash her ankles together. One hard, callused finger lingered briefly on the faint marks left by her earlier bonds. He muttered something under his breath, then turned abruptly back to the window.

8

So thoroughly restrained that she could make no movement except that necessary to breathe, Courtney watched wide-eyed as the man again withdrew the sturdy piece of metal and placed it in the crack between the shutters. For a moment he leaned his weight firmly against it. The heavy wood gave way, taking with it the bolt holding the shutters in place.

Wrenching them back, he threw open the windows and leaned forward to peer outside. Whatever he saw must have satisfied him, for he promptly returned his attention to the bed.

Crossing the room quickly, he lifted Courtney as easily as a doll. Nestled against the smooth wool covering his broad chest, she forced herself to lie limply. What little strength she had left had to be conserved. Now that she was certain the man intended to remove her from the house, she dared to wonder if she might be able to make use of his actions for her own benefit. If she could only get him to untie her, her chances of escape would be far greater than they could ever have been in the locked room under the scrutiny of Mrs. Hammond and the like.

Resolved to convince him of her compliance, Courtney offered no resistance as he swung powerful legs over the first-floor window and swiftly lowered them both to the ground. They were in a dark alley behind the house. Courtney flinched as a rat scurried by, pausing for a moment to stare at them with yellow eyes. The stench of garbage assailed her, made all the worse by the heavy miasma of fog drifting up from the nearby river. The man's cape was scant protection from the damp. She shivered helplessly.

Seeming to ignore her discomfort, he strode toward the cobblestoned street, where an enclosed carriage waited. Courtney did not catch whatever he said to the driver, but the moment they were inside, the horses were spurred to a brisk trot. Thrown against her captor, she stiffened. Despite the gag, a whimper of pain broke from her.

At once his grip eased. Fighting against the clouds of weariness that were closing in on her, Courtney tried to put some distance between them. But he would not allow it. Fatigue brought on by the ravages of the drugs deadened all her senses. She barely heard his muttered order to lie still as he began to untie her bonds.

A dull hum, like the buzzing of bees on a sultry summer day, rose in her ears. Her eyes closed relentlessly. Even as she tried desperately to stay awake, telling herself she must seize any opportunity to escape, sleep swept over her. With a despairing sigh she sagged against the dark man.

Stripping off his mask, Nigel stared down at his unconscious wife. Never in his life had he known such a tumult of conflicting emotions. Torn by profound relief that he had her safe and immense rage at the danger she had deliberately brought upon herself, he could not decide whether to beat or comfort her. The sickening fear he had felt when told of her kidnapping provoked him to at least mild cruelty. For that reason alone he had withheld the truth of his identity even after they were alone. It seemed mild enough punishment to keep her in suspense awhile longer.

But now, looking down at her ashen skin marked by the trail of her tears, he regretted not having spoken. With a low groan, he drew her closer against him, as though seeking to impart his own strength to her fragile form. Behind them he heard the clatter of the second coach, containing Sir Lloyd and several sturdy servants. They had remained out of sight to provide assistance if Nigel was followed from the house. Grimly he wished there had been an opportunity to claim immediate vengeance on those who had dared to take his wife. It was as well that Courtney slept, for her fear would have increased tenfold if she had seen the savage look in his silvery eyes as Nigel promised himself that revenge would soon be his.

The Davies town house appeared deceptively quiet, most of the servants being long abed. Only Johnson and Mary knew of their master's desperate mission. They waited up far into the night, occassionally bringing another pot of tea to Sara, who paced back and forth in the drawing room until she thought she must certainly have worn a trench in the carpet.

The clang of coach wheels coming round the corner nearest the house brought them all racing to the door. Johnson remembered himself sufficiently to stand aside, but Sara and Mary could only stare white-faced as Nigel lifted his precious bundle from the carriage and swiftly took the steps to the entry hall.

Sir Lloyd was right behind him. He made a manful effort to hide the full extent of his concern from the women, but neither was fooled. Wringing her hands, Mary hurried upstairs to prepare her mistress's room. Sara stayed behind, gazing on her dear friend's supine form with dread. All the color drained from her face as she whispered, "What did they do to her? Oh, Nigel, she is not—?"

"No," he grated, not lessening his stride toward the stairs, "but she might have preferred to be if that obscene crew had achieved its ends." Through tightly clenched teeth he added, "She was heavily drugged. I think most of the effects have worn off, but now she is exhausted. She needs rest more than anything else."

"A doctor . . ." Sir Lloyd ventured, too dazed by the night's incredible events to speak with his usual clarity.

From the moment the message had arrived from a frantic Sara, who was scouring London to get word to Nigel of his wife's fate, everything seemed to move both at top speed and with maddening slowness. After that first terrible instant when the meaning of what had happened gave Nigel the appearance of a man standing on the brink of a deadly chasm, he rallied to act with such speed and determination as to leave Sir Lloyd stunned.

Lord Nigel's upbringing as an immensely wealthy, privileged peer of the realm in no way lessened his ability to deal with a situation which would have left most others of his class mired in helpless confusion. Within minutes the idea of going to the constabulary was dismissed as useless and a waste of precious time. The carriage and driver that had conducted Nigel to the club were dispatched for several large, burly servants known for both their absolute loyalty and their skill at settling any physical dispute in their own favor.

While all this was being done, Nigel strode into White's gaming room. Without a by-your-leave, he interrupted a round of cards to speak quietly in the ear of one of the players. Whatever he said was enough to cause the gentleman to forfeit what may well have been the winning hand and follow Nigel outside. In a secluded corner of the club, they spoke for several minutes.

The man appeared at first reluctant to do Nigel's bidding. A few more words were exchanged, during which his plump, dissipated features turned bright red with mingled fury and dread. The bluster went out of him in a rush. They spoke together a brief time longer as a diagram was drawn and passed to Nigel's waiting hand. His lordship turned abruptly and went to join Sir Lloyd, who was standing just out of earshot observing the scene. Watching him go, the other man mopped his forehead and looked decidedly ill.

The diagram, Sir Lloyd now knew, was of Mrs. Hammond's notorious establishment, where, the other man had confirmed, a very special auction was rumored for that evening. The young peer still had no idea of exactly how Nigel had secured that information or of what had occurred once he got inside the brothel. He preferred not to know. His acquaintance with the terrible sorrows humans could inflict on each other was already far too great. It was enough that Courtney was safe and, God be willing, unharmed.

"About the doctor," he repeated as Nigel hastily climbed the stairs.

His lordship nodded over his shoulder. "If you know of one who is both capable and discreet, by all means send for him."

Sir Lloyd understood his concern for discretion. Courtney might recover quite well physically from her ordeal, but if it became public knowledge, her spirit would undoubtedly suffer all the more. Quickly he ran down the list of physicians he knew before being certain that he could more than fulfill both of Nigel's requirements in the person of Dr. Winston Blakeston. Writing a short note, he sent Johnson to fetch the doctor from his home, then gently urged Sara into the drawing room, where they could wait together.

"I should go upstairs," she protested, "to help take care of Courtney."

"Nigel will care for her," Sir Lloyd insisted. "I doubt he would allow anyone else to touch her just now."

The young peer was correct. Nigel went so far as to dismiss Mary from the room, despite her objections that she should be allowed to care for her mistress. Not until the door had closed behind the reluctant girl did he lay Courtney gently on the bed.

Removing the cape, he tossed it to the floor. The sight of her loveliness brought back in vivid detail the moment she was led into the viewing room to be exposed before the men. A look of black rage contorted Nigel's face. His fists clenched furiously. Only the knowledge that his wrath could do her no good forced him to shake off the almost irresistible desire for immediate retaliation. While Courtney needed him, he would remain at her side. But the moment she was sufficiently recovered . . .

A basin of warm water sat next to the bed. Dipping a towel in it, Nigel gently washed away the traces of tears from her silken skin. She murmured faintly but did not wake. He removed the vermilion dye from her lips, then gently cleaned her darkened nipples. Wrapping her bruised wrists and ankles in damp strips of fabric, he pulled the covers over her and dimmed the light.

Barely had he finished when voices alerted him to the physician's arrival. Dr. Blakeston was a man in his mid-thirties with a calm, sympathetic demeanor that inspired confidence. He listened without interruption as Nigel explained what had happened, and made no objection when his lordship indicated he would remain in the room while his wife was examined.

With deft, careful movements, the doctor ascertained much of what Nigel had already guessed. The potentially lethal drugs had left Courtney exhausted but otherwise unharmed. She would sleep far into the next day and waken with a great thirst and considerable confusion. But there should be no further aftereffects.

While Nigel blanched slightly but made no effort to interfere, the doctor also determined that the sanctity of her body had not been invaded. Neither the conscientious physician nor the concerned husband needed to acknowledge the necessity of such an examination. If Courtney had not been rescued in time to prevent her from being raped, there was the possibility of pregnancy. Prepared to take immediate steps to forestall that, the doctor was relieved to discover it was not necessary.

"Her ladyship is most fortunate," Blakeston said quietly as he packed up his instruments. "Her ordeal could have been far worse. As it is, she will undoubtedly have some frightening memories, but nothing more. When she wakes, I urge you to be kind and reassuring. Do not try to force her to speak of what happened, but be willing to listen if she needs to talk. Above all, let her know that she is safe and that you do not hold her to blame for what occurred."

"That will be difficult," Nigel muttered, "since I do hold her very much responsible. Her impulsive disregard for her own safety could have—"

"My lord," the physician interrupted sternly, "I do not mean to suggest that when your wife is fully recovered you should not have a firm discussion with her about her actions. But in these next few days it is vital that she receive only tender understanding from you. Otherwise, her emotional suffering will far outweigh the actual physical experience."

Nigel listened to him gravely. He regretted his hasty words and was embarrassed that the doctor had to explain to him what he should have understood intuitively. Though he had not intended to confront Courtney with the seriousness of her actions before she was fully recovered, he now resolved all the more firmly to refrain from making her acknowledge the folly of her actions until the shocks of the past day were completely behind her.

Assuring Dr. Blakeston that his instructions would be followed, Nigel escorted him downstairs. The two men stood in the entryway together for a moment, the grim-faced young lord trying vainly to express his appreciation for the visit, while the physician brushed aside his thanks in a way that indicated he already regarded the incident as forgotten. He vanished into the night with a final reminder to deal carefully with the lady's battered sensibilities.

Returning to his wife's room, the marquess pulled a chair close to the bed and sat down. For all his own weariness, no thought of sleep entered his mind. He was still wide-awake some hours later, his gaze fastened on Courtney's pale features, when she began to move restlessly beneath the covers. At first, Nigel's only response was surprise. He had expected her to sleep much longer.

Not until she cried out softly did he realize she was still deeply unconscious and caught in the throes of a nightmare whose origins were not difficult to guess. In an instant, Nigel was beside her on the bed. His strong arms cradled her tenderly as he murmured, "Hush, love, it's all right. There's nothing to fear. No one will harm you now."

At first he did not think his words could penetrate the horror that held her captive. She continued to sob softly, reliving her experiences at Mrs. Hammond's hands, which he could only pray she would not remember when she was conscious. Drawing her even closer, he repeated his promises of safety and protection more urgently as his hands lightly caressed her trembling form. There was no passion in his touch, only the most profound need to give comfort and reassurance. To his immense relief, his efforts succeeded. With a little sigh of release, she went limp against him.

Even then, Nigel did not let her go. Easing himself onto the bed, he continued to hold her throughout the remainder of the night, alert to any indication that her nightmare might return.

It did not, and by dawn the marquess was confident that his wife would sleep peacefully for several more hours. Leaving her in Mary's care, the maid's stony look making it clear she thought she had been dispensed with quite long enough, he went off to his own room.

Once there, the iron self-control he had exercised since first entering the brothel snapped. The full realization of what his wife had suffered, and what she had almost been forced to endure, shot through him like a knife. Even as his silvery eyes misted over at the thought of her vulnerability, rage drove out every other consideration.

Barely realizing that he did so, Nigel smashed his huge fist into the wall beside his bed, splintering the wood and sending shards of plaster in all directions. The pain of his bloodied hand had a cleansing effect.

He lay down, still fully dressed, and gave himself over to the contemplation of revenge.

Courtney woke late in the afternoon. She stirred reluctantly, unwilling to let go of the peace and contentment filling her. Dimly, on the edge of her mind, she knew she had come through a terrifying experience and feared more of the same might wait for her on the other edge of consciousness. The oblivion of sleep seemed far safer. But the restored alertness of her body was not to be denied. Hesitantly her eyelids fluttered open.

Mary sat beside the bed, stitching a piece of lace to the sleeve of a chemisette. Courtney's eyes widened as she took in this picture of domestic calm. She was back in her own world, the safety of which she had never before so thoroughly appreciated. Was it possible that the hideous events polluting her memory were nothing more than a ghastly phantasm? Clinging to that thought, wishing desperately that it might be so, she sat up slowly.

The maid dropped her sewing. Hurrying to her mistress's side, she looked down worriedly at her until the renewed color of her cheeks and her puzzled but composed gaze indicated her ladyship was once more in possession of her faculties. A long sigh of relief escaped Mary.

"Oh, ma'am, you gave us such a scare, you did!"

"S-scare . . . ?" Courtney repeated hesitantly.

"I've never seen his lordship in such a state, and God willing, I never will again! When we found out where that horrible man had taken you . . ." Mary reddened painfully, unable to even speak of such a thing.

With the fading of her hopes that the events she recalled were no more than dreams, Courtney forced herself to confront her situation. She remembered nothing of the preparations for the auction and little of the sale itself, but she did recall vividly the man who had bought her for his pleasure, only to promptly remove her from her prison.

Nigel! Of course, how could she have been so foolish as not to see it last night? Her husband had come after her, rescuing her from a fate she could hardly bear to contemplate, and restoring her safely to their home. A warm flush of gratitude spread through her.

"His lordship, is he here?" she asked tentatively.

Mary nodded toward the connecting doors of the master suite. "He's asleep, ma'am. Even after he got you back here, he wouldn't leave you until he was sure you were all right. Worn out, he is, though I'm sure he'll be back to snuff in no time." There was a grudging hint of admiration in the maid's tone. She might not approve of his lordship's insistence on caring for her lady himself, but she gave top marks to his courage and boldness.

Disappointed that she could not see her husband at once, Courtney was also a bit relieved that their interview was to be postponed. Her immense thankfulness for his actions did not blot out the realization that Nigel must be furiously angry. She could do with a few hours to gather her thoughts and prepare herself to face him.

After a light breakfast accompanied by copious amounts of lemonade for which she had a remarkable thirst, she enjoyed a leisurely bath before rejecting Mary's suggestion that she return to bed to rest.

"Nonsense," the young marchioness declared firmly. "I am hardly an invalid. I will dress and go down to the drawing room."

Relieved that her mistress at least had no thought of leaving the house, Mary grudgingly laid out clothes for her. When she was properly attired in a soft rose day dress of muslin accompanied by a cashmere shawl, she left the room eagerly.

For all her assertions to the contrary, she felt rather like someone emerging from a long illness. The return of health could not be any more dramatic than the recovery of safety, she thought as she walked down the

wide staircase and into the sun-dappled drawing room.
Never again would she take such security for granted.
The burgeoning understanding of the real world begun when she entered the East End had matured into a
profound awareness of the vast extremes of both good
and evil possible in human behavior. The world no
longer appeared a relatively placid, even sometimes
tedious place. Quite the opposite; it was an arena in
which all manner of pain and joy might be found.

- Looking around the drawing room with new eyes,
Courtney smiled faintly at herself. Everything seemed
somehow sharper and clearer. The colors were more
vibrant, the patina of polished furniture was warmer,
the fragrance of honeysuckle drifting through the open
windows was sweeter. Tempted to mock her sudden
enthusiasm, she did not. There was nothing foolish
about no longer taking anything for granted.

Sitting down at the pianoforte, Courtney ran her
hands over it lovingly. She played snatches of her favorite melodies before drifting into a sonata whose pure,
liquid tones seemed to express much of what she was
feeling. Her profile was turned toward the door, a
poignant smile curving her lovely mouth as the melody
carried her far away.

It was thus that Sara found her. Surprised by the
music, she had dismissed the footman who would have
presented her and instead found her own way to the
drawing room. The sight which greeted her was as
unexpected as it was moving. Deeply relieved to discover her friend not only apparently recovered but
looking quite content, Sara breathed a silent prayer of
thanks. Loath to interrupt, she stood quietly as the
music reached a final soaring crescendo before softly
dying away. Only then did she move forward, smiling
broadly.

"Courtney, I've never heard you play like that! How
beautiful it is."

Rising gracefully from the music bench, the marchioness greeted her friend with open arms. "Oh, Sara, I'm

so glad to see you! Yesterday . . . you must have been so worried. I'm sorry . . ." She broke off, abashed by the concern she had caused.

"You don't need to say anything more. I'm just so glad you're safe and well. If Nigel hadn't been able to find you . . ." Pain flitted across Sara's smooth face. The shadows of her dread were not completely banished. But she refused to let them darken the happiness of that moment.

Studying her friend carefully, she said, "No one looking at you would guess what you've just been through. I've always known you had spirit, but I never really appreciated how much until now."

Such approbation made Courtney acutely uncomfortable, since she felt it was completely undeserved. "Perhaps I have more room for spirit now that I've cast off folly," she suggested, then quickly drew the conversation away from herself.

"How *did* Nigel find me, Sara? The last thing I remember is being struck and losing consciousness just as I was thrown into a carriage."

"Peggy saw what happened. She ran to get me, but by the time we reached the street you had vanished. Several of the children in the shelter had also seen you taken. They must be even more appreciative of our care than we realized, because they spread out through the area, searching for the carriage. When it was spotted outside Mrs. Hammond's . . . establishment, I was told at once. Since I wasn't sure where to find Nigel, I sent messengers all over. Fortunately, he was at his club with Lloyd." Her eyes softened as she thought of the young peer. The words he had spoken to her as they waited alone in the drawing room would remain forever engraved on her heart. But this was not the time to speak of them.

Quietly she continued, "I've always thought that Nigel was an unusually strong, resourceful man, but he really proved it yesterday. Somehow, he knew exactly what to do. He didn't waste a moment, but decided immediately how to reach you. Of course, we were very worried when he insisted on going in there alone. But he made us see it was the only way. Anything else might have caused them to panic and do away with you before you could be found."

Courtney shivered as she considered the truth of this. The audacity of kidnapping a member of the aristocracy to sell into sexual bondage stunned her. Had London truly reached the point where such things could happen?

Sara echoed her thoughts. Seated close beside her friend on the settee, she said, "Hard though it may be to believe, something good could come out of all this. Nigel and Lloyd have agreed to quietly spread word of what happened to the right quarters, without of course mentioning your name. It is hoped that enough peers will be shocked and outraged to finally take action."

She smiled sadly. "It is unfortunate that no amount of cruelty to the poor seems to have any effect on most people's thinking. But let one of their own be threatened, and they see everything differently. If the program Lloyd has in mind actually becomes law, we will see some major changes that may prevent what happened to you from recurring."

"I hope you are right," Courtney said. "It won't do much good for organizations such as ours to try to help the poor if they aren't also protected from the human vermin who prey on them."

The two friends spoke awhile longer until the sight of a small dark head peering round the door interrupted them. Peggy glanced into the room, then hastily withdrew, only to be called back by Courtney's gentle summons. "Please come in. I think we need to talk."

She knew the moment she saw the child that her estimate was correct. Peggy's eyes were red-rimmed with weeping. She was pale and her shoulders were stooped. She kept her head down, unwilling to meet the marchioness's gaze.

The two women looked at each other worriedly. A

silent message passed between them. Murmuring that she had to be on her way, Sara took her leave. When she was gone, Courtney beckoned the little girl to come and sit beside her.

Peggy did so reluctantly. She perched on the edge of the settee, every muscle in her slight body rigid with misery. Several moments passed, while the marchioness tried to find the best way to approach her. Finally she decided to come straight to the point.

"I have already apologized to Lady Sara for what happened yesterday. Now I also ask your pardon. I know I put my friends through great pain and worry."

The child's mouth dropped open as she stared at her in amazement. Stunned, she forgot her misery long enough to blurt, "But it was *my* fault!"

Courtney put a gentle arm around her shoulders, blinking back tears at the thought of what Peggy must have lived through in the last few hours. "I was afraid you might think that," she said softly. "But you forget, I am a grown woman. It was my choice to run out into the street and attack that man. If I had stopped to think sensibly for a moment, I would have handled it differently. But I did not, and by my foolishness I embroiled myself and others in great danger. The only blame is mine."

"But you wouldn't have gone if I hadn't come and got you. You wouldn't have even known."

"Peggy, if you hadn't acted as you did, another little girl like yourself would have suffered terribly. Believe me, I have a far better awareness now of what I am saying, and I am absolutely convinced that what you did was right. It takes great courage and determination to fight the bad people. You showed both." Smiling down at the child, she added, "I am very proud of you."

The little girl swallowed hard. Barely able to believe that what she most fervently hoped might be true, she whispered, "Then . . . you don't want me to go away?"

Courtney's throat was tight as she shook her head.

"Never. You are part of our household now and we would be quite lost without you. Besides," she teased tenderly, "if you leave, who will teach me all the things I still need to learn if I am to go on helping the children at the shelter?"

Sniffing audibly, Peggy was unable to answer. But she did nestle close against Courtney, her arms going round her waist as the marchioness gently smoothed her hair and continued to murmur to her reassuringly.

Neither the lovely young woman nor the comforted child noticed the tall, somber-eyed man who watched them silently from the door before turning away. Nothing could persuade him to interfere with such a tender scene, but Nigel carried the memory of it with him as he left for a meeting of a far different sort.

9

To Courtney's disappointment, her husband was not at home for supper that evening. She ate a solitary meal in her room before retiring much earlier than her usual hour. Her fear that she would sleep poorly did not materialize. Barely did it seem her head touched the pillow than she was opening her eyes to morning.

The day passed slowly. Aware that if she attempted to go to the shelter, she would be goading Nigel's temper beyond all bounds, Courtney had to be content with another visit from Sara, who assured her all was going well. The marquess, with Sir Lloyd's help, had hired several large, burly young men from the neighborhood to work in very visible positions around the shelter. They were not precisely guards—that might have had the effect of keeping some of the most needy away. But they were clearly not about to stand for any further trouble.

"I do feel reassured by them," Sara admitted. "They seem quite nice and helpful. One confided to me that his sister was sold into . . . one of those places while still a child. He has no idea what happened to her, though naturally he fears the worst. I believe he is only one of many in the East End who want to see an end to such abuse."

She sipped her tea before adding, "I wonder if that sort of sentiment has anything to do with what happened early this morning."

"What was that?" Courtney inquired, nibbling on a sesame biscuit.

"There was a terrible fire in one of the buildings toward the edge of the neighborhood. I don't know exactly what burned, but I heard people saying it was an inferno. Anyone was lucky to get out alive."

"Were there casualties?"

"Quite a few. The woman who owned the building was caught inside with several men in her employ. Others who were apparently customers also died, and quite a few were severely burned." Hesitating, she murmured, "The odd thing is, it seems that a large number of other people, young women mostly, who were also in the building when the fire broke out, escaped without difficulty. It's almost as though the rest were deliberately trapped."

Listening to her, Courtney paled. She had all too clear an idea of what had happened. Even as she told herself Nigel was a civilized man who would look to the law for justice, she sensed such was not necessarily the case. Driven too far, he might lash out with all the resources of his considerable wealth and power. But was he truly capable of such ferocity? Suspecting she would not care for the answer, Courtney tried hard to distract herself, first with Sara's company and later with a new book. Neither worked. Her nerves were strained close to the breaking point when she at last heard her husband arrive home.

He went directly to his own room, where he spoke softly with Johnson. Their words were indistinguishable, but the valet's disapproving snort as he left carrying his master's discarded clothes reached her clearly. Easing open the door to the corridor, Courtney watched the man's receding back. The bundle he carried gave off a faintly charred odor that made her nostrils twitch.

She waited a few minutes, listening to Nigel moving around next door, before abruptly making up her mind. Whether he cared for her company or not, she would wait no longer. Knocking softly at the connecting door, she entered swiftly before he could make any response. "My lord, I am sorry to disturb you, but . . ."

Fastening the belt of his dressing gown, Nigel stared at her in surprise. It had been his intention to seek her out before supper. Never had he expected her to come to him. Taking in her wide, apprehension-darkened eyes and pale cheeks, he crossed the room swiftly. "You are not disturbing me, my dear. On the contrary, I am delighted to see you up and about."

"Oh . . . I thought you might . . . that is, I wasn't sure you wanted to see me."

Leading her over to the overstuffed leather couch that occupied a corner of the room, Nigel sat down beside her. "Of course I do. I am sorry not to have been here today, but pressing business required my attention. Now that it is concluded, I have every intention of remaining at home to enjoy your company."

Confused by his tender, unaccusatory demeanor, the marchioness tilted back her head to study her husband carefully. Fresh from a bath, his hair gleamed like molten gold. Against its lightness, his skin looked like bronze etched with the silver of his eyes. There were hard lines etched around his full mouth and straight nose, speaking of recent strain.

A clean male scent emanated from him. Courtney closed her eyes briefly, overwhelmed by desire that stunned. It was all she could do not to reach out and stroke the expanse of hair-roughened chest left bare by his dressing gown, to feel again the ripple of iron muscles beneath her touch.

Though she was too caught up in her own feelings to realize it, Nigel was equally moved by her nearness. Only the memory of her recent ordeal kept him from carrying her to his bed and reasserting beyond the shadow of a doubt his rights and privileges as her husband.

Seeking some time alone to control his rampaging desire, Nigel suggested, "I need to dress for dinner and

I presume you would like to change. So why don't you join me shortly downstairs?"

Before she could object, he gently but firmly eased her out of the room. Courtney was left staring at the closed door between them, wondering how she was going to ask her husband the question that had increasingly tormented her from the moment she awoke in the safety of her home.

His manner had not changed a short time later when they met again in the parlor. Prompted by instincts she did not quite understand but was still wise enough to obey, Courtney had worn one of her most beguiling gowns. The shimmering emerald silk highlighted the startling clarity of her eyes while emphasizing each delectable curve of her slender body. Worn low on the shoulders with a deep neckline, it exposed much of creamy skin to his regard. Nigel had seen the dress before, and had shown the most complimentary response to it. But now he appeared oblivious of her charms.

"Care for a drink, my dear?" he inquired as she entered the parlor. Nodding, Courtney struggled to hide her growing bewilderment. The evening clothes he had donned made him all the more compellingly attractive. She could think of little except the need to break through his inexplicable reserve. Even anger would be preferable, she thought dismally, to this distant cordiality.

Her efforts did not succeed. As she dallied with a predinner sherry and Nigel finished off his whiskey, he kept the conversation firmly on the most mundane matters. Every attempt to bring up the events of the last few days was adroitly sidestepped. Even when they went in to dinner, which Courtney barely tasted, he did not relent. Long before the sweet was served, her bewilderment had grown to frightening proportions.

Why was he doing this? Did he intend never to mention the incident? Surely Nigel was too intelligent to believe they could go along forever pretending it had not happened. But that seemed exactly what he was intent on doing. Only one possible explanation presented itself. Her sojourn in the brothel so sickened him that he could not bear to speak of it. Courtney's pallor increased as she wondered if that also meant he no longer wished to touch her.

Seeing his wife's distress, though by no means understanding the reason for it, Nigel moved swiftly. "You have rather overdone, my dear. I believe you should retire."

Courtney agreed glumly. She had no spirit left to fight. Nor did she need to be told that her husband would not be joining her in the big empty bed. Bidding him a distinctly cool good night, she withdrew hastily. Upstairs, after Mary had helped her undress and departed, the tears came hot and hard. She wept silently into her pillows, utterly unaware that just below in his study Nigel was systematically drinking himself into a stupor in a desperate effort to stay away from that which he longed for most.

Their curious estrangement continued for several days. True to his word, Nigel remained at home. He was there each morning when Courtney went down to the breakfast room, ensconced behind a newspaper, which he would politely abandon when she appeared. Not a day passed that he did not suggest some excursion, riding in the park, boating on the river, attending a match at Lord's cricket fields, or simply strolling along the elegant byways of Pall Mall.

Though he accepted no social invitations, apparently feeling that she was not yet up to it, he made certain that she was highly visible at his side. No one observing Nigel's gentle, protective attitude toward his wife would be foolish enough to give credence to the rumors about their marriage or to the few mutterings that had surfaced about the incredible events preceding the fire which destroyed Mrs. Hammond's brothel.

There was quite enough to talk about as it was, since two high-ranking lords had died in the fire and several others had suddenly taken it into their heads to depart for parts unknown. The *ton* was hard pressed to keep up with such a surfeit of scandal. The state of the Davies marriage, which on reflection seemed to be in better shape than had been generally thought, was tame in comparison.

Even as she appreciated what her husband was doing, Courtney despaired that there might never again be anything between them other than the appearance of tranquillity. She grew increasingly restless and concerned, sleeping poorly and eating little. Nigel, at a loss to understand her decline, thought it meant he was not being sufficiently solicitous and redoubled his efforts. He took to treating her like a delicate piece of porcelain that would shatter if touched.

Matters reached a peak less than a fortnight after her rescue, when Courtney at last came to the conclusion that she could endure no more. Reasonably certain that she had not been raped, since her own body seemed to tell her that much, she was still plagued by the need to know what had happened to her. However distasteful Nigel might find it, she resolved to confront him soon.

The opportunity finally came after dinner. Since that first evening, she had fallen into the habit of leaving him as soon as the meal was over. He seemed to prefer that, and she needed privacy to sob out her heartbreak. But this time she remained. Better to stand her ground and fight than to be constantly in retreat.

Nigel frowned slightly when he stood to bid her good night and she did not respond as usual. Remaining firmly in her chair, his marchioness said, "I would like to speak with you, my lord. Here or elsewhere, it matters not to me. But I suspect you would prefer that we not be overheard."

His frown deepened to genuine perplexity. "Is something wrong, Courtney—?"

She held up a hand. "Here or elsewhere, my lord? Which do you prefer?"

Sensing that her warning against being overheard was not exaggerated, he reluctantly escorted her upstairs.

Once in her room, where he had not set foot since the night of her rescue, he kept the width of the carpet between them as he said, "All right, now suppose you tell me what this is all about."

Courtney took a deep breath and came right to the point. "I want to know what happened to me that night."

Taken by surprise, Nigel still managed to respond swiftly. His face expressionless, he demanded, "Why?"

"Because it happened to *me*! Surely I have a right to know what was done to my own body."

"Isn't it enough that you are safe?" he countered, meanwhile seeking some way to bring the conversation to a speedy end. He would consult Dr. Blakeston in the morning to get his advice on how to handle her demand. But in the meantime . . .

"No, it is not enough. Would it be for you? If you were drugged insensible for hours in a den of iniquity where anything might be done to you, wouldn't you want to know what had happened?"

It occurred to him suddenly through the fog of his male arrogance just what she might be saying. A dull flush stained his high cheeks as he stumbled, "Surely you don't think . . . that is, I presumed you understood that—"

"That I was not raped," she finished for him bluntly.

"Well . . . uh . . . yes . . ."

"I managed to figure that out for myself, and I have no doubt only your intervention kept that from happening. There is no way to adequately express my gratitude to you, but—"

"Gratitude! I am your husband! What did you expect me to do? Stand by while you were passed from man to man like the most hardened whore?"

"Whether I should be grateful or not," Courtney said firmly, "is beside the point. I want to know what happened."

When he still stubbornly refused to speak, she continued with only the barest tremor in her voice. "I remember your being there. You were dressed all in black and masked. You wore a cape, which you put around me after . . . after I was sold to you."

"What else do you remember?" Nigel demanded, overcome by the need to know how much of that night remained clear in her memory. He had presumed she would be unable to recall anything except for right at the end. But perhaps he was wrong.

"Not much," Courtney admitted. "Two women, one old, the other young. The older one seemed to be in charge."

"Mrs. Hammond. She is . . . no longer in business."

"She is dead."

"How did you know that?"

"Oh, Nigel, I am not some child to be sheltered from every unpleasant or frightening truth! I knew she was dead when I heard about the fire. It was her brothel that burned, wasn't it?"

"Yes, but do not ask me to explain how that happened, because I will not!"

"I had no intention of asking you," Courtney said quietly, making it clear that any such question was unnecessary.

While Nigel struggled to come to terms with this latest evidence of her perception, she went on, "Please try to understand that not knowing what was done to me is far worse than anything you might describe." When he looked skeptical, she insisted, "Truly it is! I am stronger than you think."

Nigel's scowl deepened. The blithe insistence on her strength reminded him of just how stubborn and foolhardy she had been. Grimly he thought of the strain of the last weeks. The nerve-racking days spent trying to be no more than the congenial companion he believed she wanted were as nothing compared with the torturous nights as he tried futilely to drown his need for her in a brandy bottle or paced the floor of his room struggling against the almost irrepressible urge to tear open the door between them and reclaim her fully.

Even before the incident in the brothel, he had been on fire with need for her. His threat to seek relief with the *demimondaine* had never materialized. Rather to his chagrin, he had discovered that no woman but Courtney could satisfy him. Only his regard for her welfare had stopped him so far from seeking that release, and now it seemed that, far from appreciating his solicitude, she resented it.

His mistake seemed clear: he had put her first for too long. It was time to consider his own desires. "So," he muttered, "you are certain of this great strength you possess? I hope you are right, my lady, for it is about to be tested!"

Surprised, Courtney instinctively backed away from him. She did not like the hard glitter in his eyes or the predatory way he stalked her across the room. Always before, her bedchamber had seemed of more than adequate size, but now it appeared to shrink as she tried futilely to elude her husband.

Her knees struck the side of the bed and gave way beneath her. The carefully coiled perfection of her hair was knocked loose, sending a cascade of auburn silk over her bared shoulders. Feeling her hair come down, Courtney reached automatically to restore it. The motion further strained the satin evening dress she wore, outlining the curve of her breasts.

"N-Nigel . . . ?"

"You were telling me how strong you are, my lady," he growled, coming to a stop directly in front of her, so close that the smooth wool of his breeches brushed her trembling knees. Forced to look up at him, Courtney struggled to contain the rapid rise and fall of her breath.

"I . . . I don't understand wh-why you are acting like th-this . . ." she gasped. Always before, his lovemaking had been infinitely demanding, but hardly threatening. The change frightened her more than she cared to admit.

"You will," he promised menacingly as he undid his cravat. His jacket was next, followed rapidly by his waistcoat. Courtney's eyes widened in astonishment as he began unbuttoning his shirt.

"I have been far too patient," Nigel went on, never removing his gaze from the perturbed beauty crouched on the bed before him. "That is obvious now. I cannot undo my mistakes, but I can certainly make sure they do not recur."

"I have no idea what you are talking about," the marchioness declared stoutly, "nor do I understand why you are undressing in my room. You may leave at once!"

Nigel ignored her. His shirt joined the clothes on the floor. The sight of her husband's broad chest, the hair-roughened expanse of muscle and sinew gleaming like bronze in the soft light of the chamber, made Courtney gulp. It seemed an eternity since she had last seen him thus. Some treacherous weakness made her yearn to reach out to him. But she would not, at least not until she understood exactly what game he was playing.

In the tone of voice she had found very useful when coping with her younger brothers, she said: "Really, Nigel, I have no idea what you are thinking of, but this has gone far enough. We can continue this conversation tomorrow, in the breakfast room. But for now, I wish to retire."

She did not add *alone*, but she might as well have. A sardonic smile curved the marquess's hard mouth. "We are in accord, my lady, for I too wish to be abed."

Courtney required no explanations to understand he was not referring to his own bed. The large brown hand unfastening his breeches made his intention clear enough. After all these weeks, he meant to share hers. Even as she felt an astonishing quiver of delight, she wondered what had suddenly made him forget his vow.

"You said you would not touch me until I asked you," Courtney reminded him, hardly aware that she spoke.

"Another mistake, one I intend to rectify immediately." The rest of his clothes were removed, leaving the marquess as nature had intended him. Nature and the added inducement of his lovely wife. Any remaining doubt Courtney might have had about how he intended to spend the night vanished as she stared at his swollen manhood. A tiny flicker of remembered pleasure uncurled within her. It had been so long . . .

His hands on her shoulders forced her to stand. Without pause, Nigel turned her around and began to undo the laces of her gown. "We were speaking of your strength, my dear," he rasped as he slipped the silk from her. "Is it sufficient for you to hear how you were stripped naked before a crowd of lustful men who bid for the right to spread your thighs?"

Bile rose in Courtney's throat. She choked it back, refusing to give him the satisfaction of seeing how horrified she was. Her bold assertion that anything was worse than ignorance was not holding up before the sickening images his words unleashed in her mind.

"Would you care to hear how you looked?" her husband went on implacably. "Your hair tumbled to your waist, as it does now. Your eyes were wide and vacant because of the drugs you were given. Your lips pouted most invitingly, and your nipples were dark, ripe fruits begging to be suckled."

Remembering far more than she had ever thought to, Courtney paled. She could almost hear the lewd shouts of the men, smell the cloying scent of incense and opium, feel her own intense vulnerability. Despite her best efforts, a soft moan broke from her.

Nigel's hands, busy removing her corselette, were briefly stilled. He did not truly wish to hurt her, but the memory of all he had endured the last few weeks spurred him on. Once before, he had made the mistake of walking away from her, believing she would come to him. He would not do so again.

"Are you also sufficiently strong," he demanded, sliding the light whalebone-and-linen garment from her, "to face some truths about your station in life and the purposes for which God intended you?"

"I . . . I don't understand what you mean."

Giving in to overwhelming temptation, Nigel pressed his lips to the scented nape of her neck before responding. "I have done you a disservice, my sweet, in being too tolerant of your wild schemes and unseemly actions. Because of that, you were endangered. Therefore, it is in both our best interests to clear up the misconceptions you obviously have about your role as a woman and a wife."

Easing the chemise from her shoulders, he concluded huskily, "By tomorrow morning I trust no further delusions will remain and you will be quite happily resigned to your fate."

Astonishment blotted out revulsion as she realized what he meant. *How dare he!* That pompous oaf thought he could still use physical measures to subdue her! Did he believe her to be the untried, easily controlled girl he had married? She had lived through far too much since then. It was time his lordship recognized the changes that were transforming her into a strong, forthright woman.

Taking advantage of his preoccupation with her few remaining clothes, Courtney whirled to face him. Her cheeks were flushed and her deep sea-green eyes gleamed dangerously. In a high temper made all the more glorious by her *déshabille*, she exclaimed, "So that is your plan! To use man's age-old weapon to bring me to heel! You make yourself just like those other men who bid for me! Pray tell me, my lord, what acts must I perform before you will feel you have gotten your money's worth?" This last was said with such bitter sarcasm that Nigel flinched.

"C-Courtney . . ." he murmured, not quite relenting but at least determined to blot out any thought she might have that this encounter could be likened to what she would have experienced in the brothel. They were man and wife, he reminded himself fiercely. Their intimacy was beautiful and sanctified by their mutual commitment to one another.

About to say as much, he was stopped by his outraged spouse. "Or do you expect me to cower and plead for mercy? If so, you will be disappointed. I am no more whore than terrified virgin! I am a woman and you would do well to remember that!"

Despite himself, Nigel could not quite control his admiration of her courage. He had deliberately set out to intimidate her, but far from succeeding, he had only awakened the full fury of her glorious femininity. A tremor of anticipation ran through him as he contemplated the upheaval of his plans.

Softly he said, "You may be right to remind me, Courtney. But even if that is the case, you are all the woman I will ever want. Do not blame me for forcing you to accept your fate."

"*My* fate! Hah! Do you think me some passive vessel for your will? I am not! My desires are a match for yours any day, my lord!"

Refusing to be deterred by what she had just admitted, Courtney banished the last remnants of modesty and hurtled on, "When we were first wed, I was completely unprepared for the way you made me feel. Even though I could not help but enjoy it physically, I was very resentful of the ease with which you seemed able to control me. That feeling was uppermost in my mind when I sent you from this room, only to deeply regret my foolishness. I robbed myself of what I wanted most, out of some silly, stiff-necked idea that the world should suddenly be perfect because I willed it so. I was guilty of the same error you make now, my lord. There is no sense in trying to force another person to see everything your own way or act in every case as you would. It is enough that you and I have found much joy together. I will deny myself that happiness no longer!"

"Wh-what are you saying?" the flustered marquess demanded. He did not precisely understand how his wife had turned the entire situation in on him, nor was he absolutely certain that he minded. Any effort to muster indignation faded swiftly as Courtney slipped the chemise from her body and stood before him proudly naked.

"I am saying, husband," she declared succinctly, "that I wish to resume our marital intimacy."

When he continued to stare at her dumbfounded, she lost all patience. "I wish you to share my bed, Nigel! Must I put it more clearly than that?" Recovering himself at last, the marquess took a quick step toward her. Her body was honeyed velvet against his. Her slender curves filled his arms. Her taut breasts, rubbing against his chest, drove him near mad with need.

"Oh, Courtney," he groaned into her hair, "you are the most damnable woman! Here I had every intention of delivering a salutary lesson on the proper role of a wife, and you manage to upset everything!"

"If you wish to debate social roles, my lord," she murmured as her eager hands stroked the bulging muscles of his back, "confine yourself to the drawing room. This is the setting for more intimate discussion."

Her husband laughed throatily. Lifting her easily, he carried her to the bed, where he laid her down tenderly. Courtney's touch never left him. As a blatantly provocative smile curved her lips, she drew her husband to her. Their bodies merged as eagerly as darting flames melding into an inferno.

Nigel groaned with delight as his wife fought to take the lead in their lovemaking. He yielded graciously, allowing her her way as she coaxed and tempted and teased until he could bear it no longer. Returning her swiftly to her back, he penetrated the depths of her womanhood in a single thrust. A moan of pleasure tore from her as they were both engulfed in ecstasy.

When the storm had subsided, Courtney nestled against her husband. She smiled faintly and reached out a small pink tongue to lick the salty elixir of his skin. He shivered delightedly. "Wench!"

Arms and legs entwined, they slept briefly, only to waken with their bodies already reaching out to each other once again. A wicked smile lit the marchioness's eyes as she said, "I set your account at two hundred guineas, my lord. We have another four to spend. Do you think you have the stamina?"

"Hah! Have no fear of that, my lady." His hands and mouth confirmed his confidence as Courtney wiggled deliciously. Against the fragrant silk of her breasts he muttered, "I will undoubtedly be heavily in debt by morning!"

— 10 —

"Of course you should go with him," Sara insisted. "This is no time for you and Nigel to be apart."

Courtney was inclined to agree with her. In the weeks since the scene in her bedroom, she and the marquess had kept busy exploring the nature of marital compromise. They were getting rather good at it, but that was no reason to tempt their luck with a separation.

With her new sensitivity to Nigel's concern for her, Courtney restricted her work at the shelter to four days a week under the careful eyes of the young men he had hired. In return, he supplied ample funds to engage additional staff, purchase supplies, and generally meet her highest hopes for the help they would be able to offer.

Though Nigel said frankly that his financial support was in the nature of a bribe, Courtney did not mind. The welfare of the many children now coming to them for aid, and her own security in herself as a woman who no longer had to prove her independence, made all contributions welcome, no matter why they were given.

In the back of her mind she might wish that he truly understood and shared her concern for those so much less fortunate than they themselves. But whenever such a thought arose, she reminded herself of how far they had come since their marriage and determinedly counted her blessings.

In part because she wanted Nigel to know of her appreciation, but mainly because she could not endure the thought of being away from him, she had viewed his projected trip to Manchester gloomily.

"I don't want to go," he explained as they lay in bed the night before, sated with the pleasure of their lovemaking, "but I must. There is a limit to the authority I will relinquish to others. Occasionally, I have to take a look at things for myself."

Courtney could hardly complain. She knew that Nigel had not visited the mills that provided a large measure of their wealth since before their marriage. Whereas other lords might consider it beneath them to give a moment's thought to affairs of business, the marquess was far too intelligent and realistic to leave such essential matters completely in the hands of a trustee, regardless of how experienced or trustworthy he might be. Several times a year he bestirred himself to visit the sources of their income. Such a trip was now overdue.

"Will you be gone long?" she asked glumly.

"A fortnight, perhaps slightly more." Nigel hesitated before tipping her chin back to look at her as he said, "Courtney . . . you could come with me."

Of course, why hadn't she thought of that? Though hardly on a par with their wedding trip to the Continent, any journey with Nigel would be delightful. She could imagine them exploring new places together, talking over his business concerns, making love behind the locked door of their hotel room. . . .

It was really rather embarrassing how her mind kept returning to that single topic she was once unable to contemplate at all. Determinedly Courtney forced her attention back to Sara. Her friend smiled patiently as she repeated herself. "Lloyd mentioned to me that there is a lady in Manchester, a Mrs. Wilson, who is providing considerable help to the poor of that town. Perhaps while you are there you could meet with her. She might be able to give us some excellent advice."

The last of Courtney's hesitation about the journey

vanished. She could go with Nigel without disregarding any of her responsibility to the shelter. While he was busy at the mills, she would look up Mrs. Wilson. With all the questions she was accumulating about the needs of the poor and the best way to meet them, they would undoubtedly have a great deal to talk about.

The marquess's party set out the following day. It included both Johnson and Mary, as well as two coachmen and a bevy of footmen. Leaving the open barouche at home, Courtney and Nigel occupied a well-fitted brougham, while the valet and maid made do with a somewhat less luxurious version of the same sort of carriage to transport both themselves and the ample amount of baggage.

Although the weather was fair, the snug coach was a blessing, since it protected them from the dirt and dust of the road. Her ladyship's upturned nose wrinkled as she surveyed the shower of debris sent up by their horses' pounding hooves. "Mr. McAdam's services are needed here."

That estimable gentleman had recently drawn national attention to Bristol by covering the surfaces of all roads passing through his city with crushed stone, which both improved drainage and reduced dust. But his influence had not yet been felt on the London–Manchester route.

Nigel groaned in mock dismay. "I trust you are not considering yet another cause, my dear. Were you to take up the challenge of paving the kingdom's roads, I would fear greatly for our rustic ways. Within a year or two, at the most, Britain would be *macadamized* from end to end."

Though her face warmed at the loving look she saw in his eyes, Courtney merely sniffed in response. Resigning herself to a long, stuffy trip, she tried to divert herself with one of the books she had brought along. Nigel was busy with reports concerning the mills, which he wished to read before beginning his inspection tour. She was loath to interrupt him, knowing that if they were not read now, they would have to be attended to that evening at the inn where they would stop for the night, when she would much prefer his undivided attention.

As the book failed to hold her interest, Courtney gazed absently out the window. Having not traveled north of London in years, she was curious to see what changes might have occurred.

They were more drastic than she had expected. The lumbering coach passed barren fields where once wheat had ripened, mute reminders of the official policy to keep supply low and prices high. Enormous profits were made by the landowners, who were not put to the expense of seeding all their property or hiring laborers to tend it.

In the villages they passed, ragged men and women stood mutely watching the coach go by. There was a vacant hopelessness in their eyes Courtney had not seen before. She noticed it again in the farm workers who lined up to one side of the crossroads where they stopped to water the carriage horses.

When she suggested she would like to stretch her legs, Nigel seemed at first predisposed to agree. But after a quick glance out the window, he shook his head. "We will be at the inn before dark. You can take a stroll then."

Although she suspected the answer, Courtney asked, "Is it because of those men?"

Nigel hesitated a moment before nodding. "They are waiting for work, probably have been since before dawn, and by now their chances of finding anything for the day are very slim. Tempers grow short in such circumstances. There is no sense in provoking belligerence."

Her gaze moved to the brace of pistols beneath his seat. She had wondered why he was bringing them along, but had not thought to question him. Now it was no longer necessary. Even the large crowd of farm workers with their crude implements would be helpless before such weapons. Nigel had anticipated the possibility of a confrontation, and was prepared to deal with it expeditiously.

"Has there been trouble on the roads?" she asked softly.

He shrugged. "Not very much. Highwaymen still plague certain remote areas, but are too clever to attack a pair of coaches traveling by day. There have been a few incidents of unrest, though. For that reason, it is wise to be cautious."

Unrest. Courtney turned the word over in her mind. It could mean a great deal, or very little. Certainly England seemed more at peace than it had in some time. There had been no recent repetitions of the hostile crowds that greeted the Prince Regent two years before when he went to open Parliament. The firm measures put into effect then seemed to have put an end to disquiet.

Or had they? An England in which *habeas corpus* was suspended, any criticism of government could be labeled seditious, and magistrates throughout the country were handing down the harshest possible penalties, for even minor offenses might give the misleading impression of serenity. Much as a teakettle does in the moments before it suddenly begins to whistle and shake.

A shiver darted through her as the carriage moved on past the sullen group of men. They looked tired and hungry and desperate. Not unlike the children she saw in the shelter. If such inhumanity was no longer confined to the cities, but was spreading through the rural heart of the nation, surely intolerable pressures for change must be building.

She wanted to say as much to Nigel, but he was once again emeshed in the neat columns of figures detailing mill production. So many looms in use. So many workers employed in their operation. So much spent for materials, wages, and shipping costs. So much earned as profit for his lordship.

The numbers meant nothing to Courtney except that they represented the way of life she had always presumed would continue. It surprised her to discover she was no longer certain she wanted it to.

Lulled by the rhythmic sway of the coach, she had almost drifted to sleep when they pulled up before the Red Rooster Inn. A popular stopping point on the Manchester–London route, it was larger and better appointed than most inns. A fact which was clearly a source of pride to the plump proprietor, who hastened out to greet them.

"A great honor, my lord, my lady. Our humble establishment is proud to have you."

The man's unctuousness grated. Nigel must have thought so as well, for he was unusually cool. A mere nod sufficed to acknowledge the proprietor's presence before he said, "Her ladyship is fatigued and would like to rest before dinner. Kindly show us to our quarters."

Nearly tripping over himself in his haste to obey, the proprietor escorted them inside. As stableboys hurried to unhitch the horses and lead them away for a brisk rubdown under the careful eyes of the carriage drivers, Mary and Johnson stayed behind to supervise the footmen unloading the luggage. Although little would be needed during their overnight stay, it was best to leave no belongings in the coach. Not with thievery so common despite the horrific penalties.

The room set aside for their lord and ladyship was small but clean. A wood-frame bed occupied most of it. Covered by bleached linen sheets and a quilt, it looked comfortable enough. A chest and wardrobe took up the remaining space between the bed and a curtained window overlooking the river that ran behind the inn.

Glad that they were not above the courtyard, which was likely to be noisy no matter what the hour, Courtney pulled off her bonnet and removed her high-necked spencer. Beneath the jacket, her day dress was somewhat rumpled. But she judged it would do well enough for dinner in the private room Nigel had undoubtedly reserved.

Maids hastened in with a basin of warm water and towels. After washing her face and hands and smoothing her hair, Courtney lay down on the bed to wait while Nigel saw to his own tidying. Having assured Johnson his services could be dispensed with in such tight quarters, the marquess matter-of-factly straightened his cravat and shook the worst of the wrinkles from his frock coat.

His wife smiled faintly, wondering how many of his friends could see to their own needs as effectively. Like as not, most of the peerage was helpless without the constant care of servants. It wasn't clear to her exactly who was responsible for such ineptitude, the so-called masters or the retainers who encouraged their dependency. The thought of a vast underclass of Johnsons and Marys meticulously maintaining the nobility in a state of near-infantile helplessness made her smile widen.

"What amuses you?" her husband inquired, gazing at her gently.

Briefly she told him, adding, "It's not as outrageous as it sounds. After all, our servants decide what we will eat and wear, they see to our amusements, soothe our tempers, and are ever cautious of our health. Just as though we were perpetual children who never quite made it out of the nursery."

"Only our pastimes change," Nigel mused. "From storybooks and tag, we progress to parties, hunts, and indiscretions. Hardly an improvement."

The underlying bitterness of his tone startled Courtney. Weeks before, he had mentioned his boredom with the social whirl. But so much had happened since, that they had not discussed the matter further. Honesty compelled her to admit this was in large measure her fault. She had been so caught up in her discovery of herself as someone capable of making decisions and taking actions that she had given little thought to her husband.

Accompanying him downstairs, Courtney resolved that would have to change. But the dining room of a public inn was not the place to embark on a private discussion. Though they were apart from the common room shared by less affluent travelers, they were still constrained in their speech. Serving girls came and went with heavy trays of roast fowl, garnished potatoes, meat pies, cheeses, and savories, all very well prepared and fresher than what was usually available in town.

Discovering that she was hungrier than she had thought, Courtney thoroughly enjoyed the meal. She and Nigel shared an excellent hock. The marchioness drank rather more than usual of the white Rhine wine, heedless of the pleasant glow that quickly engulfed her.

The marquess, far more accustomed to heady drink, observed his wife tolerantly. Slightly tipsy, she made a delightful spectacle. A rosy flush emphasized the porcelain delicacy of her skin. Thick-fringed eyes sparkled invitingly. As he watched, leaping flames were reflected in emerald irises ringed with a darker midnight blue. Her lips parted slightly, a small tongue darting out to moisten them.

Nigel swallowed with difficulty. One appetite sated, he found another requiring his urgent attention. Suggesting it was time to retire, he was pleased by her ready compliance. Courtney needed no urging. Her hunger matched his own. Barely had they reached their room than she turned into his arms, nestling close.

Small hands made swift work of his cravat and shirt. Nigel shrugged them off along with his jacket and waistcoat. Courtney muttered with frustration at the ungiving stays of her dress. The mutter turned to an outraged giggle as her equally impatient husband caught the laces between lean brown fingers and snapped them apart.

What Mary would say, she could not imagine. But a pair of laces seemed singularly unimportant when weighed against the urgency of her desire. All thought faded before the delight of his caresses as the remainder of their clothes were hastily removed and they tumbled across the bed.

Neither was in the mood for long seduction. Pushing aside the sheet and quilts that were not needed on such a torpid August night, Nigel positioned her beneath him. His mouth drifted down the hardened peaks of her breasts, across the silk smoothness of her abdomen to tease her inner thighs. An anguished moan tore from Courtney as his caresses became more daring, bringing her to the edge of ecstasy.

Swiftly he moved to join them, his possession coming as joyful relief. Courtney rose to meet him, her fingers tangled in his golden hair, sensitized nipples rubbing languorously against his chest. Nigel was in no condition to long endure such torment. Grasping her buttocks, he increased the pace. With eagerness that astonished them both, Courtney urged him on. They moved as one toward an irresistible peak of fulfillment that left them both trembling with exhaustion but infinitely satisfied.

Not bothering to cover their perspiration-slicked bodies, they drifted off into dreamless sleep.

The first day set the pattern for their journey. While they traveled, Nigel studied his reports and Courtney tried to read or, more often than not, stared out the window. She saw far more than she would have liked to of rural poverty and the despair it bred. The farther they traveled from London, the clearer it was that work was scarce and food even more so.

Whole areas of the Midlands seemed deserted, the population gone to the cities in search of jobs. The property owners were undoubtedly pleased by the migration, since it served them in two ways. The countryside was freed of the potentially dangerous poor, and the factories and mills gained the cheap labor force they required.

Courtney tried to convince herself it was for the best. After all, England was moving into a new era in which the plow and hoe could not compete with the mechanized loom and steam engine. Goods were far more plentiful than ever before, and the standard of living for those who could afford to buy them was rising precipitously. That was progress, wasn't it?

But as often as she repeated this, Courtney could not dismiss the haunted, despairing looks on the faces of the poor. They were the helpless victims of change who saw everything they lived by and believed in destroyed in the name of a better future.

Coming into Manchester, past the coal mines and gas plants ringing the city, she wondered what would happen if that future did not arrive soon.

The factories themselves, when they at last arrived near them, were not as somber as Courtney had expected. Far from being dark, they were so well lit by gas lamps that even during day the interiors seen through their broad windows were brighter than the outside.

Eight or nine stories high and hundreds of feet long, the blocks of buildings making up each factory or mill were an impressive sight. Because they were supported by iron girders, the walls were unusually narrow and graceful. All signs of the destruction done several years before by the antimachine Luddites had vanished. There was an air of pristine order and cleanliness that made it difficult to believe human beings worked there. Yet they did, under the unrelenting discipline of industrialization.

The center of the city was far more humane. A verdant park bordered one side of the hotel where they would be staying. After the rigors of country inns, Courtney was happy to give herself up to the luxury of the Royale Hotel. Though hardly up to London standards, the rooms were graciously appointed and the large staff was meticulously attentive to the care of guests.

Even Mary sniffed approvingly as she accompanied her mistress to the suite of rooms their lord and ladyship would occupy during their stay. Nigel departed to visit the first of his mills with a reminder that they were invited out to dinner.

Relaxing in a warm bath, Courtney only half-listened
to her maid's chatter about how good it was to be off
the road. Her mind was on the coming evening, when
she and Nigel would be feted by the leading citizens of
Manchester.

Emerging from behind the modesty screen, she stood
patiently as Mary draped a gown of amber satin over
her. The dress was deceptively simple. Cut low in front
and back, it narrowed to a tiny waist that fortunately
owed little to her corselette. Full sleeves tightened slightly
at the elbow to taper off in a wide lace cuff. The
pleated skirt revealed panels of matching gold lace
lined with satin. A high sash further emphasized the
contrast of her small waist and generously curved breasts
and hips.

Try though she did to convince her mistress to accept a proper coiffure, Courtney refused. She allowed
Mary to do no more than brush her hair and secure it
high on the back of her head with tortoiseshell combs,
from which it fell in glorious freedom to brush against
her bare back.

Any protests the maid might have made were forgotten when she considered that the screen of hair at least
added a slight touch of modesty to what was otherwise
an utterly fashionable but nonetheless provocative gown.

She was not at all surprised when his lordship, entering the room from his own chamber, where he had
changed for dinner upon his return from the mill,
grinned appreciatively. Mary took her leave quickly,
well aware that she would not be required when the
couple returned.

The evening's entertainment was held at Manchester's
answer to the Royal Pavilion at Brighton. Gaudily replete with marble and gilt, the smaller but nonetheless
extravagant version of Prinny's pleasure dome twinkled
with a hundred crystal chandeliers recently converted
to gaslighting. Beneath their radiance, silks and satins
took on a deeper luster, heightened by a parade of

some of the most extravagant jewels Courtney had ever seen.

Barely had they stepped inside than she thanked fortune that she had worn one of her most lavish gowns. The extravaganza of wealth confronting her matched anything the *ton* could offer. Which was, she realized, precisely the point.

"Good Lord," she murmured as Nigel led her forward to meet their hosts, "I don't believe even Almack's has managed to gather such a show under one roof. Do they do this often?"

"No, just frequently enough to remind themselves and everyone else that they have just as much to be proud of as any aristocrat in London. Most of them may not as yet have noble titles, but when it comes to real power, few can match them." He gestured obliquely toward the tall, ruddy-faced man waiting at the head of the receiving line.

"That is Sir Thomas Logan and his wife, Lady Margaret. A year ago they were plain mister and missus, until Prinny saw the wisdom of ennobling them in return for a rather substantial contribution toward paying his debts. Officially, the honor is in recognition of Sir Thomas' leadership in the wool and cotton trade, which is considerable."

Courtney was not surprised by this practice. She knew that Nigel's own title dated back no further than his great-grandfather, who had received it in reward for supplying superior arms to the forces of George II opposing the French in North America. Her own family's ascension to the aristocracy had occurred somewhat earlier, during the reign of Charles II, who granted their titles for reasons having to do with the special services of one of her ancestresses, better left undiscussed.

So she felt no hesitation about greeting Sir Thomas and his lady as courteously as she would have the most exalted member of the *ton*. Her obvious sincerity as she expressed her pleasure at meeting them quickly won over both the stern-faced mill owner and his wife.

Lady Margaret was a little bird of a woman dressed in gray not at all enlivened by a shower of pearls that drained what little color remained in her powdery complexion. But what she lacked in stature she made up for in sheer vivacity.

Extending a hand to Courtney, she said, "You are most welcome, my dear. May I congratulate you on your appearance? For any lady to look so lovely after such a grueling journey is a feat indeed. But you look positively radiant."

"Sir Nigel has always had remarkable good fortune," Sir Thomas added, not to be outdone. He meant to show he could match pleasantries with the best of them, and succeeded admirably.

Courtney enjoyed herself thoroughly as she danced first with Sir Thomas, then with several other of the gentlemen representing Manchester's ruling class. They were all unfailingly polite, if extremely reserved. There was none of the easy repartee that went on among the *ton*, but then, she had not expected it. Vividly aware of their origins, often on the deserted farms or in the early factories that could still be seen in the surrounding areas, they were not about to bend the social rules even minutely.

Moving gracefully about the dance floor, the lovely marchioness was held at a rigid one-foot distance. Conversation was understandably stilted, though she managed to ease it considerably through gracious questions about the city that drew gratified replies.

Before the evening was far progressed, word had already gone round the Pavilion that Lady Courtney was an unexpectedly lovely and amenable gentlewoman. So great was the praise for her beauty and charm that Nigel could not resist teasing her.

When he was at last able to claim his wife for a dance, he murmured in her ear, "I can see now that I should have stayed in London and left you to conduct

my affairs here. A few days of this and I would have no
more business competitors. Only eager gentlemen more
than happy to grant your every wish."

Tapping him lightly on the arm with her fan, Courtney
chuckled. "That is an excellent idea. I only wish you
had thought of it sooner. Obviously I have missed a
great career in business."

The thought of his lovely wife engaged in trade was
so amusing that Nigel almost burst out laughing. Only
the realization that a few months before he could not
have imagined her working among the children of the
East End stopped him. Cautiously he said, "Disabuse
yourself of any such notion, my sweet. Your penchant
for getting your own way is too dangerous to inflict on
my fellowman. Besides, I think you have quite enough
to concern yourself with as it is."

Pleasantly surprised that he seemed quite sincere in
his appraisal of her abilities, Courtney shot him a tender look. Its impact was such that Nigel sighed inwardly,
wondering how much longer it would be before they
could properly take their leave.

There was still the supper to get through, followed
by more dancing. Courtney entered the vast dining
room on Sir Thomas' arm as Nigel escorted Lady
Margaret.

The meal was as sumptuous as any served to Prinny
himself. Turtle soup, salmon, smelts, and turbot were
followed by beef roasts, saddles of mutton, fowls, cold
tongue, and ham. Boiled potatoes seemed to accompany every course, arriving at the table as tepid as everything else. Cauliflower and pickles rounded off the
vegetables, with the idea being to get as many different
kinds of food as possible on one's fork at the same time
and daintily hoist it into the mouth without spillage.

The results were not always what one hoped. Courtney
found it far simpler to take solitary bites of a few
courses and let most of the rest go by. In this way she
even managed to have room for the meringue, which
was her favorite sweet.

Throughout the meal, the talk was light and congenial. Until two gentlemen began to discuss their conviction that the poor were getting above themselves and the topic quickly spread from one end of the table to the other.

"I don't understand how those people have such effrontery," Lady Margaret marveled. "It was bad enough when they dared to demonstrate in small groups, but now I hear they are drilling with staves and planning some sort of major rally."

Perplexed, Courtney looked from her hosts to her husband, who seemed to understand what Lady Margaret was referring to. "I wouldn't put too much credence in those reports of drilling," he soothed. "They come from the yeoman militia, a rather unreliable source."

"The men of the militia mean well," Sir Thomas conceded, "but they have been known to get a bit too fired up."

"You can hardly blame them," Lady Margaret insisted. Turning to Courtney, she explained, "Most of the militia consists of small property owners who may have a share in a single factory or mill. They view the discontent of the laborers as especially threatening and are inclined to deal with them harshly."

"But surely these people have a right to express their views," Courtney ventured, "so long as they do it peacefully."

"That is the problem," Sir Thomas murmured. "Thus far, their meetings have been law-abiding. Oh, there are always a few firebrands, especially among the speakers, but nothing has ever come of it. But that may not last."

"Why not?" Nigel asked, appearing to give more attention to his sherry than he did to the question. Courtney was not misled by his seeming casualness. Though they were seated across the table from each other, she could almost feel the tension in his lean, hard body as he waited for Sir Thomas' response.

"Because Orator Hunt will be at their next meeting," the older man said tightly.

Nigel frowned. He made no further comment, instead adroitly turning the conversation back to safer ground. The party continued on most successfully to the early hours of the morning. But for Courtney, at least, the earlier carefree atmosphere did not return. She continued to wonder who Orator Hunt might be and why the mention of his name troubled her husband.

— 11 —

"Our major problems here in Manchester," Emily Wilson explained, "are malnourishment and consumption. Many of the people we see have worked in the mines or the mills, both of which seem to cause lung ailments."

Following the soft-spoken young lady through the women's dormitory of the Samaritan Shelter, Courtney was as much impressed by Emily Wilson herself as by what she saw. She had never before encountered anyone so quietly purposeful and resolute. Within a body slender enough to hint at frailty lived a spirit that would not bow down before the greatest human misery or cruelty. At twenty-eight, Emily had seen more suffering than Courtney could imagine. Yet she still persevered and was willing to share her knowledge generously.

"We began three years ago," Emily explained, "with a single room offering food and shelter to homeless mothers and their babies. I had a small income left to me by my late husband. That was enough to get us started, but it quickly became apparent that the need was far greater than our resources could meet."

"What did you do?"

"I approached the leading citizens of Manchester." Emily smiled faintly, remembering. "They were quite scandalized. Many had known my father and husband and thought I was behaving most improperly for a woman of my class. We aren't supposed to be aware of the grimmer side of life, you know."

158

"So I've been told. It seemed that we can either argue about what we should or should not be allowed to do, or simply ignore the subject and get on with what we know is right. I have tried to do the latter."

Emily nodded approvingly. "From your letter, I gathered you have a practical turn of mind. You show no sign of being inflicted with the maudlin sentimentality common to so many who claim they wish to do good works. Frankly, that is the only reason I agreed to see you."

"I know how busy you must be," Courtney began quickly, anxious to make it clear that she greatly appreciated the lady's time and effort.

"It isn't that. No matter how much needs to be done in a day, I can always make room to talk about what we are doing here. No, the difficulty is that too many wealthy ladies and gentlemen are more interested in indulging their curiosity than in actually helping."

Glancing around the neat, sunlit dormitory lined with two rows of beds separated by small chests, Emily added, "I take the view that our residents are entitled to as much privacy as possible. They are not exhibitions in a zoo, to be studied by the callously inquisitive. If there is a genuine desire to understand the misfortunes of the poor and work to improve their lives, then I will do everything possible to assist. Otherwise, I will not permit them to be pricked and proded by so-called do-gooders who don't even think of them as human beings."

Though Emily never raised her voice above the mild tone heard in drawing rooms, there was no mistaking the fiery determination behind her words. Courtney did not doubt she was an able champion of the downtrodden. She even felt a slight twinge of sympathy for those leading citizens of Manchester who had felt the full force of her resolution. No wonder they had donated the funds she required. Had they not, Emily would certainly have kept after them tenaciously.

"Whatever illusions I had about the poor and my capacity to help them," the marchioness said levelly, "were quickly cured. If there is nobility in poverty, I have yet to encounter it. If there is a limit to the potential venality of man, I have not found it. Accepting that, I am doing what I can."

Emily surveyed the calm, somber-eyed woman beside her astutely. Beneath the lovely face and form, she recognized a strength akin to her own. Whatever last doubts she had about Lady Davies' sincerity and ability disappeared.

The first smile Courtney had seen lit her hostess's face. Black eyes sparkled vibrantly. The effect was startling. From a pale, mouse-haired nonentity in a shapeless gray frock, she was transformed into a compellingly vital woman far more attractive than any vapid society beauty.

So great was the change that Courtney could only stare at her in amazement as Emily said, "Good, then we can cut through all the nonsense about why people are poor and whether or not they are really capable of being helped. I gather we both understand that but for the grace of God, we could share their plight. So the question is, what do we do about it? You have started with a children's shelter?"

"Yes, in the East End. In addition to illnesses caused by chronic lack of food and alcoholism, we face several other problems there. Chief among them is the abuse of children, which often takes the form of prostitution. Combating that is our first objective."

Courtney watched carefully to see how this blunt statement would be received. To her relief, Emily only nodded. "Prostitution, especially of children, is fortunately limited here. Far more widespread are harmful labor practices."

As she spoke, she approached one of the beds, on which a young woman lay. Spectrally thin, with the ashen pallor that precedes death, the girl could not have been more than eighteen. A hoarse, gasping sound came from her as she struggled to breathe. The effort exhausted her. She seemed barely able to lift blue-veined eyelids to gaze at her visitors.

"Hello, Harriet," Emily said softly, taking one of the girl's translucent hands in her own. "How are you feeling today?"

"A-all right . . ." The tortured whisper belied her brave assertion. Courtney had to blink hard to clear her vision before Emily drew her forward.

"Harriet, I would like you to meet a visitor, Lady Courtney Davies. She is from London, where she has just opened a shelter for children."

Harriet nodded, studying the beautiful apparition before her in mingled bewilderment and awe. As she did so, Emily murmured, "Harriet worked in a mill for ten years. Her lungs were infected with flax dust. I am trying to get her into the small free medical clinic which opened a few months ago, but it is already badly overcrowded."

Unspoken was the realization that the clinic could do Harriet no good. She was beyond help, as soon as she would be beyond life itself. The narrow metal-frame bed in the Samaritan Shelter was her last refuge.

"A mill. . . . Not one of my husband's?"

"No," Emily assured her quickly. "Lord Davies' mills are unusually clean and the women who tend the machines are allowed more rest periods than is customary. Mind you, I am not saying they are wonderful places to work, but they are better than most."

"Are there many here like Harriet?"

Emily did not answer at once. She smoothed the dying girl's limp hair back from her forehead and assured her she would return later in the day before leading Courtney out of earshot. At last she said, "There are far too many. Each day, dozens more girls and women come from the countryside to try to find work. They know few men are hired for the mills, it being thought that women's hands are better suited to the labor and at far lower cost. Most of them end up standing twelve to sixteen hours a day in airless rooms, breathing in the flax and wool dust, rushing from machine to machine to make sure no thread snaps or becomes tangled, and all for a pittance that barely keeps body and soul together. Very few survive past their twenties. Many, like Harriet, don't make it that far."

"Why do they endure it?"

"Most have no choice. The bolder among them immigrate to America or the Crown Colonies. But there is no guarantee of a better life even then. Many of those who stay may have plans to leave, but time passes and they grow increasingly weak. After a while, they give up their hopes and resign themselves."

Despite the bright sunshine and the warmth of the day, Courtney shivered. The evidence of man's inhumanity struck her forcibly, as did its ultimate imprudence.

"But surely," she ventured, "they will not go on enduring these conditions forever? England has only begun to industrialize. Beyond the rantings of the Luddites, who only knew they wanted no change, there must be opposition stirring."

Emily glanced over her shoulder, confirming that except for the now sleeping Harriet, they were alone in the dormitory. Even so, she kept her voice so soft as to be barely audible. "Of course there is. And when it comes, Manchester is likely to be at the center. God help us then, for there are many among the city fathers who would like nothing better than to have an excuse to strike out at those they consider inferior."

Leaving the dormitory, the two women proceeded through the small courtyard that led to the dining hall, where preparations for the evening meal were already under way. Large stew pots bubbled under the careful eyes of several women. Courtney noted distantly that all ingredients were meticulously peeled and chopped so that there was no waste. Her mind was on what Emily had just revealed, and how it tied in with the events of the previous evening.

"Last night," she began uncertainly, "Lord Davies and I attended a dinner at which someone named Orator Hunt was mentioned. Do you know of him?"

Emily's back stiffened. She shot Courtney an assessing gaze, as though to gauge the extent of her ignorance. Finally she said, "Yes, the name is familiar to me. He is more correctly known as Mr. Howard Hunt, an outspoken proponent of parliamentary reform and repeal of the Corn Laws."

"And he is coming here?"

Emily nodded reluctantly. "Tomorrow, to address a rally at St. Peter's Fields. He is a fiery speaker. Many will turn out to hear him."

"Surely as long as he makes no statement advocating violence or sedition, he has the right to speak?"

"By law he does," Emily acknowledged. "Our respect for that right has protected him in the past. I can only pray it will continue to do so."

Pondering these words, Courtney accompanied her to the small office where Emily met each afternoon with individuals seeking assistance. One after another, they entered the tiny office from the anteroom where others were patiently waiting. Their problems were all different, yet all linked by the shared burden of poverty.

"It's my missus, ma'am," a grizzled miner explained, twisting his cloth cap between scarred hands. "She has a pain in the stomach and can't keep down any food. We tried the clinic, but they're full. None of the church hospitals would take 'er, said there wasn't anything they could do. Now we don't know where to turn."

Emily nodded compassionately. She asked several questions about the woman's age and overall health before reaching for a battered wooden box on her desk. Flipping through it, she found the name she was looking for and wrote it down on a slip of paper in large block letters the miner would be able to read. "This man is a physician who occasionally donates his services to patients who cannot afford to pay. Tell him that I sent you."

When the man had left, after thanking her fervently, she explained, "I have to be careful whom I send to this doctor. He is one of the few who will give any time at all to the poor. If he felt he was being asked to do too much, he would stop altogether. So I have to be sure the case is both serious enough to warrant his attention and has at least some chance of being successfully treated."

"Then you have to know something about medicine yourself, if only to be aware of what questions to ask?"

"That's right," Emily agreed. "As you become more involved with your own shelter, you will find you must acquire all sorts of information and skills you never expected to have. I used to lie awake at night wondering how I would ever be able to handle all the different problems. Finally I just decided to concentrate my energies on doing the best I could. In the end, that is all anyone can expect."

Courtney was still pondering what Emily had said, comparing it to her own tendency to try to do everything for everyone, when a small boy entered the office. He was no more than nine, and scrawny, with the pale skin of a child who rarely sees the sun. His clothes were thin and torn at the elbows and knees, where, despite the evidence of frequent patchings, his knobby joints stuck out.

Timidly accepting Emily's invitation to sit down, the boy kept his eyes lowered as he said, "Begging your pardon, ma'am, but I was wondering if you'd know of a place where me and my brothers and sisters could stay."

"I might," Emily said gently. "How many of you are there?"

"Five, ma'am, counting me." With a hint of pride, he added: "I'm the eldest."

"And your parents?"

Thin shoulders shrugged resignedly. "They're gone, ma'am. Me mother died two years ago when Tessa, that's the youngest, was born. Pa took off before then. I'm the only one can even remember 'im much."

"Have you a job?"

The boy nodded. "In the gas plant. I bring home five shillings a week, and we usually get one or two more from Maggie and Billy working in the markets. We were making out all right, living in the basement of a building over near the river. But now the man what owns it says we have to get out, to make room for another family who's able to pay more. We never made any trouble, but we still got to go. Problem is, I don't know where. Aren't many places we can afford that will take a bunch of kids."

Having gotten all this out, he coughed convulsively as though the effort to explain his plight had shaken his thin body.

Emily waited until he was once again still before saying, "I wish I could suggest a place to you right now, but I cannot. You are right to believe lodging will be hard to find. However, I will make every effort to help." Gently she suggested, "In the meantime, it might be wise to ask the orphanage if the younger children could stay there."

The boy grimaced, shaking his head firmly. "We're a family. We stay together."

"I understand why you don't want to be separated, but if the alternative is sleeping on the street . . ."

"At least I'd still be able to look after the youngest ones, ma'am. In the orphanage, there'll be no one to 'elp them. They'll be scared and lonely, the older kids'll beat 'em up, and they won't get their share of food or blankets or anything. They're better off on the streets."

Emily sighed, aware that what the boy said might well be true. The orphanage was not an alternative she recommended very often. Small and crowded, poorly funded, it was a cesspool of violence and cruelty from which no child emerged unscarred. But the streets were, if anything, worse. The little boy who faced her so bravely would have to fight long and hard to keep his siblings even moderately safe.

"How much longer do you have in your present lodgings?" she asked, giving up the struggle to convince him.

"Two days."

"Very well. Come back here tomorrow when you have finished work. I will hope by then to have something for you."

"Can you help him?" Courtney asked when they were once again alone.

"I don't know. He is right to believe few with lodging to rent of even the poorest sort will let it go for what he can afford to pay. Added to that, no landlord will be anxious to take in a family of children."

"But they can't just live on the streets."

"Many do, here as in London." Leaning back wearily in her chair, Emily spread her hands. "We have one small filthy orphanage that is nothing more than a training ground for thieves. A few of the churches run soup kitchens for children, but they don't offer them shelter. Our facilities here are strained to the limit."

She glanced around the tiny room crowded with barrels of supplies, stacks of paper, and boxes of cast-off clothes. "Even so, we will have to find something for them. It is very unusual for a family to remain together in the face of such adversity. That suggests they may be especially worth saving."

She wrote a note to herself to pursue the matter promptly, then signaled the next person in. So it went for several hours as Courtney got a close look at a cross section of the problems she was likely to face in her own shelter. By the time it was over, she was more aware than ever of how much work lay ahead of her, and her admiration for Emily was greater than ever.

Before leaving, Courtney thanked her hostess warmly. "You have been most generous with your time and knowledge. Both are very much appreciated. I will make every effort to put your insights to good use back in London." Hesitantly she added, "Would it be all right if I came back tomorrow? There is still so much I need to learn."

Pleased by what she no longer doubted was genuine sincerity, Emily assured her she would be most welcome.

Returning to the carriage, where she had prudently left Mary, Courtney ignored her abigail's stiff-lipped disapproval as she thought over the scenes she had witnessed in the shelter. Emily's efforts were so much better organized and funded than her own. But considering that the East End shelter had only just opened, they were not doing too badly. If only they could get more money—

Her thoughts were abruptly interrupted by a boisterous group of horsemen rounding the corner before the coach. As the driver was forced to rein in abruptly, the hacks shied. For a terrifying moment the carriage shook and quaked as though it might break free.

Courtney's heart was in her throat when several of the riders swiftly seized the horses' bridles and forced them back under control. Their leader doffed his hat in apology.

"I beg your pardon, my lady. We did not hear your carriage approaching."

Nerves strained by the close brush with what might have been a serious accident, Courtney snapped, "Had you been less hasty in your progress and shown more concern for the safety of a public thoroughfare, this would not have happened."

The man reddened. He was in his twenties and sturdily built, wearing a well-tailored frock coat and breeches that proclaimed him a member of the middle class. Not by any means as wealthy as those at the dinner the evening before, he was still far more prosperous than the vast majority of people. He was also, quite clearly, not accustomed to being criticized. Only Courtney's great beauty coupled with her obvious nobility forced him to swallow his pride.

"You are quite right, my lady. But as there was no harm done—"

"My coachman must have been shaken, as was my maid. If they show further harm, you can be certain this matter will be reported to the authorities."

That was more than the man could bear. Resentfully he declared, "The authorities? Think twice before you attempt that, your ladyship. *We* are the law here."

Shocked by such an assertion from a strutting popinjay, Courtney said, "*You*! The constabulary might have something to say about that."

"Not likely." The young man sneered. "No one challenges the Manchester Militia, and you'd do well to remember it!"

Without waiting for her reply, he spurred his mount viciously. The riders vanished in a flurry of dust that made Courtney choke. She raised a handkerchief to her mouth as Mary exclaimed, "Oh, ma'am, what horrible men! They can't really be the law here, can they?"

Much as she would have liked to reassure her abigail, Courtney could not. Given what she had heard both the previous evening and that day, she very much suspected that law in Manchester was not what it should be. If the police were giving way before armed thugs, anything might happen.

By the time they reached the Royale Hotel a short while later, it was difficult to believe the altercation had even taken place. Were it not for the skittish behavior of the horses and the coachman's angry glare, Courtney might have thought she had imagined it.

Only a close look revealed the ominous differences that had occurred in the streets surrounding the hotel during her absence. Sturdy wooden shutters were being erected on some shop windows. Passersby were not enjoying their usual leisurely strolls, but were hurrying along as though they did not think it wise to linger. And on the street corners beneath the wrought-iron gas lamps, men were gathering who wore the same red armbands as those who had accosted her carriage.

"I'll be back shortly. Don't leave the hotel while I'm gone." Courtney sighed as she remembered Nigel's words before he left their suite that morning. His lingering inclination to order her about was bothersome. She certainly had no intention of obeying. Emily was expecting her at the shelter, and there seemed no good reason to disappoint her.

After so many years of being insulated from all but the most pleasant aspects of life, Courtney took her newfound responsibilities very seriously. Not even Mary's outraged shock had prevented her from summoning a hired carriage and setting off for the poorer section of town. The abigail's dismay, however, had provided a perfect excuse for not taking her along. When she realized her mistress intended to go alone, Mary's agitation knew no bounds. She tried frantically to convince Courtney that proper young ladies did not go out without some sort of chaperon, but her attempt was brushed aside.

"Emily Wilson goes about in hired carriages by herself all the time," the marchioness declared. "If she can do it, so can I."

And so she could, although with rather more trepidation than she cared to admit. Glancing round at the interior of the brougham which was transporting her to Emily's, she was somewhat reassured. The carriage was neat and clean, the driver respectful and able. Though the streets were crowded with workers and their families heading toward the rally scheduled for later that day, the horses made good progress. Before she had time to dwell on the possible folly of her actions, they were pulling up before the Samaritan Shelter.

Alighting from the carriage, Courtney paid the driver with what she hoped looked like accustomed ease. He doffed his hat, thanking her for the tip, as Emily came out to greet her.

"I thought you might change your mind," she said softly, her wide-set black eyes faintly shadowed. "Many people, ladies especially, will be staying home today."

"So much the better reason to be out," Courtney declared stoutly. "If we all hide in our drawing rooms, we will seem like no more than frightened children. Besides," she added as they entered the shelter, "I promised to be here."

Emily did not pursue the matter. Her approving look was enough to make it clear she admired Courtney's determination. Together the two women spent a busy morning. They were hardly aware of the passing hours until increased noise from the street signaled that the rally was about to begin.

Glancing out the window at the crowds of men, women, and children still streaming toward St. Peter's Fields, Courtney found herself thinking how much she would like to be with them. It was far too lovely a day to be stuck inside, and this might be her only opportunity to hear an orator of such renown.

"Why don't we go to the meeting?" she asked suddenly.

Emily put down the list of supplies she was consulting and stared at her. "You're not serious?"

"Of course I am. Why shouldn't we go?"

"I can think of any number of reasons. Oh, it might be perfectly all right for *me* to go. But it is quite another matter for a marchioness to attend. Your husband would be furious."

"You mean," Courtney said, "that if I were not here, you would go."

"Well . . . I hadn't actually planned to."

"But you might?"

Reluctantly Emily nodded. "It's possible, but that is not to say I will be sorry to miss it."

"I would," Courtney declared. "It's not likely I will ever get another chance to be part of such a meeting. I would like very much to attend."

Emily hesitated. She really did not want to miss the meeting, and now that she thought about it, there was no reason not to go. No one they were likely to meet would know who Courtney was, so her reputation would be quite safe.

When she agreed to go, Courtney smiled eagerly. She was clearly looking forward to the event. Emily was less sanguine. At best, Orator Hunt would give an interesting speech which she might far more easily have read about in the newspaper. And at worst . . .

That did not bear thinking about. Putting away her files, Emily smoothed her plain muslin dress and put on her bonnet. A spark of amusement flared in her as she considered that as alike as she and Courtney were in their shared concern for the poor, their personalities were totally different. The marchioness was confident, vibrant, outgoing, whereas she herself tended to be a bit of a mouse, preferring to stay in her familiar world and rarely taking a glimpse outside.

Not today, Emily decided. Today she was going to let herself be swept along by the younger woman's excitement. Smiling broadly, she took Courtney's arm as together they joined the throng heading toward St. Peter's Fields.

Whatever expectations there had been about how many people would attend the rally were already far surpassed. Courtney had never seen so many men, women, and children gathered together in a single place, not even in London, where large crowds were not unusual.

The ladies were quickly absorbed into the teeming mass of humanity. Dressed in their Sunday best, workers from the mines, mills, and gas plants were out to enjoy the balmy weather as much as the meeting itself. They had brought their families with them, many carrying baskets of food and blankets. The children were particularly eager. The small ones who had to be carried squirmed every which way in their determination to see everything, while the older boys and girls bobbed up and down impatiently as the crowd slowly moved along toward the open swath of land where the meeting would take place. There was a holiday mood over all, which banished Courtney's last doubts about the wisdom of going along.

"Why, it's like a giant party!" she exclaimed to Emily. "I thought everyone would be rather dour and serious, but they aren't at all."

Smiling at the marchioness's naiveté, the older woman said, "Look a little closer." Quietly she pointed out the large, stern-faced men wearing red caps standing at regular intervals all along the route to St. Peter's Fields. "Those are marshals of the worker organizations, which, strictly speaking, are illegal. They are here to keep order."

Courtney stared at them in surprise. They all showed the marks of long years of hard work, though none was more than thirty. Stronger and more muscular than most of the other men, they looked more than able to handle any problem, even though they were unarmed. Despite the crowd's jovial mood, she was glad to see precautions were being taken and said as much to Emily. "No one can accuse these people of being poorly organized. They seem to have thought of everything. Look over there."

She pointed toward a copse of trees which marked the border of the rallying point. A horse-drawn wagon was pulled up, ready to dispense medical aid to those who might be overcome with excitement. There were even barrels of water on hand in case the unusually warm day proved too much for some, and a large hand-lettered sign indicated where lost children would be gathered. It was all reassuringly sensible. Surely men intent on rioting would not show such concern for the simple comforts, nor bring their families along.

"How could anyone believe they mean to make trouble?" Courtney asked indignantly. "It's perfectly obvious that these are just nice, ordinary people out to hear a few speeches and enjoy the day."

"I'm sure you are right," Emily agreed, "but not everyone sees it that way. To many property owners in Manchester, the simple fact that such a crowd of workers can get together in one place to express their common beliefs is terrifying."

A large stage was set up at the far end of the field. Thousands were already gathered in front of it, with the new arrivals settling for spots progressively farther back. Courtney and Emily got as close as they could, then looked around for a place to sit. They glanced at each other ruefully, wishing that one of them had thought to bring a blanket.

A woman seated nearby nursing a baby noticed their predicament. It took her a moment to realize that the two well-dressed ladies were not an apparition. They looked singularly out of place amid the crowd of roughly garbed workers. The older one seemed somehow familiar. When the woman recognized her as Emily Wilson, whose generous spirit and kind heart were known to all the poor of Manchester, she smiled broadly.

"Fancy you being here, Mrs. Wilson! Going to be a grand day, isn't it? Here, I've got an extra blanket we won't be needing 'less it rains, which praise God it doesn't look about to do. Sit yourselves down."

Thanking the woman for her generosity, Courtney and Emily joined the little family. A boy of about five and a girl of about three stared at them shyly, prompting their mother to laugh. "I don't suppose they've ever seen anyone dressed so grand," she said to Courtney, looking at her outfit curiously.

The marchioness, who had thought herself dressed quite plainly, flushed. Out of the corner of her eye she caught a glimpse of Emily trying hard not to grin. Amusement at her own silliness in wearing a paisley silk to a labor rally bubbled out of Courtney. After a moment, the children joined in, uncertain of what was so funny but willing enough to share a joke on such a wonderfully exciting day.

"When I said I still had a lot to learn," she sputtered, "I hope you appreciate how truthful I was being!"

Emily patted her hand soothingly. "You're doing wonderfully well. Never mind about not being dressed appropriately. If anyone from Almack's or the *Lady's Magazine* asks me who that strangely garbed person is, I'll claim not to know you."

The thought of those twin bastions of the *ton* turning up at the rally set Courtney off into fresh gales. By the time the father of the little group returned, carrying precious bottles of orange squash he had purchased for his children, they were all giggling gaily.

The tall, lean man whose seamed face bore the pallor of the mines stared at the spectacle before him in bewilderment. He was glad his wife and children were having such a good time, and he thought he knew who the woman in the gray dress was, but as for the other . . . He shook his head dazedly even as innate courtesy caused him to tip his hat.

Emily, who had so far managed to avoid introducing Courtney, was greatly relieved when the first speech started up, preventing her from responding to the miner's obvious curiosity.

As far as they were from the stage, it was difficult to hear anything. But it seemed that a clergyman was asking God's mercy on the gathering. That done, the first of the speakers stood to address the crowd on the purpose of the rally and the iniquities they must all join together to fight.

Courtney could make out snatches about the Corn Laws and parliamentary reform, and something about poor working conditions. But most of what was said was lost on the soft summer air. The crowd, though certainly polite, was no more attentive than most people gathered together on a balmy day and enjoying each other's company. As friends greeted each other and strangers became acquainted, the low hum of conversations became a persistent rumble which not even the most determined speaker could entirely drown out.

That changed abruptly when a plump red-haired man stepped to the podium and a drumroll signaled the need for silence. The crowd fell hushed, stirring expectantly, as the main attraction of the afternoon was introduced.

"I have the high honor and distinct privilege," the round little man intoned, "to present to you the esteemed organizer, spokeman for the people, bastion of the rights of man, Orator Hunt!"

The roar of approval that swept through the crowd was a wave of sound that crested, only to begin again. For long moments it was impossible to hear anything but the outpouring of tens of thousands of human beings giving vent to their most deeply held feelings. Even as she stood with all the rest to catch a glimpse of the man responsible for such furor, Courtney shivered. The potential power of these people was awesome. If they ever came to recognize it, they could reshape the world.

Swept up by the excitement that was a living thing around her, she stared intently at the slim frock-coated man who was its source. Orator Hunt was in his midforties and of medium height. Beneath a broad forehead and intent dark eyes, a pugnacious nose kept company with the stubborn set of his chin. His light brown hair was combed forward in the Corinthian style, each razored strand carefully shaped to his powerful head. If he possessed the common touch, it did not show in his appearance. Rather he looked better suited to the men's club or drawing room than to a rickety stage set above an expectant throng of laborers.

Yet when he spoke, Courtney quickly understood his appeal to men and women who would never be able to afford so much as the cost of his coat and yet who still considered him one of their own. Despite the vast size of the field, Orator Hunt's resonant tones were audible to all. He had the range and projection of a seasoned actor and he wasted no time bringing the crowd to a fever pitch.

"Let the property owners and merchant princes of Manchester take heed! Their day is ending! No longer will honest men and women toil in despair for greedy lordlings who usurp their most basic rights!"

He let the shout of approval which greeted this ride for several moments before holding up his hands. The swiftness with which the crowd obeyed this summons for silence was eloquent evidence of his power.

"The age of the aristocrat is over!" Orator Hunt boomed. "The age of the common man has begun! Throw off the tethers of subjugation and declare yourselves free!"

"Is he calling for a revolution as in France?" Courtney asked tremulously. She shared the deeply rooted horror all her class felt for the bloody upheaval across the Channel in which the very cornerstones of society had been shattered.

Emily shook her head reassuringly. "He has never gone quite that far. Instead, he supports reform of Parliament to give commoners a greater say in the government."

That sounded far more modest than the firebrand exhortations she was listening to. But as Orator Hunt continued to speak, Courtney began to notice that he was in fact very careful to say nothing that might be construed as a call to violence. Instead, he urged his listeners to organize to make their influence felt. He spoke of the need to win a fairer share of the wealth and privilege currently held by so few. And far from advocating an overthrow of the established system, he geared his entire program to working within it.

That, however, meant nothing to the grim-faced horsemen appearing on the periphery of the crowd.

The workers became aware of them slowly. Murmured warnings reached in from the edges, shifting the focus of attention from the orator himself to the intruders.

"Trouble," the miner muttered under his breath. He and his wife glanced at each other anxiously, then quickly gathered their children together. With the crowd so densely packed, there was no hope of moving away. Nor was there anywhere to go, for more horsemen had come out of the cobblestoned streets and were surrounding the entire field.

"Wh-what . . . ?" Courtney began, only to be stopped by Emily's gasp. She had recognized the meaning of the red armbands the riders wore.

"The militia. . . . Please, God, they can't mean to . . ."

Whatever she had meant to say was lost when the horsemen suddenly charged. Courtney watched in stunned horror as powerful steeds were pushed into the crowd, their deadly hooves flashing high. Sabers were drawn and clubs rained down on the helpless. Within minutes, victims lay bleeding on the ground, some ominously still.

Screams of panic replaced the earlier confident cheers. Those on the edge of the crowd took the assault first, but the militia quickly penetrated to the center of the rally. Whirling in all directions, the horsemen attacked in full ferocity. Several men who tried in vain to protect a banner proclaiming the workers' cause were cut through remorselessly. Women and children who tried to escape were trampled, their terrified pleas only a further incentive to violence.

Confronted by horror beyond any she had ever imagined, Courtney stood frozen in place. Only Emily's quick action in pulling her from the path of a rampaging horseman saved her from the fate already shared by so many scattered across the field. Grabbing her young friend's arm, Emily yelled, "Come on! We must get out of here!"

Turning dazedly to obey, Courtney caught sight of the miner fighting to shield his family. Blood trickled down his cheek from a saber cut to the head. His eyes were dark with terror, but he kept his own large body between his wife and children and the attackers as he resolutely shepherded them to safety.

Others, fleeing in panic, were less fortunate. Screams rent the air as still more victims fell, only to be trampled by the terror-stricken mob. Barely moments after the horsemen first appeared, the center of the field was empty except for the dead and wounded.

Courtney and Emily instinctively ran away from the stage that was the main target of the attackers. Turning round for an instant, the marchioness caught sight of Orator Hunt being hauled from the platform by several of the militia. He vanished beneath their flailing clubs.

Pressed together in the mass of humanity, they were pushed out toward the surrounding streets. Wedged so tightly that they could hardly breathe, they still managed to hold on to each other. Emily had lost her bonnet, and a sleeve of her dress was ripped. Courtney's reticule had vanished along with her shawl and gloves. Her paisley silk was stained and bedraggled and her hair had come down. She looked less the young noblewoman than simply a horrified victim.

At the foot of Watson Street, the crowd was stopped. Crammed against the buildings, no one could move. Those in the back continued to push forward as their panic grew. Beseeching cries were to no avail. Sobs rose in Courtney's throat as she saw a woman near her go down. The child she managed to hold above her head cried piteously. A man, who had tried but failed to help the woman, seized the little boy just in time to prevent him from also being trampled.

"My God!" Emily moaned. "This can't be happening! Not here . . . not to us. . . ."

Her disbelief was shared by the thousands of men and women surrounding them. The hideous incongruity of such an attack being perpetrated by their own countrymen left them stunned. It was all they could do to flee, and in so doing to be further trapped in the warren of streets.

The clatter of pursuing horsemen stirred the crowd to fresh panic. Courtney lost her footing and would have fallen but for Emily's iron grip around her waist. The other woman might look small and slender, but her life of hard work had endowed her with wiry strength. For the marchioness's part, her devotion to riding and long walks gave her the agility necessary to regain her balance. Just in time to see the militia appear at the end of the street and prepare to charge them again.

Looking round frantically, Courtney realized there was no way out of the narrow street. The houses on either side were locked against them, most of the windows shuttered. From the few left uncovered, shadowy figures looked down, making no effort to intervene in the acts of savagery being played out before them.

Screams tore from those closest to the attacking horsemen. Fresh blood splashed over the cobblestones. Courtney and Emily were rammed back against a stone wall so tightly that they could hardly breathe. Holding on to each other, they tried bravely to face what now seemed inevitable.

Flecks of foam spewing from one of the attackers' mounts struck Courtney. The man was so close she could see the red flush of his face, hear the exalted grunts he emitted as he struck back and forth with his saber, leaving a trail of death and injury on either side. When he spied the women huddled against the wall, his small eyes gleamed. Striking forward, he was barely a few feet from them when a trumpet blast cleaved the air.

Members of the Manchester constabulary, the professional guardians of the law, galloped into the crowd. Their leader was a white-faced young man who had at first refused to believe the incredible reports of violence coming from St. Peter's Fields. But now he had no choice but to accept the evidence of his own eyes.

Confronting the militia, he demanded, "What madness has taken you? These people are unarmed and helpless! Desist at once!"

Grudgingly the riders appeared to obey. The sons of yeoman farmers and small factory owners were accustomed to taking orders. They might not like being subject to authority, but they were not willing to challenge it directly.

"Quickly!" Emily urged. "While the constables are here, we must get away. As soon as they leave, the attacks will begin again."

Courtney wanted to believe the horror was over, but she sensed her friend knew better. Together they managed to wiggle between the attackers' horses toward the path cleared by the constabulary. Fleeing into an alley leading off Watson Street, they could hear the young officer ordering the militia to withdraw. Confident he would be obeyed, he hurried his own men on toward the field, where the main fighting continued. No sooner had they disappeared than the militia regrouped.

"Run!" Courtney screamed as clubs and swords again clashed against flesh and bone.

Yanking their skirts up, the women stumbled down the alley. The cobblestones cut into their feet and they came close to falling several times. But they kept going, spurred by the desperate screams behind them.

Courtney was gasping for breath, her heart slamming against her ribs, when they finally stopped for a moment. Though they were almost a mile from the scene of the rally, shrieks of pain and terror still reached them. The attackers had followed their quarries into the city proper, where the constables were hard pressed to contain them.

Smoke from fires lit by the militia stained the sky. The proud banners of the workers were going up in flames, along with the speakers' stage, medical wagon, and anything else remotely associated with the meeting. Those fortunate enough not to be injured were hiding where they could. Hundreds lay dead and thousands

more were wounded. Victims wandered dazedly holding bloody heads or huddling at the roadsides with
broken ribs and limbs. Many were in shock, unable to
understand where they were or what had happened to
them.

Forcing themselves to go on, Courtney and Emily
managed to get within a few blocks of the shelter.
There they were stopped as a fresh wave of rampaging
militia rode past. As the two women crouched behind a
lorry, Courtney's wide green eyes filled with terrified
tears. Had they come this far only to be killed within
sight of sanctuary?

Unable to witness further horror, she ducked her
head. Her slender body, kneeling next to Emily's, was
almost completely hidden. But the wide skirt of her day
dress, ruffling out in the breeze, gave them away.

With a shout, one of the riders was on them. He bent
down to grasp Emily by the arm, hauling her into the
street. She screamed and struck out at him, but to no
avail. Vastly stronger and inflamed by blood, he was
impervious to her blows.

Courtney was on her feet in an instant. With no
thought for herself, aware only that her friend was in
mortal danger, she sprang at the man. Seizing one
booted foot, she yanked it from the stirrup and twisted
hard. A shout of surprise and pain broke from him. He
kicked out, narrowly missing Courtney's breasts. The
attack only served to further stiffen her determination.
Throwing all her strength at the man, she succeeded in
making him drop Emily. Roaring in rage, the militiaman lashed out at his new target. A club flashed in the
air, heading straight down toward Courtney.

Emily shouted a warning. Ignoring her bruised arm,
she threw herself straight toward the marchioness,
knocking her off balance and into the street. The blow,
meant for Courtney, struck Emily full in the head.

Seeing the two women prostrate on the ground, the
man was satisfied. He spurred his horse viciously and
rode off to catch his companions. When he was gone,

Courtney sat up dazedly. She was winded but unhurt. Her stomach lurched as she spied the small unconscious figure before her.

The tattered skirt of Emily's sensible gray dress spread like the petals of a mourning flower around her. She lay facedown, one arm caught under her body and the other extended in unconscious supplication. Her face was ashen and no sign of breath escaped her parted lips. Blood poured from her broken skull, running darkly between the cobblestones.

Much later Courtney was to wonder at how she reacted to the sight of Emily's broken body lying before her. From the instant she realized the militia meant to attack, she had been acutely terrified. But now, as she stood looking down at Emily, all fear vanished. In its place was cold, implacable determination.

She could not give in to horror or grief. She could not surrender to the hysteria lurking at the edge of her consciousness. All emotion was ruthlessly reined in, locked away in some hidden part of her mind where she could not hear her own screams. Generations of forebears who had faced the most profound dangers without yielding came to her rescue. The heritage of centuries gave her the courage to lift Emily into her arms and slowly, laboriously, inch her way toward the shelter.

— 13 —

Courtney straightened slowly, one hand at the small of her back. Her body ached, but she was barely aware of the discomfort. The sights and sounds surrounding her occupied all her attention, as they had ever since she stumbled into the shelter with Emily.

She had no idea how much time had passed since then, nor did she know when she had crossed over from trembling exhaustion to blessed numbness. She only knew that she had to keep going, for the steady stream of wounded had not abated and there was almost no one else to help care for them.

Bodies crowded the corridors, overflowing from every room. Some were covered by sheets, and she tried not to look at them. Most were suffering from a wide range of injuries, everything from broken legs and arms to concussions and stabbings. Piteous cries mingled with tormented screams as those few who were unharmed struggled to cope with what looked very much like the outpourings of a battlefield.

"Hold that tighter," Mr. Penwarren ordered. Courtney obeyed automatically, as she had followed all the physician's instructions since he arrived at the shelter. The doctor Emily had described as one of a very small number willing to give of his time and skill to the poor was also one of the few of his calling to venture into the streets in the aftermath of the militia's rampage.

Making his way to the shelter, where he rightly pre-

sumed many of the injured would be brought, he found
Emily herself among his first patients. His arrival provided the only chance of saving her life, for her condition was extremely grave. Whether or not she could
fight off the combined effects of blood loss and inter-
nal injuries remained to be seen.

Courtney struggled to keep her mind on the doctor
as she accompanied him to the next form stretched out
on the hall floor. Penwarren was in his forties, pale and
sharp-featured, with lank black hair and flat eyes that
suggested he found much about the world to disdain.
His arrogant, punctilious manner made it clear he had
no patience with those who failed to instantly recognize
his superior status and respond accordingly. Yet he
had left his safe home in one of the most affluent areas
of Manchester to come here.

She puzzled over that seeming contradiction deliberately, determined to think of anything other than the
grimy, blood-soaked linen he was removing from a
whimpering child. After inspecting the wound closely,
Penwarren secured fresh gauze over it. That done, he
stood briskly. "The tot will most likely lose that arm,
but there's nothing to be done for it. Saber went through
most of the ligaments." He shook his head, as though
mildly annoyed. "No, I'm afraid there's no alternative
but amputation. Not here, of course. That can wait a
bit until we've cleared off some of the others."

Courtney swallowed hard. Though very little was
getting through the blanket of shock surrounding her,
she could still ache for the child whose life would have
been difficult enough even whole and strong. Glancing
up at Penwarren, she thought she saw a glimmer of the
same pain she felt pass through his bloodshot eyes. But
it was gone instantly, replaced by an emotionless mask.
Telling herself it must have been a trick of the lighting,
she dismissed the thought.

When the supply of bandages on the tray she carried
ran low, Courtney excused herself long enough to fetch
more. In the small stockroom, she methodically ripped

sheets into strips, noting that there was very little linen left. All the beds in the dormitories were now taken by wounded, and many more lay on the floor. The last blankets were in use and the tiny hoard of medications Emily had so meticulously maintained was long since gone. Laudanum in particular was desperately needed, but she had no idea where they might find some.

On her way back to continue helping Penwarren, she stopped briefly in the small room where Emily lay. Her head was heavily bandaged, the white gauze wrappings as pale as her skin. Freed of the frame of her hair, the ashen features had the purity of sculptured alabaster. The lines of care and compassion that had marked her face were gone. She looked young and lovely, but frozen beyond human touch. Stroking her hand gently, Courtney felt the coldness of ebbing life. She might have been looking at an effigy on some ancient tomb.

Her slender shoulders shook as she gazed at the woman she had met only the day before but whom circumstances and shared convictions had already made a friend. There were so few people like Emily in the world. It seemed the height of injustice that she should be taken just when her work was so desperately needed.

Silent tears slipped down Courtney's cheeks as she confronted her own helplessness. Emily lay only inches from her, yet she could do nothing to stem the seemingly inexorable approach of death. Guilt warred with anguish as she remembered how the blow that wreaked such damage had been meant for her. The vagaries of fate that decreed a selfless, giving woman such as Emily should be taken instead of herself proved too much for Courtney. She buried her face in her hands, weeping softly.

She barely noticed when strong arms came around her to draw her close against a hard chest. The overwhelming need for comfort that engulfed her blocked out all else. She did not resist, but instead accepted the infinitely tender embrace with all the frantic urgency of a child waking from a nightmare.

"Hush, now . . ." a low voice soothed. "It's all right. . . ."

The hard plank floor dug into her knees, but Courtney was unaware of it. She knew only that she was being rocked gently back and forth, stroked and consoled in exactly the way she needed most. Her sobs died away, the desperate beating of her heart receding to a steadier rhythm.

Slowly she looked up into Nigel's compassion-filled eyes. Her husband's sudden presence evoked no surprise from her numbed senses. Of course Nigel would come. Wasn't he invariably there when she needed him most? Not even the fact that he was most probably enraged by her failure to obey his instructions and remain in the hotel dimmed the relief that surged through her. It was as though the other half of herself had appeared to renew her strength and restore her courage.

Leaning her head against his shoulder, she murmured, "I was so frightened . . ."

A pulse beat in Nigel's throat. His hands tightened around her waist. Beneath his habitual tan, his face was gray. The agony he had felt when she was taken to Mrs. Hammond's had not proved the ultimate in fear after all. Nothing had prepared him for the sheer gut-wrenching terror that stabbed through him when he learned from a petrified Mary that her mistress was somewhere in the riot-torn streets of Manchester. In its aftermath, there was no room left even for recriminations.

"Are you hurt?" he asked tautly.

"No . . . but Emily . . ." Her voice broke, fresh tears turning her emerald eyes to haunted pools.

Upon his arrival at the shelter, Nigel had been directed to Penwarren, with whom he spoke briefly. He was aware of Emily's condition and knew the outlook for her was not good. Gently he tried to give his wife what comfort he could. But Courtney was not to be consoled. She was becoming more convinced with every passing moment that she was at least partially responsible for what had happened. If she had not cajoled the other woman into accompanying her to the rally, Emily would never have been out on the street in the path of the militiaman's blow.

When she said as much to Nigel, he quickly shook his head. "I don't approve of what you did, but you can't blame yourself for Emily's injury. She made her own decision to go with you."

"But perhaps only because I asked her to. It was bad enough when my impulsiveness got me into trouble, but now I've led someone else into danger." Remorse made Courtney's voice shake. She bent her head, weeping softly.

Compassion blocked out every other consideration as the marquess drew his wife closer against him. She felt so small in his arms, yet she possessed such extraordinary spirit. Even as he told himself he should be angered by her foolish disobedience, he could not deny his pride at her courage and determination.

His big hand was on her tumbled hair, gently stroking the auburn curls, when a sound from the doorway made him glance up. Dr. Penwarren stood there, hands on his hips and a definite look of chagrin darkening his austere features.

"If you don't mind," he said waspishly, "this is hardly the time to be conducting a private *tête-à-tête*."

The sarcasm in his tone made it clear he had no idea whom he was addressing. Having never bothered to ask the name of the bedraggled young woman assisting him, he was equally ignorant as to her companion's identity. The man who had approached him in the corridor did not look precisely like a gentleman. He was without a jacket, and his trousers, though quite well cut, were stained with dust and grime. His shirt sleeves were rolled up to expose powerful forearms which could not have belonged to any languid aristocrat. As Nigel rose to face the doctor, Penwarren was struck by the lithe grace of his movement and wondered in the back of his mind if the man might be an athlete of some sort, perhaps a boxer.

He was disabused of that notion at once.

"I am Lord Nigel Davies, Marquess of Glendale," the deep voice intoned. "This is my wife, Lady Courtney. She is very concerned about the condition of her friend Mrs. Emily Wilson."

The doctor paled. The last thing he would have expected to encounter amid the dead and wounded crowding the humble shelter was a member of the aristocracy whose wealth and power were all too well known to him. And the marchioness . . . She had worked beside him for hours without a word of complaint, not even when he snapped instructions at her and complained several times because she was not more adept at tasks that must have been utterly new to her.

Swallowing hard, Penwarren struggled to make amends for his rudeness. "M-my lord . . . my lady . . . pray forgive me. I had no idea who you were. No idea at all. Really it is most extraordinary that you should be here!"

Nigel inclined his head graciously. He recognized the physician as a man of undoubted intelligence and, for all his aloofness, unusual kindness. The awe with which the good doctor regarded those he considered above him was not new to the marquess. He had encountered it all his life, and though he had never shared the view of his peers that such respect was no more than their due, he had learned to tolerate it with a certain wry patience.

"I quite agree. Now, if you could just tell us how Mrs. Wilson is doing . . ."

"Oh, yes. . . . O-of course." Kneeling swiftly beside Emily, the doctor checked her over carefully. Nigel noted that his touch was properly gentle but thorough. When he had checked her pulse, skin tone, and temperature, Penwarren said, "She is holding her own, but beyond that I cannot say. The injury to her head is quite serious. I believe there was some bleeding beneath the skull. The pressure that causes should be relieved, but . . ."

"But what?" the marquess demanded.

"I have never performed such a procedure. It is extremely difficult and must be done with absolute accuracy or the patient ends up even worse off than before." Glancing down at Emily, he sighed. "If I thought there was any chance of being able to help her, I would attempt it. But I would only be hastening her demise."

Nigel nodded, glad that the man was professional enough not to insist on his competence in all areas. "Who could do it properly?"

"There are no physicians in Manchester trained in this procedure. The only ones I know of are in London."

It was a commonly accepted characteristic of the nobility that they should be given to prompt decisions backed by the authority to get them carried out. In this, Nigel did not disappoint. "Then I will send to London at once. My coachman is outside. If you will come with me, we will give him an appropriate letter."

Nodding rather dazedly, Penwarren obeyed. A short time later the coachman was dispatched, charged to ride posthaste to the capital, and supplied with sufficient coin to assure he would be able to get relay horses at the inns along the way. Informed of the reason for his urgent task, the man was determined to succeed. In his short time in Manchester, he had heard of Emily Wilson and the assistance she gave to those in need. If he could help save her life, he would consider himself honored.

With the man gone in a flurry of dust, Nigel stood for a moment looking up and down the street. It was deserted except for a few last stragglers emerging from their hiding places to creep fearfully home. A pallor of smoke hung over the city. He fancied he could smell the stench of blood, and for just a moment he was transported back to another time and place where he had stared out over a battlefield counting the dead and trying to convince himself to join his brother officers in

celebrating their great victory. The horrors of Waterloo still burned in Nigel's mind. But now they were
rivaled by new proof of man's inhumanity, delivered
on his own doorstep.

Anger burned through him at the thought that anyone would dare to commit such an atrocity in England.
That the perpetrators would be punished, he did not
doubt. But no amount of punishment could wipe out
the effect of their crimes.

Brushing a weary hand across his face, Nigel went
back inside the shelter. He drew Courtney and Penwarren aside and spoke to them firmly. "There is little
point in trying to help these people without proper
supplies. Tell me what you need and I will get it."

Neither doubted he would do exactly that. If anyone
could find bandages and medications in riot-torn
Manchester, it was the marquess. With Courtney's help,
the doctor swiftly drew up a list. He presented it
diffidently. "It's rather long, I'm afraid. The most urgent items are at the top."

Nigel only nodded. Slipping the paper into his pocket,
he touched his wife's hand lightly and departed.

While he was gone, Courtney had little time to worry
over him. Word came that a temporary morgue was
being set up a few blocks away. The dead were moved
there, making more room for the living. The man who
transported the corpses in his wagon came back to say
he had counted more than two hundred bodies, with
more still coming in. Estimates of the number of
wounded were harder to come by, since there were far
more and they were scattered all over the city. But
already it was believed more than ten thousand men,
women, and children had been hurt in the militia's
brutal assault.

Learning the extent of the tragedy only strengthened
Courtney's sense of unreality. She moved about her
tasks with apparent calm, all the horror she felt buried
deep inside.

When Nigel returned, he found her holding the hand

of a young boy whose face had been cut open by a saber. Barring infection, the boy would survive. But he would be maimed for life. The knowledge of this shone in his eyes, which brightened slightly as Courtney said, "Do you know that in Prussia the nobles vie with each other to see who can acquire the best dueling scar? They are considered a mark of distinction, and a lord who does not have one is thought a coward." Quietly she added, "Now you, too, will bear proof of your courage. When people find out where you got it, they will admire you greatly."

More than willing to believe the beautiful, angelic creature before him, the boy nodded gratefully. He fell asleep smiling, his hand still clasped in Courtney's.

She put it down gently and turned to find her husband watching her. He looked even tireder and grimier than before, but to Courtney he was the loveliest sight imaginable. Rising swiftly, she walked into his arms.

Nigel held her tightly, burying his face in the silken strands of her hair. Despite all she had gone through, she still smelled of lemon soap and sunshine. He breathed in the scent lingeringly, hard pressed to put even an inch of space between them.

When at last he let her go far enough to look at her, he could not help but laugh. "God's blood, my lady, if the doyennes of Almack's could see you now, they would think the world had truly ended! A marchioness looking as disheveled as any scullery maid!"

Courtney felt no rancor at his teasing. Rather it was a welcome break from the unrelentingly grim events of that terrible day. Smiling up at him, she challenged, "And what about you, my lord? I've seen the dandies who like to masquerade as coachmen, or highway robbers, or pugilists. Is this a new look? Lord Muckabout, perhaps?"

"Ungrateful wench!" Nigel exclaimed in mock anger. "Here I've brought you all manner of exotic treasures and you don't show me the least favor."

Abruptly serious, Courtney glanced toward the door,

where a wagon waited. In the gathering dusk, she could make out little except boxes and bundles. Hastily she stepped closer for a better view. What she saw made her gasp.

In a city on the edge of madness, Nigel had somehow managed to secure not simply the bandages and medicines Dr. Penwarren had asked for, but also surgical instruments, foodstuffs, bedding, and many other items essential to the care of the injured. How, precisely, he had done so, she did not care to ask. One glance at the armed men accompanying him, including an astonishingly uncouth Johnson, was enough to convince her there was much she did not want to know.

Nodding to her politely, the valet hopped down and began unloading the wagon. Everyone, including Nigel, pitched in. If any thought it was odd that a lord and a servant should be working side by side assisted by various gentlemen whose professions were better left unexplored, such a sentiment was not expressed.

Within minutes the supplies were being brought inside, where an astounded but nonetheless delighted Penwarren received them warmly. "My heavens, this is marvelous! Now we can really do something!" Turning to Courtney, he moderated his enthusiasm with extreme courtesy. "Uh . . . my lady . . . if you wouldn't mind . . . I think we should get the medicine unpacked first."

Courtney's small hands, the carefully buffed nails already torn, were little match for the tough wooden boxes. But she managed nonetheless to force them open, revealing vials of opiates and anti-inflammatory salves, as well as potions intended to prevent fever and alleviate swellings. Nigel must have raided every pharmacopoeia and physicians' office in Manchester, she thought as the precious supplies were quickly sorted.

The laudanum, Penwarren cautioned, had to be used sparingly. He believed it could do as much harm as good, particularly in the case of patients weakened by blood loss and shock. Emily received a small dose intended to preserve her strength, and others who were suffering with broken limbs were relieved of their pain. As the low moans and sobs that had filled the shelter for hours slowly diminished, blessed quiet descended.

Inured now to the sight of torn flesh, Courtney helped the doctor apply medications and replace bandages. Nigel and the men he had brought lifted the patients as fresh bedding was eased under them. Splints were at last available for the bone fractures, most of which could not have healed properly without them.

By the time the last victim was seen to, Courtney could no longer deny her own exhaustion. She slumped wearily against a cabinet, a bloodstained towel clutched in her hand. Nigel took it from her gently. Ignoring his own fatigue, he lifted her into his arms. She murmured a faint protest, something about wanting to check on Emily.

"I've just been in to see her," he murmured softly. "She's resting more peacefully and her color is better. There's nothing more to be done for her until the surgeon gets here from London. In the meantime, you must rest."

Aching in every bone and muscle, Courtney did not object further. She was almost asleep in his arms as Nigel carried her into a small supply room where he had spread out a mattress and blankets. Laying her there, he unfastened her torn, stained dress and slid her shoes off. The impromptu bed was hard and narrow, but it felt like heaven. Easing himself down beside her, Nigel spread the covers over them both.

Aware of his presence even in her deep slumber, Courtney moved closer to him. His broad chest became her pillow. Tucking her head in under his chin, Nigel smiled tenderly. He lifted one roughened little hand to his lips in a loving salute.

Never in his wildest dreams could he have imagined that his beautiful, elegant marchioness would be transformed into a woman of such strength and selflessness. The extraordinary changes in her had sent him through a tumult of emotions. He had passed from bewilderment to anger and finally to wholehearted admiration. This was a woman to match the greatest of men, and she was his. Irrevocably and absolutely his. A slight frown marred the marquess's features as he considered that, in his own opinion at least, he had yet to prove worthy of her.

—— 14 ——

"I don't really remember much of what happened," Emily murmured. "I know that horrible man tried to grab you when you made him let go of me, but after that . . ."

A bewildered frown compounded by lingering pain creased her forehead beneath the dark brown hair Courtney had just gently brushed. Though still very pale and weak, Emily seemed a different person from the unconscious woman who had lain on the pallet in the same room less than a week before. Thanks to the ministrations of the London surgeon who had responded with such haste to Nigel's authoritative summons, she was well on the road to recovery.

"Don't try to force yourself to remember," Courtney advised. "You know the doctor said you should just rest and concentrate on getting better."

Emily smiled faintly. Her friend's concern touched her deeply. The worried young marchioness was her first sight when she regained consciousness, an admittedly incongruous figure in a worn cotton dress and apron, but still unmistakable. Emily suspected she had been there a great deal during the crisis following her injury, but Courtney said little of this. Instead, she told her briefly what had happened in the city, how the shelter had become a beacon to hundreds of injured and those seeking lost members of their families, and how Nigel had mustered assistance for them.

Though she was able to reassure Emily that everything possible was being done for the victims of the attack, she could not convince her to leave the shelter. Her hopes of transferring Emily to the hotel where she could be cared for amid far more comfortable surroundings could make no headway against the older woman's quiet but unshakable determination. Though she could not yet move from her bed, she would not leave those she regarded as her own people.

"I feel so helpless." Emily sighed, her slender hands plucking unhappily at the blanket. "Surely there is something I can do . . ."

Courtney smothered a groan of impatience. For a woman who had only recently come through an experience that would have kept most strong men in their beds for weeks, Emily was being incredibly obdurate. Despite the bandage covering the back of her head where the surgeon's deft incision had released the potentially deadly pressure on her brain, she looked perfectly capable of demanding to be allowed back to work.

Determined to prevent that, Courtney cast round for some way to keep her friend occupied without tasking her still limited strength. "Perhaps you could organize the appeals for aid we are sending out," she ventured. "So much more is needed that we are asking for help from all over the kingdom. I can suggest some possible sources, but I'm sure there are many more you can recommend."

Emily nodded eagerly. "If you could just get me some paper and a pen, I will make a list."

"I'll send someone to do the writing for you," Courtney said firmly. "The doctor said you must not strain your eyes."

"Oh, very well, but please send someone soon." An ingratiating grin lit her wan face. "I fear I am a bad patient, Courtney. Don't think that means I lack appreciation for all you are doing. Nothing could be further from the truth. It's just that if I lie here much longer without occupation, I will begin to believe the cure is worse than the illness itself."

She was still shaking her head over her friend's stubbornness an hour later as she stood stirring a pot of stew. Just as she was satisfied it was thick enough, a young man stuck his head in the kitchen door and demanded her attention.

" 'Scuse me, luv, I'm looking for her nibs, the Marchioness of Glendale. Is she about somewhere?"

Boldly eyeing the lovely young woman who turned to face him, Peter Hastings decided perhaps this assignment wouldn't be so bad after all. He hadn't been the least bit keen about trekking all the way up to Manchester because of some set-to between workers and the gentry, but now that he was there he might as well make the most of it.

Wiping her hands on her apron, Courtney gazed at the tall, thin personage before her. Dressed in a wool frock coat and trousers of good quality whose tailoring was rather spoiled by the myriad accumulation of papers and pens jammed into the pockets, the young man looked like an eager greyhound at the starting gate.

He was making no attempt to hide his scrutiny of her, or his blatantly male appreciation. Several months before, Courtney would have found such behavior abominably rude. But now, after all she had been through, she could not manage the slightest glimmer of indignation. Instead, she felt only amusement as she considered the picture she must make with her hair in disarray, a smudge of flour on her cheek, and her dress simple to the point of austerity. When added to her anticipation of how the young man would look when he learned the identity of the woman he obviously considered an appropriate target for his amorous intent, she had to fight down a wicked urge to laugh.

"I am Lady Courtney Davies," she said quietly. "How may I help you?"

The young man looked at her sideways. "Really," he drawled, "then I must be Prinny himself." Before

Courtney could respond, he went on, "Look, luv, I like
a joke as much as the next man, but the fact is, I've got
to find her nibs. My editor's got some idea there's a
story here and that she's the one to give it to me.
Sooner I get straight with her, sooner you and me can
have a little fun. What do you say?"

"I say," a deep voice injected, "that the quality of
London journalists must be in a sorry state indeed for
anyone to send such a scatterwag as yourself, sir. Either
your manners improve instantly or you will be removed
by the scruff of your neck!"

"What the . . . !" Whirling, the young man confronted
an irate Nigel. The marquess was getting rather tired
of people failing to recognize his wife. Not that he
could blame them, given her present mode of dress
and occupation, but he was damned if he would stand
for this young puppy sniffing about her like a mongrel
in heat.

Mr. Peter Hastings, some two years out of a moderately good boys' school and with two questionable terms
at university behind him, was forced to rapidly reassess
his position. He might enjoy affecting the familiarity of
the lower class, particularly when he believed it was
likely to help him get his own way. But he was perfectly
aware of the inappropriateness of ever daring such
behavior with the aristocracy.

Rubbing the back of his neck nervously, he stared at
the man before him. The large, muscular, sweat-stained
fellow carrying an ax he had apparently been using to
chop firewood in the yard hardly looked like a lord.
But nowadays it wasn't always easy to tell. So many of
the richest swells liked to dress up as commoners and
then amuse themselves with the reactions of those unfortunate enough not to tumble to the truth. Weighing
Nigel's incongruous appearance against the unmistakable authority and arrogance of his manner, Mr. Hastings decided to err on the side of caution.

"Uh . . . look here . . . I certainly meant no offense.

How was I to know. . . ? I say, are you really Lord and Lady Davies?"

"Yes," Courtney assured him, "we are and we are both quite busy just now, as you can see. So unless you've come to help . . ."

Sensing imminent dismissal, which would be certain to bring his editor's ire down on his head, the young reporter said quickly, "Oh, but I have! That is, certainly it would be helpful to you for the *Gazette*'s readers to learn what you're doing here. Unless, that is, you didn't want anyone to know. . . ."

He had a sinking feeling that would be it. Having stumbled on what was easily the best story of his short but ambitious career, he was loath to think he might not be allowed to report it.

Nigel was familiar with the *Gazette* and was not impressed with the paper. It was one of the more sensational tabloids. But it reached a large audience among the newly affluent middle class, whom he believed would one day have substantial influence with the government.

As young Mr. Hastings waited anxiously, Nigel considered the situation and decided it would do no harm to speak with the reporter, provided of course that he did not look at Courtney again with any greater attention than he would give to a lamppost.

Leaning his ax against the door, the marquess accorded their guest a slightly chilling smile. "Do sit down, Mr. . . ."

Having hurriedly obeyed Nigel's order to take a chair, the young man darted up again to present his credentials. "Hastings. Peter Hastings, my lord."

Nigel nodded distantly. He leaned back against the counter, arms folded across his massive chest, and his long, sinewy legs stretched out before him. "Now, Mr. Hastings, suppose we begin by your telling us what exactly brought you to Manchester."

Licking his lips nervously, Hastings said, "Well, sir, you see, we began to hear rumors in London a few days ago, something about a rally up here by the work-

ers and an attack by another group that left quite a few
injured. We even heard there might be some deaths.
Naturally, most people discounted them. After all, this
isn't France or one of those other foreign places. But
the rumors kept coming. Eventually my editor heard
there were drivers of mail coaches and other people
who had reason to travel between the two cities who
not only said the stories were true but who claimed
there had been some sort of massacre. Impossible to
credit, of course, but he thought it might be worth a
look. Some of the other heads of the London papers
thought so too, because we ended up quite a contingent
of reporters all rushing north on each other's heels."
Preening slightly, he admitted, "I was one of the first to
get here, but there's a pack right behind me. Most of us
have put up at the Royale, courtesy of Sir Thomas
Logan."

"Logan!" Nigel exclaimed. "How did he get involved
in this?"

"I don't precisely know, sir. But Sir Thomas was on
the scene when we began arriving. He sort of took
charge of us, if you know what I mean. Very helpful,
he was. Assured us the reports we had heard in London were grossly exaggerated and that there wasn't
much of a story, but promised to do anything he could
nonetheless. And he's kept to his word. Not only has he
put us all up at the hotel, but he's arranged for us to
meet Manchester's leading citizens."

A faint glimmer of rebellion shone in Mr. Hastings'
pale eyes. "But I've never been one for sitting still while
someone feeds me pabulum. So I thought I'd have a
look-see for myself." Without turning his head, he managed to gesture in Courtney's direction. "I heard about
her ladyship from a street urchin who claimed she was
here at the shelter, so I decided to come round."

"And a good thing you did," Nigel muttered. "Sir
Thomas and his cronies appear well on their way to
sweeping this whole sordid mess under the carpet."

"Oh, no!" Courtney protested. "That would be terrible.

It's bad enough that all those people died, but to have lost their lives in vain . . . Nigel, we must do something!"

"*Died?*" Hastings squeaked, seeing his story take on a dimension he had not suspected. "I say, what exactly happened here?"

"More than Sir Thomas wants known," Nigel said grimly. "Come with us. We'll explain everything to you on the way to the Royale." A single order was sufficient to send Johnson scrambling for the carriage. With Hastings in tow, Nigel took the reins, urging the horses to a dizzying speed.

As the brougham careened round corners, and dashed down cobblestoned streets, Courtney murmured soothingly to the white-faced reporter, "There is really no cause for concern, Mr. Hastings. Lord Davies is a more than competent whip. I promise we shall reach the hotel in one piece."

Her confidence was not shared. The *Gazette's* intrepid correspondent was decidedly shaken when they at last screeched to a stop before the hotel. Climbing out, he did everything but get down and touch the ground.

Hiding his amusement, Nigel delivered his instructions in a tone that left no room for discussion or failure. "Go inside and find your fellow reporters. Make sure they stay together. Don't let Sir Thomas or anyone else disperse you or send you off on any wild chases. As soon as my wife and I have bathed and changed—that is to say, as soon as we have transformed ourselves back into the accepted view of a lord and lady—we will be down to speak with you. And I guarantee, the story I give you and your colleagues will be well worth any effort you had to make to get here!"

Hastings believed him. The resolute look in Lord Davies' silvery eyes made it clear he meant exactly what he said. Already rehearsing what he would tell his associates, the young reporter took himself off at a run.

Upstairs in the suite she had not seen since before the massacre, Courtney hesitated. She felt decidedly out of place, as though she had stepped into another world. The luxurious comfort of brocade walls, Persian carpets, elegant furnishings, and lush appointments contrasted sharply to the hard gray reality that had so thoroughly engulfed her over the last few days. Rich colors and textures dazzled her, as did the sheer sweep of space not crowded with other people. She took a step backward, momentarily overcome.

Nigel must have shared her reaction, for he smiled encouragingly. "It is a bit much, isn't it? But I expect we'll manage." Touching her cheek tenderly, he added, "I really shouldn't have bothered bringing you up here. You look the lady no matter what you wear or do."

Distracted from her unease, Courtney laughed. "I don't think the journalists downstairs would agree with you. Mr. Hastings was convinced only by your . . . shall we say, forceful manner."

"That young pup," Nigel snorted. "Don't expect me ever to become inured to the way other men react to you, my dear, for I shall not. When we are both quite old and gray, I expect to still be beating your admirers off with my cane."

Courtney was still giggling at the image he conjured up when Mary arrived. Overjoyed to see her mistress, who had sent her back from the shelter when the maid became exhausted by her own efforts to help, she exclaimed, "Oh, my lady, I'm so glad you're here!" Her delight faded slightly as she took in Courtney's bedraggled appearance, but she managed to maintain her smile as she said, "Now, don't you lift a finger. I'll ring for hot water and you'll be nice and comfy in a bath in no time."

"I suppose Mary would be shocked if I joined you," Nigel murmured in her ear, making Courtney blush fiercely. Chuckling, he vanished through the connecting door to where the ever-ready Johnson was already laying out fresh clothes.

Half an hour later, suitably transformed, the marquess and marchioness returned downstairs. They bore little relation to the couple who had entered the suite.

Nigel wore an impeccably tailored frock coat of dark gray linen sculptured to the broad width of his shoulders. Fawn-colored trousers hugged the long, sinewy line of his muscular thighs. A white silk shirt and diamond-studded cravat emphasized the classic ruggedness of his features. The thick pelt of his sun-warmed hair was swept back from his broad forehead. He looked the epitome of a young, vigorous lord sure of himself and his prerogatives.

Beside his compelling masculinity, Courtney looked infinitely fragile and feminine. A dark green silk dress highlighted the mysterious depths of her emerald eyes. The white lace collar clung to her slender throat, framing the delicate oval of her face. Her hair, sedately arranged into a loose chignon from which a few auburn wisps trailed, was the perfect foil for her pale beauty. The smallness of her waist made the ripe curve of her breasts and hips just visible beneath the modestly cut gown all the more alluring. She moved with exquisite grace, her arm tucked protectively into Nigel's.

Sir Thomas saw them first. The mill owner was deep in conversation with several journalists clustered together in the lobby when Nigel and Courtney descended the marble staircase. His small pursed mouth dropped open as he abruptly broke off a conversation with the gentleman from the *Times* and hastened forward.

"My lord . . . my lady . . . what a surprise! I thought you were engaged elsewhere. . . . Uh, does this mean you are returning to London?"

"Eventually," Nigel drawled, dashing the man's hopes. Tall though Sir Thomas was, the marquess topped him by several inches. He had no difficulty seeing over his head toward the curious reporters, who, spurred by Peter Hastings' cryptic promises, were already moving toward them.

"Lord Davies, if you could spare a moment . . ."

"My lord, about these rumors we've heard . . ."

"Any truth to them, sir?"

Nigel held up a hand. "Gentlemen, may I suggest we

adjourn to the salon, where I will be happy to answer all your questions."

"That isn't necessary!" Sir Thomas protested. "I've already explained what happened!"

Nigel's calm demeanor did not change in the slightest, yet he still conveyed the impression of extreme anger held barely in check. So softly that the miller had to lean forward the hear him, he said, "You have *explained* what you hope the world will believe. Now I am going to tell these gentlemen what actually happened, and if you make any attempt to interfere, you will look back on this day as the beginning of your own destruction. Do I make myself quite clear?"

Sir Thomas' normally ruddy complexion blanched. He wanted to object, to tell the marquess that he had no right to take matters into his own hands to the detriment of honest property owners who saw no reason to make a regrettable incident worse. The words were on the tip of his tongue, but he could not utter them. Generations of innate respect for aristocratic authority coupled with instinctive fear of the raw power that could explode in merciless punishment kept him silent.

The salon was large enough to hold the crush of reporters comfortably. Nigel took his place at the front, standing on a slightly raised dais with Courtney beside him. He did not relinquish her hand as he said, "Before you begin your questions, I would like to make a brief statement. In the week since the aborted rally at St. Peter's Fields, my wife and I have been working at the shelter run by Mrs. Emily Wilson, who was seriously injured in the attack but is now recovering. We have seen at first hand the suffering of the workers who were assaulted for no greater offense than attempting to peacefully express their views. My own experiences over the last few days have convinced me that serious reforms are needed to change the iniquitous system under which far too many English men and women now labor."

As Courtney stared up at him in mingled surprise and pride, he continued, "For that reason, I am willing to cooperate with you in making known exactly what happened in Manchester last week. Now, gentlemen, you may begin. . . ."

An hour later the questions were still coming in rapid-fire succession, but the journalists scribbling frantically in their notebooks were now somber and pale. Their professional objectivity had begun to waver when Nigel described in graphic detail the extent and severity of the injuries to which he personally could attest.

"Most of the wounds were caused by clubs and sabers," he explained quietly, "which the members of the yeoman militia wielded with equal zealousness against men, women, and children. Other people were killed or severely injured by being trampled by horses or panicking crowds."

"How many were killed, my lord?" the reporter from the *Times* asked.

"The final count is two hundred and twenty dead and approximately twelve thousand injured. We are relatively certain of the number killed, but some of the wounded were taken directly back to their homes, so that is only an estimate."

"Have any of the militia been arrested?"

"No, not yet. As you may have noticed, there is a certain reluctance on the part of city authorities to acknowledge what happened here and take the necessary steps to render justice. It is my opinion that action will have to be taken from a higher level."

"From Parliament, sir?"

"Precisely."

"Her ladyship, sir, what part has she played in all this?"

"My wife is a friend of Mrs. Emily Wilson, who runs a shelter in Manchester for the poor and homeless. They became acquainted through Lady Courtney's own efforts to help the children of the East End. Mrs. Wilson and my wife attended the rally at St. Peter's Fields together and were caught up in the militia's attack, during which Mrs. Wilson was injured."

At the news that Courtney had witnessed the attack, the focus of the journalists' interest shifted to her.

"What did you see, my lady?"

"How can you be sure the attackers really were members of the militia?"

"Wasn't any attempt made to stop them?"

Though Courtney had never before spoken in public, she managed to keep her voice steady as she faced the reporters. "I saw the attack from the beginning. The militia, wearing the red armbands that identify them, charged a peacefully gathered group of men, women, and children who were listening to a speech by Orator Hunt. He was dragged from the podium and severely beaten. Other members of the militia struck out indiscriminately at anyone within reach, causing the crowd to scatter in panic. We were pursued through the streets, where I did see a group of constables attempt to put a stop to what was happening. But their efforts did not succeed. As soon as they left, the assault resumed. It was only by the grace of God that I was able to reach the shelter again with Mrs. Wilson, who by then was badly hurt."

"What happened to Orator Hunt?"

Courtney looked to Nigel for that information. "He was taken to the magistrate's house," the marquess explained, "from which he was eventually released the following day. The beating by the militia when he was seized off the podium was apparently only the beginning of the attack against him. His injuries are serious and will require extensive care."

This was the first Courtney had heard about the fate of the man she had listened to only briefly but still been impressed by. She swayed slightly as the image of him being torn from the podium flashed before her. It was all too easy to imagine what had happened to him after that. The delicate apricot blossom faded from her cheeks. Though she tried desperately to maintain her composure, the events of the last few terrible days were catching up with her.

Nigel was instantly aware of her distress. A steadying arm went around her waist as he said, "I'm sure you gentlemen are anxious to get your dispatches off to London, so if you will excuse us . . ." Without waiting for their agreement, he guided Courtney from the room.

The reporters would have in fact preferred to go on questioning the marquess, who was a remarkably helpful and impressive source for an incredible story. But they realized that his concern for his lady was such that they would get nothing further from him just then. Standing aside reluctantly, they waited only until Nigel and Courtney had left the salon before rushing to get their revelations down on paper and on the way to the capital by the fastest possible route.

Upstairs in the suite, Nigel dismissed Mary and locked the door behind her. Turning to his wife, who slumped white-faced on the side of the bed, he eased her gently to her feet and began undoing the laces of her gown. Courtney stood quietly under his touch. She felt rather like an exhausted child who had spent too long in the grown-up world, until the brush of Nigel's large warm hands against her bare shoulders reminded her that she was very much a woman.

There was nothing childlike in her response as he laid her tenderly on the bed and pulled a light comforter over her before stripping off his own clothes. As his lean, hard body was revealed in the fading summer light, Courtney's breath quickened.

It was no child who welcomed him as he slid into the bed next to her. During the last few days, as they worked together at the shelter, she had discovered a side of her husband she guessed even he had never suspected might exist. In the aftermath of intense hor-

ror and fear, he had cast aside the last prejudices and
indifference of his class to emerge as a strong, caring
man capable of the greatest tenderness and compassion.

She had seen him work tirelessly to help those she
would once have believed he barely even noticed. Never
once in the endless, often frustrating days had he shown
the slightest impatience or distaste. He was a bulwark
of strength and gentleness upon whom everyone, including herself, could depend. The final proof of his
transformation had come when he addressed the journalists and firmly put himself on the side of right and
justice no matter what the consequences.

Courtney desperately needed to express how much
the changes in him meant to her. Murmuring inco-
herently, she snuggled against him, tasting the salty
elixir of his skin ardently.

Nigel bit back a groan. He had not made love to his
wife since before the massacre and was in sore need of
her. But remembering the ashen pallor of her face and
the fragility of her body, he told himself sternly that he
must wait awhile longer. Only a cur would ignore all
she had suffered in the last few days and impose his
will on her regardless of her feelings.

But it was devilish hard not to be tempted when the
woman he loved so passionately stroked his broad chest.
Her touch was light as a hummingbird's wing, and
potent as a volcanic eruption. Heedless of any discipline his mind tried to impose, his manhood rose hard
and urgent.

Annoyed at his lack of control, Nigel seized Courtney's
hand gently in his own to still her explorations. Not all
the best intentions in the world would allow him to
endure much more without tossing his resolve aside
and taking her fiercely. His only hope was to lure her
into sleep quickly.

But Courtney had her own priorities. Her need was
every bit as great as his, and growing even more so with
each passing moment. Everywhere their bodies touched,

the latent power of oak-hewn muscles and corded sinew woke her to shivering awareness of her femininity. Against the warm velvet of his chest, her dark, full nipples hardened. The brush of his long, erect manhood against her softness uncoiled a core of heat deep within her loins.

Slipping a silken leg between his, Courtney traced the steely ridge of his thigh with bemused fascination. Her lips brushed the powerful column of his throat, lingering over the pulse points that leaped to life beneath her touch.

"C-Courtney . . ."

Beyond thought, acting purely on instincts as old as time, her hand slid down his flat abdomen to caress the proof of his desire. A low groan broke from Nigel as he made a last, valiant effort to maintain his self-control.

His marchioness frowned slightly. She wanted him desperately, needing the reaffirmation of life only his lovemaking could give. Far in the back of her mind, she suspected his restraint stemmed from concern for her. With loving determination, she set herself to shatter it.

Trailing tiny kisses up along his throat, she nipped the lobe of his ear in the instant before licking away the minute hurt. Tracing the hard line of his mouth with one finger, she bent to kiss him lingeringly, her tongue joining his in an erotic duel.

When Nigel's large hand caught the back of her head, trying to hold her in place, she wiggled free. Breathlessly she murmured, "No . . . let me . . ." A quiver of anticipation ran through him as he acquiesced.

Teasing the flat male nipples which hardened at her touch, she followed the line of golden hair that tapered below his waist only to burgeon at his groin. Nigel moved ardently beneath her, delighting in her care. When her tongue again darted out to caress and provoke, he groaned. Smiling to herself, Courtney drove him onward, enchanted by his unbridled response to her.

Breathing in his musky scent, she made full use of all the skills he had so lovingly taught her. Wanting to please him to the utmost, she held nothing back as she gloried in the force of his need that only she could satisfy.

Nigel bore it as long as he could, any chance of self-denial now clearly impossible. That small portion of his mind still capable of thought marveled at her sensuality. He knew her to be an innately modest woman who shunned the more overt displays of passion not uncommon among the *ton.* Yet in the privacy of their bedchamber, with the sanctity of their love drawn around them, she emerged as unrestrainedly erotic as the most accomplished courtesan. Far more so, in fact, for her every touch was both offered and received with mutual awareness that he was the special, unique man in her life.

Acutely sensitive to his every response, she knew exactly when the driving force within him approached its peak. Lifting her head, Courtney kissed him deeply as Nigel gently seized her hips. In the dim light of the room, she could see the quicksilver flare of his eyes as he guided her to him. A low whimper of delight broke from Courtney as they became one.

For a short time she was content to remain still above him, letting only her powerful inner muscles work in a way that drove him to the brink of release. But Nigel was far too capable and considerate a lover to seek his own pleasure before being absolutely certain of hers. Smiling faintly through the red mist of his passion, he arched deeper into her, bringing a gasp of sheer physical joy.

Holding her firmly above him, he thrust first slowly and then with increasing speed as together they exploded past the boundaries of separate being and hurtled into rapturous unity.

When at last the storm of fulfillment had passed, Courtney lay curled against him. She felt at once drained to the utmost and made complete. Nigel's chest beneath her cheek was damp with sweat. The steady beat of his heart reverberated through her. Languorously replete, she murmured her love to him before slipping into healing sleep.

—— 15 ——

"Mary, I can't find my hat! Have you seen it?"

"It's on your head, ma'am," the maid answered patiently, "and here's your reticule. You should be all set now."

Courtney looked doubtful. She had been up since before dawn and felt as though she would never be able to sleep again. Intense excitement coupled with nervousness surged through her. Her eyes glowed and her cheeks were flushed, adding to her already remarkable beauty. No one looking at her would guess she was off to spend the afternoon in the peeresses' gallery of the House of Lords. That infinitely staid institution did not usually provoke such emotion. But the times, Courtney reminded herself as she hurried from her room, were changing. Oh, how they were changing!

Nigel had gone on ahead with Sir Lloyd, but Sara and Peggy were waiting in the drawing room. Little girls were not usually taken to the gallery, but this was a special occasion and Peggy had more than earned the right to attend. Simply dressed in a pretty pink day dress trimmed with white lace, she seemed unusually subdued by the grandeur of the occasion. Only the impatient wiggle of her small body gave away her own excitement.

Nor was Sara immune to the import of the day. In the midst of preparing for her wedding to Sir Lloyd the following month, she had still found time to attend.

Not for the world would she miss what promised to be a landmark occasion.

Bidding the fondly smiling servants farewell, the ladies settled into a barouche with Peggy nestled between them. The day was unusually fair for early autumn, with a brisk breeze ruffling the leaves of the chestnut and oak trees lining their route. The incessant rain of the last few weeks had given way to brilliant sunshine. Courtney could not quite suppress a smile as she thought that even nature was nodding its approval.

Only one omission made the day a little less than perfect. She had hoped Emily Wilson would be able to come down to London, but her friend was far too busy at the Manchester shelter to make the trip. She had, however, sent, along with the latest news, her sincere hopes that all would go well.

A slim gloved hand drifted to the marchioness's reticule and Emily's latest letter. "The mood here in Manchester is still very strained," she had written. "There is great animosity and suspicion between the workers and owners, although each is treading wearily at the moment. The shock and outrage engendered by this summer's terrible events have quieted, at least temporarily, the aggressiveness of the property class. Everyone seems to be waiting for the other shoe to drop."

How difficult it must be, Courtney thought, for men like Sir Thomas to admit they were no longer in control of their destinies. Their frantic efforts to hide the truth of what happened at St. Peter's Fields had failed dismally. All England, indeed all the world, now knew of the events ironically dubbed "Peterloo."

The caustic comparison to Waterloo, where glory and honor had abounded, was not missed by anyone. Throughout the late summer and early fall, a sense of shock compounded by guilt lay over the kingdom. Decent men and women, even those who instinctively distrusted the workers, were dismayed that the rule of law could be so cavalierly abandoned. Over and over, variations were heard on the same theme. "This is not France," people said, well aware of what blatant disregard for justice had led to across the channel. The assertion held as much hope as it did conviction, for its truth yet remained to be proven.

"What was the mood at Carlton House last night?" Sara asked, breaking in on her train of thought.

Courtney grimaced. She would have preferred to skip the Prince Regent's soiree, but understood that it was important for Nigel to be seen, and heard, at this crucial time.

"You were wise to remain at home," she advised, "although I imagine the pleasure of an evening alone together would have outweighed even the most exciting entertainment."

Sara blushed becomingly. "We were not quite alone. My mother kept a benign eye on us, and my brother dropped by . . . several times."

Remembering the frustrations caused by such propriety, Courtney nodded sympathetically. "It won't be much longer now. Soon you and Lloyd will have all the privacy you desire."

That could not come soon enough, so far as Sara was concerned. To distract herself, she said, "You were saying about Carlton House . . ."

"Something rather surprising happened," Courtney admitted. "I danced with His Highness."

Sara's eyebrows arched expressively. A turn around the dance floor with Prinny was a special mark of favor reserved for those he wished to especially honor. By association, such royal approval would be extended to Nigel, who had done nothing whatsoever to earn it. On the contrary, he might well be thought to have earned royal censure.

"Why on earth did Prinny do that?" Sara asked. "Did he give you any clue?"

Courtney nodded. She remembered every word of her conversation with the Prince Regent. "Tell me, my dear," Prinny had begun as they pirouetted elegantly, "whatever is Nigel thinking of? Hasn't gone over to the ragamuffins, has he?"

Somehow managing a dazzling smile, she had murmured, "Nigel is the same man he has always been, sire. It is only that he has lately come to a more serious regard for the well-being of his country, which I am sure you would prefer all the nobility to share."

Prinny, who had no serious regard for anything except himself, frowned slightly. "Of course, of course. But this reform business . . . I can't believe he means to involve himself in that."

In Courtney's estimation, too many people had for too long made a practice of telling the Prince only what he wanted to hear. While she would not trespass upon the limits of court etiquette, neither would she play the sycophant. "Nigel believes there must be changes, sire, to prevent any recurrence of what happened at Manchester as well as the inevitably violent upheavals that would come of it."

The Prince shivered fastidiously, his round cheeks jiggling. "I have been sleeping so poorly," he complained. "My dreams are plagued by visions of the mob lurking outside my bedroom window, waiting to dispatch me as they did poor old Louis."

"I doubt we are anywhere near that point, your Highness," Courtney murmured tartly. She had little sympathy for the insomniac Prince, since she had seen the sufferings of his people.

"But you think it is a possibility, and Nigel believes the same, doesn't he?"

"You would have to ask him that, sire. But I do know that my husband's actions are not governed by any fear of the people. He is simply doing what he believes is right for all concerned."

Prinny sighed, the dejected lament of a man who admires another's qualities without ever hoping to approach them. "Nigel is so . . . resolute. He used to be quite a pleasant chap, always ready for a game of cards or a romp. Now he talks of little but politics and seems stuffed full with great ideas."

Courtney bit back a laugh. In the privacy of their bedroom, Nigel did not talk of politics at all, but she could hardly tell the Prince that. Instead, she said, "He takes his position very seriously, your Highness. After all, we are living in demanding times."

"I suppose," Prinny muttered, making it clear he thought it all a plot to spoil his pleasures. His perplexity had not eased when the dance at last ended and he returned Courtney to her husband.

Nigel greeted the Prince politely, but without the slightest evidence of fawning approbation to which he was accustomed. Of course, part of Nigel's attraction to the Regent had always been his rather detached arrogance. It had both challenged and provoked him.

Courtney held her breath, hoping there would be no repetition of the dangerous insolence which marked their last encounter. She relaxed slightly when it became evident that Nigel was far too occupied with other matters to pay the Prince any but the most superficial notice.

Prinny tried briefly to engage him in conversation, but they really had nothing to say to each other and Nigel could not be stirred to engage in dilettante repartee. After a brief time, His Highness drifted away in the company of those rakehell lords he could better understand. Nigel and Courtney took their leave shortly thereafter, since he wished to go over his notes for the following day and get to bed early.

"My word!" Sara exclaimed when this was related to her. "It sounds as though you have given the *ton* enough excitement to keep tongues wagging for weeks. There will be all sorts of speculation about what passed between you and Prinny, not to mention Nigel's part in it all."

Courtney shrugged. She had no interest in the gossip of the *ton*. Anything that might be said by the matrons at Almack's or the lords at White's was singularly unimportant. What words did matter were to be uttered in a far different arena.

As the barouche swept round the corner, the stolid stone facade of Parliament came into view. Courtney leaned forward eagerly. She could see a long line of carriages drawn up in front, with many men and a few women hurrying inside. The session that was about to begin promised to be far better attended than was usual. There was no doubt in her mind as to what sparked such interest.

With the assistance of the footmen, Courtney, Sara, and Peggy descended. They stood for a moment taking in the scene until they were distracted by the arrival of yet another brougham, this one bearing the Hampson crest. Glad that she had managed to arrive first, Courtney stepped forward to greet her friend.

In the radiant light of day, so unbecoming to many women, Lady Katherine looked even more ethereally beautiful than usual. She left the carriage under the protective gaze of her husband, who hovered over her until he spotted Courtney. Only then did Lord Hampson relax slightly, certain that his wife would be well protected in the peeresses' gallery.

"You look lovely, my dear," Katherine murmured, kissing the younger woman's cheek. "The peers will be hard pressed to keep their attention on Nigel."

Courtney laughed softly. "I've heard parts of his speech, and I have no doubt at all of where attention will be firmly riveted." Without attempting to mask her pride, she added, "He's becoming something of a firebrand, you know."

"That's exactly what's needed," Lord Hampson assured her, bowing politely to Sara, who acknowledged the greeting with a soft smile. She had met Katherine and her husband several weeks before at a small party arranged by Courtney and Nigel. Impressed by their obvious intelligence, compassion, and deeply rooted sense of honor, she had no reluctance to welcome them into her own circle of friends.

Before such a panoply of beauty and nobility, Peggy hung back self-consciously. Courtney's gentle touch on her shoulder was needed to bring her forth, where she curtsied with instinctive grace. Katherine looked the child over with undisguised interest, impressed by the great changes in her.

Under the combined influences of love, security, and proper care, she was blossoming. Her slender body had filled out slightly and her delicate features had lost their pinched look. The bruises were all gone from her face, and if the delighted gleam in her eyes was anything to go by, they were also healing swiftly from her soul.

"How pretty you are," she told the little girl gently. "I'm delighted you are joining us today."

Peggy smiled up at her radiantly. Her hand held snugly in Courtney's, she accompanied the ladies inside the majestic edifice which many believed housed the very heart of England.

Part judicial center, part men's club, the House of Lords was alternately reserved to the point of inertia and riotous to an extent that made it impossible to believe anything constructive could be happening. Courtney had been there once before with her father on a day that was so somnabulantly quiet as to make her wonder why anyone would wish to serve there. But this session promised to be far different. Her pulse quickened as she observed the throng of lords beginning to take their seats. Whig and Tory alike, no one wanted to miss a word of what would be said.

Taking her seat in the peeresses' gallery, Courtney quickly spied her husband below. He stood surrounded by a cluster of supporters, including Lord Hampson and Sir Lloyd.

Somberly dressed in a dark gray frock coat and trousers, Nigel looked unusually subdued and thoughtful. Only the quicksilver gleam of his eyes hinted at the energies surging just below the surface.

For a brief time, during which Courtney fidgeted

impatiently, routine business was dealt with. At its conclusion, the floor was open to debate. As tradition required, the leaders of both parties spoke first, but only to defer to other members who had special topics they wished to raise. The spokesman for the Tories began a turgid attack on the inefficiencies of the agricultural system to which he predictably objected because of decreased revenues of property owners. He was booed good-naturedly by the Whigs and even by some members of his own party who were anxious to get on to the main event.

The presentation of a maiden speech in the House of Lords was always an anxious moment. But Nigel appeared singularly unperturbed as he rose to address his peers.

"My lords," he began so softly that the inevitable murmurings and shufflings had to die down for him to be heard. "For too long, the vast majority of men and women in our land have suffered under the harsh burden of exploitation. In a less enlightened age, this was accepted as inevitable. But we who have dared to harness the powers of nature know that nothing is inevitable, except change. The world of the steam engine and gaslight requires a new social contract which recognizes the worth of all people."

"Hear, hear!" a supporter shouted.

"Balderdash!" a red-faced lord insisted.

Various other comments, pro and con, were offered in respect for the ritual of audience participation that characterized Parliament. But they died away quickly as Nigel continued.

"Some of us prefer to believe that everything can continue as it has been. The recent tragic events in Manchester show this to be categorically untrue. The time has come for us to acknowledge the rights and privileges of all men to participate in the government of the kingdom *regardless* of birth or position."

"Rubbish!"

"Intolerable!"

"Next he'll say the dustman should be prime minister!"

"Let him finish! Or are you too afraid to hear what he has to say?"

This last came from Sir Lloyd, who looked rather surprised when he was obeyed. Many of the lords might not like what Nigel was telling them, but they could hardly deny his right to speak or their own urge to know exactly how far he would go.

"If we attempt to blindly continue as before without regard to the realities of our time, we will have only ourselves to blame. The outcry of our people will not be suppressed forever. The day will come when they rise up successfully against us to claim what is rightfully theirs. Recent experiences by our neighbor to the south indicate that such armed rebellion leads inevitably to further abuses. We will replace the tyranny of the few with the tyranny of the masses, with the result that justice will continue to be barred from this land."

Allowing that ominous prediction to settle over the chamber, Nigel continued, "I, for one, do not wish to see that day. Nor is it preordained. Simple humanity proclaims that we must cease the exploitation and suppression of the common people and welcome them as fellow countrymen with whom we share a sacred legacy of freedom under law."

Rather to the surprise of those in the gallery, this was greeted by no more than a smattering of objection. Not that there was any widespread degree of accord, but the sheer impact of Nigel's words and manner was enough to keep the lords quiet at least for the moment. They had anticipated a forceful speech, but nothing had prepared them for the tough, unadorned way he presented his views.

Those among them who were old enough or wise enough to gauge the potential of their opponents were shaken by what they heard. Hitherto, the reformers had been well-intentioned but not particularly forceful men like Sir Lloyd or potentially strong proponents like Lord Hampson who were too distracted by their personal lives to be very effective. It was only too clear that Nigel was a different matter entirely.

He possessed the intelligence and articulateness without which he could not hope to earn the respect of his peers no matter what his views. But far more important, he gave evidence of profound inner strength and determination bordering on ruthlessness that made him a dangerous adversary. Nigel was a man others would follow. He provided what the reform movement had critically lacked, a charismatic leader capable of inspiring the greatest loyalty and tenacity.

Courtney listened to him with undisguised admiration. Though she knew in principle what he intended to say, she was not prepared for the depth and forcefulness of his convictions.

For a moment she felt a surge of concern as she realized that the far simpler, more predictable man she had married was gone forever. In his place was a purposeful, resolute leader who would not rest until the horrors he had witnessed in Manchester could never again be repeated. Her anxiety vanished as she realized that she would no more want Nigel to return to the way he had been than she would wish to do so herself. Their lives would certainly never again be as serene, but neither would they ever again be subject to the gnawing discontent and futile search for distraction that plagued the *ton*.

Not for them the endless round of parties, balls, and routs that were a desperate effort to stave off the inevitable. Thanks to the tumultuous events of the last few months, they were among the few who would help shape the future, rather than clinging like graying cobwebs to the remnants of the past.

Of course, there would have to be adjustments. Just as Nigel was learning to share her with the children of the East End, she had to accept that the people for whom he now spoke would have considerable call on his time and energies. The absolute confidence she had in their love allowed her to view such a necessity without fear.

That certainty was further heightened as Nigel concluded his speech. As he made a clarion call for reform in the name of simple humanity, he faced her directly. All the power and sincerity of his love were written clearly on his leonine features as he made the words a vow of their future together.

The overwhelming approval of a significantly large number of lords threatened to shake the revered rafters. Sir Lloyd was the first to reach him, offering his hand in congratulation. Lord Hampson was close behind, his usually somber features wreathed in smiles. Dozens more pressed in, driven by the instinctive human nature to be near a man with a vision of the future and the means to achieve it.

In sharp counterpoint, the opponents of change sat in stony silence. Lady Katherine could not resist pointing out several florid gentlemen who looked in danger of erupting. Even Sara came close to giggling when one of Prinny's most trusted agents shook himself like a baited bear helpless to deal with the sudden riptide of events.

But it was Peggy who brought the occasion into sensible perspective. "I think," she intoned gravely, "Sir Nigel must be very thirsty after all that talking. Is it time for the champagne yet?"

She had to wait a short while until they were free to return home with a large contingent of well-wishers. During their absence, a large buffet had been set out with ample bottles of hock, port, and sherry brought up from the wine cellar. But it was the champagne, cold and tart, that accompanied the toast of Nigel's success.

"I have never heard a more impressive maiden speech," Lord Hampson said sincerely. "You have a brilliant future."

"I had every confidence you would do well," Sir

Lloyd confirmed, "but I did not expect such eloquence. You are exactly what we have needed for so long."

Nigel waved the compliments away modestly. "I only said what I believe." A self-deprecating smile lit his eyes. "It's a rather nice feeling to have convictions. I think I'll stick with them."

Appreciative laughter rang through the drawing room. No one there doubted that Nigel would do exactly that. Excitement ran through them all as they sensed they were in at the beginning of something that would one day be looked back on as very important. A man of immense abilities had at last found his direction. His potential was truly unlimited.

Courtney waited patiently on the outskirts of the admiring group. She had no wish to intrude on what was quite rightly Nigel's moment. He had worked so hard that she felt only gladness at his success. But she was all the happier when, having slipped out briefly to ease the ever-bothersome pins from her hair, she found him waiting for her in the corridor.

"There you are," he murmured. "I wondered where you had gone to."

Standing so close to him that she could feel the warmth emanating from his body, Courtney found herself too distracted for all but the briefest explanation. "My hair . . ."

Nigel nodded in quick understanding. He stroked a strand of the auburn silk. "Of course . . ." Drawing her closer, he kissed her lingeringly, heedless of the guests waiting for them.

When they at last broke apart, Courtney whispered, "I am so proud of you."

Gazing down at her lovingly, Nigel said, "As I am of you. Without your courage and insight, I would never have reached this point."

A teasing gleam came into her eyes. She could not resist the urge to challenge him. "Do you never regret that the sheltered girl you married took it in her head to develop a mind of her own?"

Nigel laughed appreciatively. His eyes were infinitely tender. "No, I can't say that I do. That girl was very lovely, but the woman she has become is far more so. Although," he added provocatively, "I must admit the lady has given me more than a few sleepless nights."

"You have caused some yourself," his marchioness reminded him archly. "Although usually for quite pleasant reasons."

The recollection of sweetly passionate hours they had spent together further distracted them both. Heedless of the lords and ladies gathered in the drawing room, they embraced in tender reaffirmation of all they shared. Passion, never far from the surface, flared between them. But now it was made all the more intense by profound love capable of triumphing over any challenge.

A young maid, on her way downstairs after changing into her best uniform, stopped in mid-step. Blushing, she backed away hastily. Such a moment deserved privacy. Ruefully she reminded herself to tread more cautiously in the future. The way their lord and lady-ship were going, they would be up to similar carryings-on in their nineties!

That was a rather pleasant thought to warm her on a decidedly chill autumn evening when the last leaves were falling from the trees and a new, clean wind was blowing over the land. By the time the maid reached the kitchen, where most of the other servants were gathered to enjoy their own celebration, she was smiling broadly.

About the Author

Anne MacNeill is a pen name for a well-known author of both contemporary and historical romances. Born and raised in New York City, Ms. MacNeill graduated from the City University of New York with a BA in Liberal Arts/History and became a full-time romance writer. She is married and lives in Connecticut.